SPECTRAL
SOUNDS

SPECTRAL SOUNDS

Unquiet Tales of Acoustic Weird

edited by

MANON BURZ-LABRANDE

This edition published 2022 by
The British Library
96 Euston Road
London NW1 2DB

Cataloguing in Publication Data
A catalogue record for this publication is available from the British Library

ISBN 978 0 7123 5417 2
e-ISBN 978 0 7123 6805 6

Frontispiece illustration by Harry Clarke, for 'Silence — A Fable' in Edgar
Allan Poe's *Tales of Mystery and Imagination*, G. G. Harrap and Co., London,
1923. Illustration on page 320 from *Planches anatomiques du corps humain executées
d'après les dimensions naturelles*, F. Antommarchi, Cte de Lasteyrie, Paris, 1826.

Cover design by Mauricio Villamayor with illustration by Mag Ruhig
Text design and typesetting by Tetragon, London
Printed in England by CPI Group (UK) Ltd, Croydon, CR0 4YY

CONTENTS

IV · SOUNDS AND SILENCE:
ACOUSTIC WEIRD BEYOND THE GHOSTLY

INTRODUCTION

Inexplicable noises have long been at the heart of fear-inducing fiction—questions such as whether the sound is identifiable or strange, who hears it and who does not, and what it means, are still key tropes of contemporary popular fiction, whether on the page or on screen. Sound, as the scholar Isabella van Elferen has recently explained, is imbued with uncanniness. After all, the famous tagline "in space, no one can hear you scream" points towards a particular note of horror in the science-fiction film *Alien* (1979): terror arises when the right kind of noise cannot be heard, and when others, such as floorboards mysteriously creaking or disconnected phones ringing, invade our personal space. This is what *Spectral Sounds: Unquiet Tales of Acoustic Weird* offers to explore, in the context of the ghost story and beyond.

When critics of the Gothic published articles in 1797 denouncing the repetitive formula of contemporary novels, ghosts were associated with many sounds. In a piece entitled "Terrorist Novel Writing" published in *The Spirit of the Public Journals for 1797*, spectres were depicted as appearing with the rattling of thunder, the whistling of wind "louder than one of Handel's choruses", and more importantly, "noises, whispers, and groans, threescore at least". In *The Universal Magazine of Knowledge and Pleasure*, "A Recipe for a Modern Romance" described the creaking of doors and the clanking of chains that accompany spectral manifestations. But beyond the classical Gothic décor of an old castle on a stormy night, populated with standing armours and ghosts with ball and chain, popular culture over the past two hundred and fifty years has continuously experimented with acoustic manifestations to create an atmosphere of unease, of suspense and of fear. Stories of haunted houses in which strange sounds can be heard have been written during virtually every decade since at least Horace Walpole's formative Gothic work *The Castle of Otranto* (1764), in many different guises; we can all think of at least one novel, short story, radio drama, film, TV episode or video game which draws on the trope of unexplained noises. It is the ambiguity of the aural that explains why there exists a myriad of stories where sound is terror—whether voice, noise, whisper or knock—up to this day.

In terms of perceived objectivity, the visual has long been culturally prevalent, held to be more reliable. As the saying goes, seeing is believing. This, in turn, has endowed the unseen with a particularly strong potential for terror, and aural cues of spectral presence become all the more powerful as they heighten the fear felt by characters and readers alike. Who has not jumped at some inexplicable sound while engrossed in the reading of a story? Beyond the realm of fiction, acoustic phenomena have a particular importance in relation to ghostly presences. Audio recorders and microphones are, after all, part of the modern equipment consistently used within parapsychology and ghost-hunting. The hope to capture otherwise inaudible or unintelligible communications from spirits is an attempt to control the unreliability and the subjectivity of sound, through supposedly objective technology. But it also betrays the uneasiness that is triggered by aural cues and phenomena that potentially cannot be explained; and this concern is what underpins a great many ghost stories of the nineteenth and early-twentieth centuries, as they attempt to negotiate the fast-changing world around them.

In her cultural history of ghosts, the art historian Susan Owens explores how ghosts reflect changing attitudes, hopes and fears:

ghosts, she says, "personify the layers of history beneath our feet, the old stories that refuse to be erased". Ghost stories do not merely reflect anxieties about death and its permanence, about an afterlife, and about life itself; they also express contemporary concerns, as well as long-standing questions. They represent attempts to make sense of the unknown, and to keep exploring our fears. This helps elucidate why ghost stories rely so often on the sense of hearing. Sounds are experienced internally, as the translation of acoustic waves into nerve signals, i.e. the language of the brain; they do not leave any physical trace in the world. There is no proof that one heard a strange noise. It is, quite literally, all in our heads—and this subjectivity connects particularly well with the figure of the ghost as the expression of anxieties ranging from individual to society-wide.

Building on the metaphorical potential of ghosts, I have chosen to include stories in this collection which focus on a sound or a noise that is haunting, more than on literal ghosts. Though many do feature ghostly revenants, the acoustic phenomena—and their potential consequences—upon which the selected stories hinge often bear more importance than the spectre itself. In this, I have tried to place the emphasis on the stories' *soundscapes*, a term theorised by composer R. Murray Schafer to designate sonic environments as perceived by humans. In fiction, soundscapes can be rich, with many noises resounding throughout the text, or they can be more focused, with one reoccurring sound in the story that never leaves the characters. For instance, the recipe proposed by critics of the Gothic evokes the many sounds of an old castle during a storm; but perhaps the most famous of all haunting sounds in a short story is Edgar Allan Poe's "The Tell-Tale Heart" (1843), in which a heart keeps beating and resounding from under the floorboards of the narrator's house. What matters is the significance of the aural. By gathering these stories and dedicating crucial attention to aurality as a potential marker for terror, *Spectral Sounds* inscribes itself within the relatively recent but vibrant field of literary sound studies. The unexplained noises take centre stage, helping us to reconsider the themes of presence and absence in the ghost story through the emergence and echoes of sound and silence.

This collection features fourteen tales, mostly ghost stories but not exclusively, by authors from both sides of the Atlantic. All were published within a hundred years, from the nineteenth century to shortly after the First World War. In the tradition of the Tales of the Weird series, *Spectral Sounds* includes both household names of the ghost story or of the weird alongside more obscure authors or texts. Such famously sonorous tales as Poe's "The Tell-Tale Heart", but also Vernon Lee's "A Wicked Voice" (1890), M. R. James's "Oh, Whistle, and I'll Come to You, My Lad" (1904) or Algernon Blackwood's "The Whisperers" (1914) have been intentionally left out, as they can be read in other British Library Publishing anthologies. I do, however, encourage the readers of *Spectral Sounds* to go back to previous volumes and reread their favourite tales, perhaps with special attention to the soundscapes that they contain.

Spectral Sounds contains four thematic sections, chosen based on the main spectral manifestation(s) at the heart of the various stories. Of course, many of them have complex soundscapes and feature both voice and noise, for instance; but this organisation is intended to help showcase different thematic and cultural concerns. The scholar Fred Botting once noted that "often overlooked, sound remains prominent in the technical repertoire of gothic production"—and this prominence, also in literature of the weird, takes on many forms. We begin with a classic haunted house story, which opens the first part on living with audible presences. Then, we move on to perceiving ghostly voices in the second section; the third gathers tales of sonorous objects and haunting technology. Finally, the last section proposes a different form of acoustic weird, beyond the ghostly, through two stories that reconsider the impact of sounds and silence on human beings. From terrifyingly unquiet spectres and disconnected bells ringing to aural cues traced back to their source, from omens of death to redeeming encounters, I hope that this collection will allow you to enjoy a healthy dose of spookiness—and to reconsider whether you *did*, perhaps, hear that strange noise after all.

MANON BURZ-LABRANDE, 2022

WORKS CITED

Botting, Fred, "Poe, Voice and the Origin of Horror Fiction", *Sound Effects: The Object Voice in Fiction*, Ed. Jorge Sacido-Romero and Sylvia Mieszkowski (Rodopi, 2015), pp. 73–100.

Owens, Susan, *The Ghost: A Cultural History* (Tate Publishing, 2017).

"A Recipe for a Modern Romance", *The Universal Magazine of Knowledge and Pleasure* (London: W. Bent, 1797), pp. 232–233.

Schafer, R. Murray, *The Soundscape: Our Sonic Environment and the Tuning of the World* (Destiny, 1994).

"Terrorist Novel Writing", *The Spirit of the Public Journals for 1797* (London: R. Phillips, 1798), pp. 223–225.

Van Elferen, Isabella, *Gothic Music: The Sounds of the Uncanny* (University of Wales Press, 2012).

FURTHER READING

Archambault, Angela M., "The Function of Sound in the Gothic Novels of Ann Radcliffe, Matthew Lewis and Charles Maturin", *Études Épistémè* 29 (2016). <https://doi.org/10.4000/episteme.965>.

Foley, Matt, "Voices of Terror and Horror: Towards an Acoustics of Modern Gothic", *Sound Effects: The Object Voice in Fiction*, Ed. Jorge Sacido-Romero and Sylvia Mieszkowski (Rodopi, 2015), pp. 217–242.

Glotova, Elena, "Soundscapes in nineteenth-century Gothic short stories", *Umeå studies in language and literature* 45 (Umeå University, 2021).

Levin, David Michael, ed., *Modernity and the Hegemony of Vision* (University of California Press, 1993).

Schlauraff, Kristie A., "Victorian gothic soundscapes", *Literature Compass* 15.4 (2018): e12445.

ACKNOWLEDGMENTS

I would like to thank my PhD supervisor, Sylvia Mieszkowski, for introducing me to the fascinating world of literary sound studies. This collection began to take shape in my mind after a conference organised in Vienna and a co-edited journal issue entitled "More than Meets the Ear", and the connection between the ghost story and sounds soon became so clear to me that I launched myself into this project—and I am so glad I did. It is a real privilege to have been able to edit this volume of the Tales of the Weird collection, and I wholeheartedly thank Jonny Davidson for his support, as well as the whole British Library publishing team for their hard work. Finally, thanks are due to Jen Baker, for her feedback and her help, and to my husband Andi, for his constant encouragements.

This collection is dedicated to my mum, and the (many, many) hours spent together at the British Library.

A NOTE FROM THE PUBLISHER

The original short stories reprinted in the British Library Tales of the Weird series were written and published in a period ranging across the nineteenth and twentieth centuries. There are many elements of these stories which continue to entertain modern readers; however, in some cases there are also uses of language, instances of stereotyping and some attitudes expressed by narrators or characters which may not be endorsed by the publishing standards of today. We acknowledge therefore that some elements in the stories selected for reprinting may continue to make uncomfortable reading for some of our audience. With this series British Library Publishing aims to offer a new readership a chance to read some of the rare material of the British Library's collections in an affordable paperback format, to enjoy their merits and to look back into the worlds of the past two centuries as portrayed by their writers. It is not possible to separate these stories from the history of their writing and as such the following stories are presented as they were originally published with minor edits only, made for consistency of style and sense. We welcome feedback from our readers, which can be sent to the following address:

British Library Publishing
The British Library
96 Euston Road
London, NW1 2DB
United Kingdom

I.

"I heard a noise, sure enough": Living with audible presences

THE INVISIBLE TENANTS
OF RUSHMERE

Florence Marryat

Florence Marryat (1833–1899) was an author, playwright, editor, singer and actress. Born in Brighton, she was the daughter of the novelist and mariner Captain Frederick Marryat and his wife Catherine (née Shairp). In many ways, Marryat dedicated her professional life to entertainment: from the 1860s onwards, she wrote no fewer than 68 novels (from sensation novels to Gothic works), along with short story collections, memoirs and children's stories. At times working as a journalist and editor, too, her large body of written work nevertheless only forms part of her career. She also performed on stage for over a decade, touring with piano sketch entertainment and later starring in comedies, dramas, and in Gilbert and Sullivan operettas with the D'Oyly Carte Opera Company. Marryat also had a particular interest in spiritualism: known to have attended many séances and frequented celebrated mediums of the late nineteenth century, she translated her ardent beliefs and her experiences into literary output—for instance, in *There is No Death* (1891), which was an account of a séance.

"The Invisible Tenants of Rushmere" was originally published in her short story collection *The Ghost of Charlotte Cray and other stories* (1883). The tale was chosen as the first of this collection because it is a classic haunted house story, in which characters move into a charming mansion only to begin hearing a variety of spectral sounds resonate through the house. Presences manifest acoustically rather than visually, and it soon becomes obvious that "no one who lives in Rushmere lives there alone"...

" n the banks of the Wye, Monmouthshire.—To be Let, furnished, a commodious Family Mansion, surrounded with park-like grounds. Stabling and every convenience. Only two and a-half miles from station, church, and post-office. Excellent fishing to be procured in the neighbourhood. Rent nominal to a responsible tenant."

Such, with a few trifling additions, was the advertisement that caught my eye in the spring of 18—.

"My dear Jane," I said, as I handed the paper over to my wife, "this, I think, is the very thing we want."

I was a London practitioner, with a numerous family and a large circle of patients; but the two facts, though blessings in themselves, were not without their disadvantages.

The hostages which I had given to fortune had made that strenuous action which attention to my numerous patients supplied incumbent on me; but the consequent anxiety and want of rest had drawn so largely on my mental and physical resources, that there was no need for my professional brethren to warn me of the necessity of change and country air. I felt myself that I was breaking down, and had already made arrangements with a friend to take my practice for a few months, and set me at liberty to attend to my own health. And being passionately fond of fishing, and all country pleasures and pursuits, and looking forward with zest to a period of complete quiet, the residence alluded to (if it fulfilled the promise of its advertisement) appeared to be all that I could desire.

"Park-like grounds!" exclaimed my wife, with animation. "How the dear children will enjoy themselves."

"And two and a-half miles from church or station," I responded eagerly. "No neighbours, excellent fishing, and at a nominal rent. It sounds too good to be true."

"Oh, Arthur! you must write, and obtain all the particulars this very day. If you put it off, some one will be sure to take the house before we have time to do so."

"I shall go and see the city agents at once," I replied, resolutely. "It is too rare an opportunity to be lost. Only, don't raise your hopes too high, my dear. Advertisements are apt to be deceptive."

But when I had seen Messrs. Quibble & Lye on the subject, it really seemed as though for once they had spoken the truth. Rushmere, the house in question, had been built and furnished for his own use by an old gentleman, who died shortly afterwards, and his heirs, not liking the situation, had placed the property in the agents' hands for letting. The owners were wealthy, cared little for money, and had authorised the agents to let the house on any reasonable terms, and it was really a bargain to anyone that wanted it. They frankly admitted that the loneliness of the position of Rushmere was the reason of its cheapness; but when I heard the rent at which they offered to let me take it, if approved of, for three months, I was quite ready to agree with Messrs. Quibble & Lye in their idea of a bargain, and that, for those who liked solitude, Rushmere offered extraordinary advantages.

Armed with the necessary authority, I found my way down into Monmouthshire, to inspect the premises on the following day; and when I saw Rushmere, I felt still more disposed to be surprised at the opportunity afforded me, and to congratulate myself on the promptitude with which I had embraced it. I found it to be a good-sized country house, comfortably furnished, and, to all appearance, well built, standing in enclosed grounds, and on a healthy elevation; but, notwithstanding its isolated situation, I was too much a man of the world to believe, under the circumstances, that its greatest disadvantage lay in that fact. Accordingly, I peered eagerly about for damp walls, covered cesspools, unsteady joists, or tottering foundations, but I could find none.

"The chimneys smoke, I suppose?" I remarked, in a would-be careless tone, to the old woman whom I found in charge of the house, and who crept after me wherever I went.

"Chimbleys smoke, sir? Not as I knows of."

"The roof leaks, perhaps?"

"Deary me, no. You won't find a spot of damp, look where you may."

"Then there's been a fever, or some infectious disorder in the house?"

"A fever, sir? Why, the place has been empty, these six months. The last tenants left at Christmas."

"Empty for six months!" I exclaimed. "How long is it, then, since the gentleman who built it died?"

"Old Mr. Bennett, sir? He's been dead a matter of fifteen years or more."

"Indeed! Then why don't the owners of the place sell it, instead of letting it stand vacant?" thought I to myself.

But I did not say so to the old woman, who was looking up in my face, as though anxious to learn what my decision would be.

"No vermin, I hope?" I suggested, as a last resource. "You are not troubled with rats or mice at night, are you?"

"Oh, I don't sleep here at night, sir, thank heaven!" she answered in a manner which appeared to me unnecessarily energetic. "I am only employed by day to air the house, and show it to strangers. I go home to my own people at night."

"And where do your people live?"

"Better than half a mile from here, sir, and ours is the nearest cottage to Rushmere."

And then—apprehensive, perhaps, that her information might prove a drawback to the letting of the property—she added, quickly,—

"Not but what it's a nice place to live in, is Rushmere, and very convenient, though a bit lonesome."

I perfectly agreed with her, the "lonesomeness" of the situation proving no detraction in my eyes.

On my return to London I gave my wife so glowing a description of the house and its surroundings, that she urged me to conclude the bargain at once; and, in the course of a few weeks, I and my family were transplanted from the purlieus of Bayswater to the banks of the Wye. It was the middle of May when we took possession, and the country wore its most attractive garb. The children were wild with delight at being let loose in the flower-bespangled fields, and, as I watched the tributaries of the river, and perceived the excellent sport they promised me, I felt scarcely less excited than the children. Only my wife, I thought, became inoculated with some of the absurd fears of the domestics we had brought with us from town, and seemed to consider the locality more lonely and unprotected than she had expected to find it.

"It's a charming place, Arthur," she acknowledged, "and marvellously cheap; but it is certainly a long way from other houses. I find we shall have to send for everything to the town. Not even the country carts, with butter and poultry, seem to call at Rushmere."

"My dear Jane, I told you distinctly that it was two and a-half miles from church or station, and you read it for yourself in the paper. But

I thought we looked out for a retreat where we should run no risk of being intruded on by strangers."

"Oh yes, of course; only there are not even any farmhouses or cottages near Rushmere, you see; and it would be so very easy for anyone to break in at night, and rob us."

"Pooh, nonsense! What will you be afraid of next? The locks and bolts are perfectly secure, and both Dawson and I have firearms, and are ready to use them. Your fears are childish, Janie."

But all my arguments were unavailing, and each day my wife grew more nervous, and less willing to be left alone. So much so, indeed, that I made a practice of seeing that the house fastenings were properly secured each night myself, and of keeping a loaded revolver close to my hand, in case of need. But it damped my pleasure, to find that Jane was not enjoying herself; and the country looked less beautiful to me than it had done at first. One night I suddenly awoke, to find that she was sitting up in bed, and in an attitude of expectation.

"My dear, what is the matter with you?"

"Oh, hush! I am sure that I hear footsteps on the stairs—footsteps creeping up and down."

I listened with her, but could detect no sound whatever.

"Lie down again, Jane—it is only your imagination. Every one is fast asleep in bed."

"I assure you, Arthur, I am not mistaken. Once they came quite near the door."

"If so, it can only be one of the servants. You don't wish me to get up and encounter Mary or Susan in her night-dress, do you? Consider my morals!"

"Oh no, of course not," she replied with a faint smile; yet it was some time before she fell to sleep again.

It was not many nights before my wife roused me again with the same complaint.

"Arthur, don't call me silly, but I am *certain* I heard something."

To appease her fears, I shook off my drowsiness, and, with a lighted candle, made a tour of the house; but all was as I had left it.

Once, indeed, I imagined that I heard at my side the sound of a quick breathing; but that I knew must be sheer fancy, since I was alone.

The only circumstance that startled me was finding Dawson, the man servant, who slept on the ground floor, also awake, and listening at his door.

"What roused you, Dawson?"

"Well, sir, I can hardly say; but I fancied I heard some one going up the stairs a little while ago."

"You heard me coming down, you mean."

"No, sir, begging your pardon, it was footsteps going up—lighter than yours, sir. More like those of a woman."

Yet, though I privately interrogated the female servants on the following day, I could not discover that any of them had been out of their beds; and I forbore to tell my wife what Dawson had said in corroboration of her statement.

Only I was as much annoyed as astonished when, as I finished my catechism of Mary, our head nurse, she informed me that she had made up her mind to leave our service. Mary—my wife's right hand—who had been with us ever since the birth of our first child! The announcement took me completely aback.

"What on earth is your reason for leaving us?" I demanded angrily; for I knew what a blow her decision would be to Jane. "What have you to find fault with?"

"Nothing with you or the mistress, sir; but I can't remain in this house. I wouldn't stay in it a night longer, if it were possible to get away; and I do hope you and Mrs. Delamere will let me go as soon as ever you can, sir, as it will be the death of me."

"What will be the death of you?"

"The footsteps, sir, and the voices," she answered, crying. "I can hear them about the nurseries all night long, and it's more than any mortal can stand—it is, indeed."

"Are you infected with the same folly?" I exclaimed. "I see what it is, Dawson has been talking to you. I didn't know I had such a couple of fools in my establishment."

"Mr. Dawson has said nothing to me about nothing, sir," she answered. "I hear what I hear with my own ears; and I wouldn't stay a week longer in this 'aunted place, not if you was to strew the floor with golden guineas for me."

Not possessing either the capability or the inclination to test Mary's fidelity by the means she alluded to, and finding her determination unalterable, I gave her the desired permission to depart; only making it a stipulation that she should not tell her mistress the real reason for her leaving us, but ascribe it to bad news from home, or any other cause.

But though I could not but believe that the woman's idiotic terrors had blinded her judgment, I was extremely surprised to find she should have been so led astray, as I had always considered Mary to possess a remarkably clear head and good moral sense. The wailing and lamentation, from both mother and children, at the announcement of her departure made me still more angry with her obstinacy and folly. But she continued resolute; and we were driven to try and secure some one to fulfil her duties from the neighbouring town. But here a strange difficulty met us. We saw several fresh, rosy-cheeked maidens, who appeared quite willing to undertake our service, until they heard where we resided, when by an extraordinary coincidence, one and all discovered that some insurmountable obstacle prevented their coming at all. When the same thing had occurred several times in succession, and Jane appeared worn out with disappointment and fatigue, the landlord of the inn where we had put up for the day appeared at the door, and beckoned me out.

"May I make bold enough to ask if you want a servant to go to Rushmere?" he inquired of me in a whisper.

"Certainly, we do. Our nurse has been obliged to leave us suddenly, and we want some one to supply her place."

"Then you may give it up as a bad job, sir; for you'll never get one of the country people here about to set a foot in Rushmere—not if you were to live there till the day of your death."

"And why not?" I demanded, with affected ignorance.

"What, haven't you heard nothing since you've been there, sir?"

"Heard? What should I have heard, except the ordinary noises of the household?"

"Well, you're lucky if you've escaped so far," returned the landlord, mysteriously; "but it ain't for long. No one who lives in Rushmere lives there *alone*. I can tell you the whole story if you like?"

"I have no desire to listen to any such folly," I replied, testily. "I am not superstitious, and do not believe in supernatural sights or sounds. If the people round about here are foolish enough to do so, I cannot help it; but I will not have the minds of my wife or family imbued with their nonsense."

"Very good, sir; I hope you may be able to say as much two months hence," said the man, civilly.

And so we parted.

I returned to Janie, and persuaded her he had told me that all the girls of that town had a strong objection to leave it, which was the reason they refused to take service in the country. I reminded her that Susan was quite competent to take charge of the whole flock until we returned to London; and it would be better after all to put up with a little inconvenience than to introduce a stranger to the nursery. So my wife, who was disappointed with the failure of her enterprise, fell in with my ideas, and we returned to Rushmere, determined to do as best we could with Susan only.

But I could not forget the landlord's earnestness, and, notwithstanding my incredulity, began to wish we were well out of Rushmere.

For a few days after Mary's departure we slept in peace; but then the question of the mysterious footsteps assumed a graver aspect, for my wife and I were roused from deep slumber one night by a loud knock upon the bedroom door, and springing up to answer it, I encountered, on the threshold, Dawson, pale with fright, and trembling in every limb.

"What do you mean by alarming your mistress in this way?" I inquired, angrily.

"I'm very sorry, sir," he replied, with chattering teeth, "but I thought it my duty to let you know. There's some one in the house tonight, sir. I can hear them whispering together at this moment; and so can you, if you will but listen."

I advanced at once to the banisters, and certainly heard what seemed to be the sound of distant voices engaged in altercation; and, light in hand, followed by Dawson, I dashed down the staircase without further ceremony, in hopes of trapping the intruders.

But all in vain. Though we entered every room in turn, not a soul was visible.

I came to the conclusion that the whole alarm was due to Dawson's cowardice.

"You contemptible fool, you are as chicken-hearted as a woman!" I said, contemptuously. "You hear the frogs croaking in the mere, or the wind blowing through the rushes, and you immediately conclude the house is full of thieves."

"I didn't say it was thieves," the man interposed, sullenly; but I took no notice of the muttered remark.

"If you are afraid to sleep downstairs by yourself," I continued, "say so; but don't come alarming your mistress again, in the middle of the night, for I won't allow it."

The man slunk back into his room, with a reiteration that he had not been mistaken; and I returned to bed, full of complaints at having been so unnecessarily roused.

"If this kind of thing goes on," I remarked to my wife, "I shall regret ever having set eyes on Rushmere. That a pack of silly maid-servants should see a robber in every bush is only to be expected; but how a sensible man like Dawson, and a woman of education like yourself, can permit your imagination to betray you into such foolish fears, is quite past my comprehension."

Yet, notwithstanding my dose of philosophy, poor Jane looked so pale upon the following morning, that I was fain to devise and carry into execution a little excursion into the neighbouring country before she regained her usual composure.

Some time passed without any further disturbance, and though upon several occasions I blamed myself for having brought a family, used to a populous city like London, to vegetate in so isolated a spot as Rushmere, I had almost forgotten the circumstances that had so much annoyed me.

We had now spent a month in our temporary home. The fields and hedgerows were bright with summer flowers, and the children passed most of their time tumbling amongst the new-mown hay. Janie had once more regained courage to sit by herself in the dusk, and to rest with tolerable security when she went to bed. I was rejoicing in the idea that all the folly that had marred the pleasure of our arrival at Rushmere had died a natural death, when it was vividly and painfully recalled to my mind by its actual recurrence.

Our second girl, a delicate little creature of about six years old, who, since the departure of her nurse, had slept in a cot in the same room as ourselves, woke me up in the middle of the night by exclaiming, in a frightened, plaintive voice, close to my ear,—

"Papa! papa! do you hear the footsteps? Some one is coming up the stairs!"

The tone was one of terror, and it roused my wife and myself instantly. The child was cold, and shaking all over with alarm, and I placed her by her mother's side before I left the room to ascertain if there was any truth in her assertion.

"Arthur, Arthur! I hear them as plainly as can be," exclaimed my wife, who was as terrified as the child. "They are on the second landing. There is no mistake about it this time."

I listened at the half-opened door, and was compelled to agree with her. From whatever cause they arose, footsteps were to be distinctly heard upon the staircase—sometimes advancing, and then retreating, as though afraid to venture farther; but, still, not to be mistaken for anything but the sound of feet.

With a muttered exclamation, I seized my revolver.

"Don't be alarmed," I said, hurriedly; "there is not the slightest occasion for it. And, whatever happens, do not venture on the landing. I shall be quite safe."

And without further preamble, only desirous to settle the business once for all, and give the intruders on my domains a sharp lesson on the laws of *meum* and *tuum*, I sprang down the staircase. I had not stayed to strike a light; but the moon was shining blandly in at the uncurtained passage window, and the landing was as bright as day. Yet I saw no one there. The thief (if thief it were) must have already taken the alarm, and descended to the lowest regions. I fancied I could detect the same footsteps, but more distinctly marked, walk by me with a hurried, frightened movement, accompanied by a quick, sobbing breath; and, as I paused to consider what such a mystery could indicate, a pair of heavily-shod feet rushed past me, or seemed to rush, upon the stairs. I heard an angry shout commingle with a faint cry of terror below the landing whereon I stood; then, the discharge of a firearm, followed by a low groan of pain—and all was still.

Dark and mysterious though it appeared to be, I did not dream of ascribing the circumstance to any but a natural cause. But there was evidently no time for hesitation, and in another moment I had flown down the stairs, and stood in the moonlighted hall. It was empty! Chairs, table, hatstand, stood in their accustomed places; the children's garden hats and my fishing tackle were strewn about; but of animated nature there was not a sign, of the recent scuffle not a trace!

All was quiet, calm, and undisturbed, and, as I gazed around in mute bewilderment, the perspiration stood in thick drops upon my brow and chin.

My first collected thought was for my wife and the best means by which to prevent her sharing the mystification and dread which I have no hesitation in confessing that I now experienced; but as I turned to remount the staircase, I caught sight of some dark mass lying at the further end of the passage, and going up to it, found to my surprise the body of Dawson, cold and insensible.

The explanation of the mystery was before me—so I immediately determined. The man, whom I knew to be replete with superstitious terror, imagining he heard the unaccountable noise of footsteps, had evidently supplied that which had reached my ear, and in his alarm at my approach had discharged his firearm at the supposed marauder. Pleasant for me if he had taken a better aim: So I thought as I dragged his unconscious body into his bedroom, and busied myself by restoring it to sensation.

As soon as he opened his eyes, and was sufficiently recovered to answer me, I asked,—

"What on earth made you discharge your gun, Dawson? I must take it out of your keeping, if you are so careless about using it."

"I didn't fire, sir."

"Nonsense! you don't know what you are talking about. I heard the shot distinctly as I came downstairs."

"I am only telling you the truth, sir. There is the fowling-piece in that corner. I have not drawn the trigger since you last loaded it."

I went up and examined the weapon. What Dawson had said was correct. It had not been used.

"Then who did fire?" I said, impatiently. "I could swear to having heard the report."

"And so could I, sir. It was that that knocked me over."

"What do you mean?"

"Oh, sir, pray take the mistress and the children away from this place as soon as possible. It's no robbers that go up and down these stairs of nights, sir. It's something much worse than that."

"Dawson, if you begin to talk such folly to me, I'll discharge you on the spot. I believe the whole lot of you have gone mad."

"But listen to my story, sir. I had gone to bed last night, as tired as possible, and thinking of nothing but getting a good long sleep. The first thing that roused me was some one trying the handle of my door. I lay and listened to it for some time before I was fully awake,

33

and then I thought maybe you wanted something out of my room, and was trying not to wake me; so I got out of bed and opened the door. But there was nobody there, though I fancied I heard some one breathing hard a few yards off from me. Well, I thought to myself, sir, this is all nonsense; so I came back to bed again, and lay down. But I couldn't sleep; for directly the door was closed, I heard the footsteps again, creep, creeping along the passage and the wall, as though some one was crouching and feeling his way as he went. Then the handle of the door began to creak and turn again—I see it turn, sir, with my own eyes, backwards and forwards, a dozen times in the moonlight; and then I heard a heavier step come stumbling downstairs, and there seemed to be a kind of scuffle. I couldn't stand it no longer, so I opened the door again; and then, as I'm a living Christian, sir, I heard a woman's voice say 'Father!' with a kind of sob, and as the sound was uttered there came a report from the first landing, and the sound of a fall, and a deep groan in the passage below. And it seemed to go right through me, and curdle my blood, and I fell all of a heap where you found me. And it's nothing natural, sir, you may take my word for it; and harm will come of your stopping in this house."

So saying, poor Dawson, who seemed in real earnest, fell back on his pillow with a heavy sigh.

"Dawson," I said, critically, "what did you eat for supper last night?"

"You're never going to put down what I've told you, sir, to supper. I took nothing but a little cold meat, upon my word. And I was as sensible, till that shot knocked me over, as you are this moment."

"Do you mean to tell me that you seriously believe the report of a firearm could have reached your ears without one having been discharged?"

"But didn't you say you heard it yourself, sir?"

This knocked me over, and I did not know what to answer him. In the attempt to allay what I considered his unreasonable fear, I had forgotten my own experience in the matter. And I knew that I had heard, or imagined I heard, a shot fired, and it would be very difficult for any one to persuade me I was mistaken. Still, though I held no belief in supernatural agencies, I was an earnest student of the philosophical and metaphysical school of Germany, and acquainted with all the revealed wonders of magnetism and animal electricity. It was impossible to say whether some such effect as I have described might not have been produced upon my brain by the reflection of the fear or fancy on that of my servant; and that as he had imagined the concussion of firearms, so I might have instantaneously received the impression of his mind. It was a nice question for argument, and not one to be thought over at that moment. All my present business lay in the effort to disabuse Dawson's mind of the reality of the shock it had received.

"I said I fancied I heard something like the report of a firearm; but as none had been fired, of course I must have been mistaken. Come, Dawson, I must go back, or Mrs. Delamere will wonder what has become of me. I conclude you are not such a coward as to be afraid to be left by yourself?"

"I never feared a man in my life, sir; but the strongest heart can't stand up against spirits."

"Spirits!" I exclaimed, angrily. "I wonder what on earth you will talk to me about next? Now, I'll tell you what it is, Dawson—if I hear anything more of this, or am disturbed again at night by your folly, I'll pack you back to London without a character. Do you understand me?"

"I understand you, sir," the man answered, humbly; and thereupon I left him to himself.

But, as I reascended the staircase, I was not satisfied either with my own half-formed solution of the mystery, or my servant's reception of my rebuke. He evidently would prefer dismissal to passing such another night. I could read the resolution in his face, although he had not expressed it in so many words. When I reached my wife's room, I was still more surprised. Janie and the child lay in a profound slumber. I had expected to find both of them in a state of anxious terror to learn the meaning of the noise that was going on below; but they had evidently heard nothing. This welcome fact, however, only tended to confirm me in the belief I had commenced to entertain, of the whole circumstance being due to some, perhaps yet undiscovered, phase of brain reading, and I fell to sleep, resolved to make a deeper study of the marvels propounded by Mesmer and Kant. When I awoke, with the bright June sun streaming in at the windows, I had naturally parted with much of the impression of the night before. It is hard to associate any gloomy or unnatural thoughts with the unlimited glory of the summer's sunshine, that streams into every nook and cranny, and leaves no shadows anywhere. On this particular morning it seemed to have cleared the cobwebs off all our brains. The child had forgotten all about the occurrence of the night. I was, as usual, ready to laugh away all ghostly fears and fancies; and even Janie seemed to regard the matter as one of little moment.

"What was the matter last night, Arthur, dear?" she asked, when the subject recurred to her memory. "I was so sleepy I couldn't keep awake till you came up again."

"Didn't you hear the fearful battle I held with the goblins in the hall?" I demanded, gaily, though I put the question with a purpose—"the shots that were exchanged between us, and the groans of the defeated, as they slunk away into their haunted coal-cellars and cupboards?"

"Arthur, what nonsense! Was there any noise?"

"Well, I frightened Dawson, and Dawson frightened me; and we squabbled over it for the best part of an hour. I thought our talking might have disturbed you."

"Indeed, it didn't, then. But don't mention it before Cissy, Arthur, even in fun, for she declares she heard some one walking about the room, and I want her to forget it."

I dropped the subject; but meeting Dawson as I was smoking my pipe in the garden that afternoon, I ventured to rally him on his fright of the night before, and to ask if he hadn't got over it by that time.

"No, sir; and I never shall," he replied, with a sort of shiver. "And I only hope you may come to be convinced of the truth of it before it's too late to prevent harm you may never cease to repent of."

There was so much respectful earnestness in the man's manner, that I could not resent his words nor laugh at them, as I had done before; and I passed by him in thoughtful silence.

What if there were more in all this than I had ever permitted myself to imagine? What if the assertions of my man-servant, the unaffected terror of my wife and child, the fears of my nurse, the evident shrinking of the old woman who had charge of the house, the opposition from the servants of the neighbouring town, combined with what I had heard myself, were not simple chimeras of the brain—fancies engendered by superstition or timidity or ignorance; but indications of a power beyond our control, the beginning and the end of which may alike remain unknown until all things are revealed? I had, with the majority of educated men, manfully resisted all temptation to believe in the possibility of spirits, of whatever grade, making themselves either seen or heard by mortal senses. I use the word "manfully," although I now believe it to be the height of manliness to refuse to discredit that which we cannot disprove, and to have sufficient humility to accept the belief that there are more things in heaven and earth than are dreamt of in our philosophy. But at that juncture I should have considered such a concession both childish and cowardly. Yet, there was sufficient doubt in my mind, notwithstanding the glorious June sun, respecting my adventure of the night before, that I resolved, whatever happened, that I would satisfy myself as to the value of the fears of those about me.

I could not keep my wife and children in a house where they might be liable at any moment to be frightened out of their seven senses, from whatever cause, without ascertaining the reason of it. Some reason there must be, either natural or otherwise; and I determined, if possible, to learn it that very night. I would not tell Dawson or anyone of my intention; but I would keep watch and ward in the old parlour on the ground floor, so as to be ready to rush out at a moment's notice, and seize any intruder who might attempt to disturb us. I still believed—I could not but believe—that the footsteps which so many of us had heard were due to some trickster, who wished to play upon our nerves in that lonely old house. I had heard of such things being done, purposely to keep visitors away; and I determined, whosoever it might be, whether our own servants or strangers, that they must take their chance of being shot down like any other robber.

According to my resolution, I said nothing to Janie, but tried to render the evening as cheerful and merry a one as possible.

I ordered strawberries and cream into the hay-field, and played with my troop of little ones there, until they were so tired they could hardly walk for the short distance that lay between them and their beds. As soon as they were dismissed, and we had returned to the house, I laid aside the newspapers that had arrived by that morning's post, and which I usually reserved for the evening's delectation, and taking my wife upon my knee, as in the dear old courting days, talked to her until she had forgotten everything but the topics on which we conversed, and had no time to brood upon the coming night, and the fears it usually engendered. Then, as a last duty, I carried to Dawson with my own hands a strong decoction of brandy and water, with which I had mixed something that I knew, under ordinary circumstances, must make him sleep till daylight.

"Drink this," I said to him. "From whatever cause, our nerves were both shaken last night, and a little stimulant will do neither of us harm."

"Thank you, sir," he replied, as he finished the tumbler at a draught; "I don't deny I'm glad to have it. I dread the thoughts of the night before us."

"Lock your door on the inside," I added as I left him, "and don't get up whether the handle moves or not. Then, at all events, you will feel secure till the morrow."

"Keys won't keep *them* out," muttered Dawson, as he entered his sleeping apartment.

But I would not notice the allusion, though I understood it.

I went up to bed with my wife as usual; and it was not until I saw she was sound asleep that, habited in my dressing-gown and slippers, I ventured to creep softly out of the room and take my way downstairs again.

It was then about twelve o'clock. The moonlight was as bright as it had been the night before, and made every object distinctly visible. From the loud snoring which proceeded from Dawson's room, I concluded that my opiate had taken due effect, and that I should be permitted to hold my vigil undisturbed. In one hand I grasped a loaded revolver, and in the other a huge knotted stick, so determined was I not to be taken by my tormentors at a disadvantage. I turned into the general sitting-room, which opened on the hall. All was as we had left it; and I ensconced myself on one of the large old-fashioned sofas, trusting to my curiosity to keep me awake.

It was weary waiting. I heard one and then two sound from the big clock in the hall; still there was no other noise to break the silence. I began to relapse into my first belief that the whole business was due to imagination. From this I passed to self-satisfaction; self-satisfaction induced inertion, and inertion brought on heavy sleep. How long I slept I do not know, but I had reason afterwards to think, not more than half-an-hour.

However, that point is immaterial. But what waked me—waked me so completely that in a moment all my faculties were as clear as daylight—was the sound of a hoarse breathing. I sat up on the sofa and rubbed my eyes.

The room was fully lighted by the moon. I could see into each corner. Nothing was visible. The sound I had heard must then have proceeded from outside the door, which was open; and I turned towards it, fully expecting to see Dawson enter in a somnambulistic condition, brought on by his dreams and my soporific.

But he did not appear. I rose and looked into the hall. It was empty, as before. Still the breathing continued, and (as I, with now fully-awakened faculties, discovered) proceeded from a corner of the parlour where stood an old-fashioned secretary and a chair. Not daring to believe my senses, I advanced to the spot and listened attentively. The sound continued, and was unmistakably palpable. The breathing was hoarse and laboured, like that of an old man who was suffering from bronchitis or asthma. Every now and then it was interrupted by a short, roupy cough. What I suffered under this mysterious influence I can hardly tell. Interest and curiosity got the better of my natural horror; but even then I could not but feel that there was something very awful in this strange contact of sound without sight. Presently my eyes were attracted by the chair, which was pushed, without any visible agency, towards the wall. Something rose—I could hear the action of the feet. Something moved—I could hear it approaching the spot where I stood motionless. Something brushed past me, almost roughly—I could feel the contact of a cloth garment against my dressing-gown, and heard the sound of coarsely shod feet leaving the room. My hair was almost standing on end with terror; but I was determined to follow the mystery to its utmost limits, whether my curiosity were satisfied by the attempt or not.

I rushed after the clumping feet into the hall; and I heard them slowly and painfully, and yet most distinctly, commence to toil up the staircase. But before they had reached the first landing, and just as I was about to follow in their wake, my attention was distracted by another sound, which appeared to be close at my elbow—the sound of which Dawson had complained the night before—that of a creeping step, and a stifled sobbing, as though a woman were feeling her way along the passage in the dark. I could discern the feeble touch as it felt along the wall, and then placed an uncertain hold upon the banisters—could hear the catching breath, which dared not rise into a cry, and detect the fear which caused the feet to advance and retreat, and advance a little way again, and then stop, as though dread of some unknown calamity overpowered every other feeling. Meanwhile, the clumping steps, that had died away in the distance, turned, and appeared to be coming downstairs again. The moon streamed brightly in at the landing window. Had a form been visible, it would have been as distinctly seen as by day. I experienced a sense of coming horror, and drew back in the shadow of the wall. As the heavy footsteps gained the lower landing, I heard a start—a scuffle—a faint cry of "Father!" and then a curse—the flash of a firearm—a groan—and I remember nothing more.

When I recovered my consciousness, I was lying on the flat of my back in the passage, as I had found poor Dawson the night before, and the morning sun was shining full upon my face. I sat up, rubbed my eyes, and tried to remember how I had come there. Surely the moon had looked in at that window when I saw it last. Then in a moment came back upon my mind all that I had heard whilst holding my vigil during the past night; and I sprang to my feet, to see if I could discover any traces of the tragedy which seemed to have been enacted in my very presence.

But it was in vain I searched the parlour, the passage, and the stairs. Everything remained in its usual place. Even the chair, which I could swear I saw pushed against the wall, was now standing primly before the secretary, and the door of the room was closed, as it usually was when we retired for the night. I slunk up to my dressing-room, anxious that my wife should not discover that I had never retired to rest; and having plunged my head and face into cold water, took my way across the sunlighted fields, to see if the fresh morning air might not be successful in clearing away the confusion with which my brain was oppressed. But I had made up my mind on one point, and that was that we would move out of Rushmere as soon as it was possible to do so. After a stroll of a couple of hours, I re-approached the house. The first person I encountered was the under nurse, Susan, who ran to meet me with a perturbed countenance.

"Oh, sir, I'm so thankful you've come back! Dawson has been looking for you for the last hour, for poor missus is so ill, and we don't know what on earth to do with her."

"Ill! In what way?" I demanded quickly.

"That's what we can't make out, sir. Miss Cissy came up crying to the nursery, the first thing this morning, to tell me that her mamma had tumbled out of bed, and wouldn't speak to her; and she couldn't find her papa. So I ran downstairs directly, sir; and there I found my mistress on the ground, quite insensible, and she hasn't moved a limb since."

"Good heavens!" I inwardly exclaimed, as I ran towards the house, "is it possible she can have been affected by the same cause?"

I found Janie, as the nurse had said, unconscious; and it was some time before my remedies had any effect on her. When she opened her eyes, and understood the condition she had been in, she was seized with such a fit of nervous terror that she could do nothing but cling to me, and entreat me to take her away from Rushmere.

Remembering my own experience, I readily promised her that she should not sleep another night in the house if she did not desire it. Soothed by my words, she gradually calmed down, and was at last able to relate the circumstance which had so terrified her.

"Did you sleep in my room last night, dear Arthur?" she asked, curiously.

"I did not. But since you awoke, you surely must have been aware of my absence."

"I know nothing, and remember nothing, except the awful horror that overpowered me. I had gone to sleep very happy last night, and none of my silly fears, as you have called them, ever entered my head. Indeed, I think I was in the midst of some pleasant dream, when I was awakened by the sound of a low sobbing by the bedside. Oh, such a strange, unearthly sobbing" (with a shudder). "I thought at first it must be poor little Cissy, who had been frightened again, and I put out my hand to her, saying,—

"'Don't be afraid, dear. I am here.'

"Directly, a hand was placed in mine—a cold, damp hand, with a deathlike, clayey feel about it that made me tremble. I knew at once it was not the child's hand, and I started up in bed, exclaiming,—

"'Who are you?'

"The room was quite dark, for I had pinned my shawl across the blind to keep the moon out of my eyes before I went to bed, and I could distinguish nothing. Yet still the cold, damp hand clung to mine, and seemed to strike the chill of death into my very bones. When I said, 'Who are you?' something replied to me. I cannot say it was a voice. It was more like some one hissing at me through closed teeth, but I could distinguish the name 'Emily.'

"I was so frightened, Arthur, I did not know what to do. I wrenched my hand away from the dead hand. You were not there, and I called out loudly. I would have leaped out of bed, but that I heard the creeping footsteps, accompanied by the sobbing breath, go round the room, crying, 'Father, father!'

"My blood seemed to curdle in my veins. I could not stir until it was gone. I heard it leave the room distinctly, although the door was never opened, and walk upon the landing as though to go downstairs. I was still sitting up in bed listening—listening—only waiting till the dreadful thing had quite gone away, to seek your presence, when I heard a heavy step clumping downstairs, then the report of a gun. I don't know *what* I thought. I remember nothing that followed; but I suppose I jumped out of bed with the intention of finding you, and fainted before I could reach the dressing-room. Oh, Arthur! what was it? What is it that haunts this house, and makes even the sunshine look as gloomy as night? Oh, take us away from it, or I am sure that something terrible will happen!"

"I *will* take you away from it, my dear. We will none of us sleep another night beneath its roof. What curse hangs over it, I cannot tell; but whether the strange sounds we have heard proceed from natural or supernatural causes, they alike render Rushmere no home for us. We will go to the hotel at —— this very day, Janie, and deliver up the keys of Rushmere again to Messrs. Quibble & Lye."

I then related to her my own experience, and that of Dawson; and though she trembled a little whilst listening to me, the idea of leaving the place before nightfall rendered the heavy fear less alarming than it would otherwise have been.

The servants, upon learning the resolution we had arrived at, were only too ready to help us to carry it out. Our personal possessions were packed in an incredibly short time, and we sat down that evening to a comfortable family dinner in the good old-fashioned inn at ——. As soon as the meal was concluded, and the children sent to bed, I said to my wife,—

"Janie, I am going to ring for the landlord, to see if he can throw any light on the cause of our experiences. I never told you that, when we came to this inn to try for a nurse to supply Mary's place, he informed me that nobody from his countryside would live at Rushmere; and asked me, in a manner which assured me he could have said more if he had chosen, if we had not heard anything whilst there. I laughed at the question then, but I do not feel so disposed to laugh at it now; and I am going to beg him to tell me all he may know. If nothing more, his story may form the stratum of a curious psychological study. Would you like to be present at our interview?"

"Oh yes, Arthur; I have quite recovered my nerves since I've lost sight of Rushmere, and I feel even curious to learn all I can upon the subject. That poor, sobbing voice that whispered 'Emily'—I shall not forget its sound to my dying day."

"Ring the bell, dear, and let us ask if the landlord is at leisure. To my mind, your experience of the details of this little tragedy appears the most interesting of all."

The landlord, a Mr. Browser, entered at once; and as soon as he heard my request, made himself completely at home with us.

"After the little rebuff you gave me t'other day, I shouldn't have ventured to say nothing, sir; but when I see your family getting out of the fly this afternoon, I says to Mrs. Browser, 'If that don't mean that they can't stand Rushmere another night, I'm a pumpkin.' And I suppose, now, it did mean it, sir?"

"You are quite right, Mr. Browser. The noises and voices about the house have become so intolerable, that it is quite impossible I can keep my family there. Still, I must tell you that, though I have been unable to account for the disturbances, I do not necessarily believe they are attributable to spirits. It is because I do not believe so that I wish to hear all you may be able to tell us, in order, if possible, to find a reason for what appears at present to be unreasonable."

"Well, sir, you shall hear, as you say, all we have to tell you, and then you can believe what you like. But it ain't I as can relate the story, sir. Mrs. Browser knows a deal more than I do; and with your leave, and that of this good lady here, I'll call her to give you the history of Rushmere."

At this information, we displayed an amount of interest that resulted in a hasty summons for Mrs. Browser. She was a fat, fair woman, of middle age, with ruddy cheeks, and a clear blue eye—not at all like a creature haunted by her own weak imagination, or who would be likely to mistake a shadow for a substance. Her appearance inspired me with confidence. I trusted that her relation might furnish me with some clue to the solution of the occurrences that had so confounded us. Safe out of the precincts of Rushmere, and with the lapse of twelve hours since the unaccountable swoon I had been seized with, my practical virtues were once more in the ascendant, and I was inclined to attribute our fright to anything but association with the marvellous.

"Be I to tell the story from the beginning, Browser?" was the first sentence that dropped from Mrs. Browser's lips.

Her lord and master nodded an affirmative, whereupon she began:—

"When the gentleman as built Rushmere for his own gratification, sir, died, the house let well enough. But the place proved lonely, and there was more than one attempt at robbery, and people grew tired of taking it. And above all, the girls of the village began to refuse to go to service there. Well, it had been standing empty for some months, when a gentleman and his wife came to look after it. Browser and I—we didn't own this inn at that time, you will understand, sir, but kept a general shop in the village, and were but poorly off altogether, although we had the post-office at our place, and did the best business thereabouts. The key of Rushmere used always to be left in our keeping, too, and our boy would go up to show folks over the house. Well, one damp autumn day—I mind the day as if 'twere yesterday, for Browser had been ailing sadly with the rheumatics for weeks past, and not able to lift his hand to his head—this gentleman and lady, who went by the name of Greenslade, came for the keys of Rushmere. I remember thinking Mr. Greenslade had a nasty, curious look about his eyes, and that his wife seemed a poor, brow-beaten creature; but that was no business of mine, and I sent Bill up with them to show the house. They took it, and entered on possession at once; and then came the difficulty about the servants. Not a soul would enter the place at first. Then a girl or two tried it, and came away when their month was up, saying the house was so lonesome, they couldn't sleep at nights, and the master was so queer-spoken and mannered, they were afraid of him."

"Don't forget to say what he was used to do at nights," here put in the landlord.

"La, Browser, I'm a-coming to it. Everything in its time. Well, sir, at last it came to this, that Mrs. Greenslade hadn't a creature to help her in anythink, and down she came to ask if I would go to them for a few days. I stared; for there was the shop to be tended, and the post-office looked after, and I hadn't been used to odd jobs like that. But my husband said that he could do all that was wanted in the business; and we were very hard drove just then, and the lady offered such liberal pay, he over-persuaded me to go, if only on trial. So I put my pride in my pocket, and went out charing. I hadn't been at Rushmere many days, sir, before I found something was very wrong there. Mr. Greenslade hardly ever spoke a word, but shut himself up in a room all day, or went mooning about the fields and common, where he couldn't meet a soul; and as for the poor lady, la! my heart bled for her, she seemed so wretched and broken-down and hopeless. I used often to say to her—

"'Now, ma'am, do let me cook you a bit of something nice, for you've eaten nothing since yesterday, and you'll bring yourself down to death's door at this rate.'

"And she'd answer,—

"'No, thank you, Mrs. Browser: I couldn't touch it. I feel sometimes as if I'd never care to eat or drink again.'

"And Mr. Greenslade, he was just as bad. They didn't eat enough to keep a well-grown child between the two of them."

"What-aged people were they?" I asked.

"Well, sir, I can hardly say; they weren't young nor yet old. Mr. Greenslade, he may have been about fifty, and his lady a year or two younger; but I never took much count of that. But the gentleman looked much the oldest of the two, by reason of a stoop in his shoulders and a constant cough that seemed to tear his chest to pieces. I've known him shut himself up in the parlour the whole night long, coughing away fit to keep the whole house awake. And his breathing, sir—you could hear it half a mile off."

"He was *assmatical*, poor man! that's where it was," interposed Mr. Browser.

"Well, I don't know what his complaint was called, Browser; but he made noise enough over it to wake the dead. But don't you go interrupting me no more after that fashion, or the gentleman and lady will never understand the half of my story, and I'm just coming to the cream of it."

"I assure you we are deeply interested in what you are telling us," I said, politely.

"It's very good of you to compliment me, sir, but I expect it will make matters clearer to you by-and-by. You're not the first tenants of Rushmere I've had to tell this tale to, I can tell you, and you won't be the last, either. One night, when I couldn't sleep for his nasty cough, and lay awake, wishing to goodness he'd go to bed like a Christian, I made sure I heard footsteps in the hall, a-creeping and a-creeping about like, as though some one was feeling their way round the house. 'It can't be the mistress,' I thought, 'and maybe it's robbers, as have little idea the master's shut up in the study.' So I opened the door quickly, but I could see nothing."

"Exactly my own experience," I exclaimed.

"Ah, sir, maybe; but they weren't the same footsteps, poor dear. I wish they had been, and she had the same power to tread now she had then. The hall was empty; but at the same time I heard the master groaning and cursing most awful in the parlour, and I went into my own room again, that I mightn't listen to his wicked oaths and words. I always hated and distrusted that man from the beginning.

The next day I mentioned I had heard footsteps, before 'em both, and the rage Mr. Greenslade put himself into was terrible. He said no robbers had better break into his house, or he'd shoot them dead as dogs. Afterwards his wife came to me and asked me what sort of footsteps they seemed; and when I told her, she cried upon my neck, and begged me if I ever heard a woman's step to say nothing of it to her husband.

"'A woman's step, ma'am,' I replied; 'why, what woman would dare break into a house?'

"But she only cried the more, and held her tongue.

"But that evening I heard their voices loud in the parlour, and there was a regular dispute between them.

"'If ever she could come, Henry,' Mrs. Greenslade said, 'promise me you won't speak to her unless you can say words of pity or of comfort.'

"'Pity!' he yelled, 'what pity has she had for me? If ever she or any emissary of hers should dare to set foot upon these premises, I shall treat them as house-breakers, and shoot them down like dogs.'

"'Oh no! Henry, no!' screamed the poor woman; 'think who she is. Think of her youth, her temptation, and forgive her.'

"'I'll never forgive her—I'll never own her,' the wretch answered loudly; 'but I'll treat her, or any of the cursed crew she associates with, as I would treat strangers who forced their way in to rob me by night. 'Twill be an evil day for them when they attempt to set foot in my house.'

"Well, sir, I must cut this long story short, or you and your good lady will never get to bed tonight.

"The conversation I had overheard made me feel very uncomfortable, and I was certain some great misfortune or disgrace had happened to the parties I was serving; but I didn't let it rest upon my mind, till a few nights after, when I was wakened up by the same sound of creeping footsteps along the passage. As I sat up in bed and listened to them, I heard the master leave the parlour and go upstairs. At the same moment something crouched beside my door, and tried to turn the handle; but it was locked, and wouldn't open. I felt very uneasy. I knew my door stood in the shadow, and that who-ever crouched there must have been hidden from Mr. Greenslade as he walked across the hall. Presently I heard his footsteps coming downstairs again, as though he had forgotten something. He used to wear such thick boots, sir, you might hear his step all over the house. His loaded gun always stood on the first landing; when he reached there he stopped, I suppose it was his bad angel made him stop. Anyway, there was a low cry of 'Father, father!'—a rush, the report of the gun, a low groan, and then all was still.

"La! sir, I trembled so in my bed, you might have seen it shake under me."

"I've seen it shake under you many a time," said Browser.

"Perhaps you would like to tell the lady and gentleman my exact weight, though I don't see what that's got to do with the story," replied his better half, majestically.

"I don't think I should ever have had the courage to leave my room, sir, unless I had heard my poor mistress fly down the staircase, with a loud scream. Then I got up, and joined her. Oh, it was an awful sight! There, stretched on the floorcloth, lay the dead body of a young girl; and my mistress had fainted dead away across her, and was covered with the blood that was pouring from a great hole in her forehead. On the landing stood my master, white as a sheet, and shaking like an aspen leaf.

"'So, this is your doing!' I cried, angrily. 'You're a nice man to have charge of a gun. Do you see what you've done? Killed a poor girl in mistake for a robber, and nearly killed your wife into the bargain. Who is this poor murdered young creature? Do you know her?'

"'Know her!' he repeated, with a groan. 'Woman, don't torture me with your questions. *She is my own daughter!*'

"He rushed upstairs as he spoke, and I was in a nice quandary, left alone with the two unconscious women. When my poor mistress woke up again, she wanted me to fetch a doctor; but it would have been of no use. She was past all human help.

"We carried the corpse upstairs between us, and laid it gently on the bed. I've often wondered since where the poor mother's strength came from, but it was lent her for the need. Then, sitting close to me for the remainder of the night, she told me her story—how the poor girl had led such an unhappy life with her harsh, ill-tempered father, that she had been tempted into a foolish marriage by the first lover that offered her affection and a peaceful home.

"'I always hoped she would come back to us,'" said Mrs. Greenslade, 'for her husband had deserted her, leaving her destitute; and yet, although she knew how to enter the house unobserved, I dreaded her doing so, because of her father's bitter enmity. Only last night, Mrs. Browser, I awoke from sleep, and fancied I heard a sobbing in my room. I whispered, "Who is there?" And a voice replied "Emily!" But I thought it was a dream. If I had known—if I had but known!'

"She lay so quiet and uncomplaining on my knee, only moving now and then, that she frightened me; and when the morning broke, I tried to shift her, and said,—

"'Hadn't I better go and see after the master, ma'am?'

"As I mentioned his name, I could see the shudder that ran through her frame, but she motioned me away with her hand.

"I went upstairs to a room Mr. Greenslade called his dressing-room, and where I guessed he'd gone; and you'll never believe, sir, the awful sight as met my eyes. I didn't get over it for a month—did I, Browser?"

"You haven't got over it to this day, I'm sometimes thinking, missus."

"That means I'm off my head; but if it wasn't for my head, I wonder where the business would go to. No, sir—if you'll believe me, when I entered the room, there was the old man dead as mutton, hanging from a beam in the ceiling. I gave one shriek, and down I fell."

"I don't wonder at it," cried Janie.

"Well, ma'am, when I came to again, all was confusion and misery. We had the perlice in, and the crowner's inquest, and there was such a fuss, you never see. Some of Mrs. Greenslade's friends came and fetched her away; but I heard she didn't live many months afterwards. As for myself, I was only too glad to get back to the shop and my old man, and the first words I said to him was,—

"'No more charing for me.'"

"And now, sir, if I may make so bold, what do you think of the story?" demanded the landlord. "Can you put this and that together now?"

"It is marvellous," I replied. "Your wife has simply repeated the scene which we have heard enacted a dozen times in Rushmere. The footsteps were a nightly occurrence."

"I heard the voice!" exclaimed Janie, "and it whispered '*Emily*.'"

"The handle of my servant's door was turned. The report of the gun was as distinct as possible."

"That is what everybody says as goes to Rushmere, sir. No one can abide the place since that awful murder was committed there," said Mrs. Browser.

"And can you account for it in any way, sir?" demanded her husband, slyly. "Do you think, now that you've heard the story, that the noises are mortal, or that it's the spirits of the dead that causes them?"

"I don't know what to think, Browser. There is a theory that no uttered sound is ever lost, but drifts as an eddying circle into space, until in course of time it must be heard again. Thus our evil words, too often accompanied by evil deeds, live for ever, to testify against us in eternity. It may be that the Universal Father ordains that some of His guilty children shall expurgate their crimes by re-acting them until they become sensible of their enormity; but this can be but a matter for speculation. This story leaves us, as such stories usually do, as perplexed as we were before. We cannot tell—we probably never *shall* tell—what irrefragable laws of the universe these mysterious circumstances fulfil; but we know that spirit and matter alike are in higher hands than ours; and, whilst nature cannot help trembling when brought in contact with the supernatural, we have no need to fear that it will ever be permitted to work us harm."

This little analysis was evidently too much for Mr. and Mrs. Browser, who, with a look of complete mystification on their countenances, rose from their seats, and wished us respectfully goodnight; leaving Janie and me to evolve what theories we chose from the true story of the Invisible Tenants of Rushmere.

THE FIRST COMER

B. M. Croker

Bithia Mary Croker, née Sheppard (c.1849–1920) was a prolific Irish writer of short stories and novels. Born in County Roscommon, Ireland, Bithia Sheppard took her husband's last name after their wedding in 1871. An officer of the British Army, he was posted abroad for long periods of time; Croker accompanied him, which led to her spending fourteen years in India and Burma. As a result, many of her novels are concerned with life in the Anglo-Indian colonial society, while others focus on an Irish context. Croker was also a notable writer of ghost stories, and her work has undergone crucial re-evaluation over the past decades.

"The First Comer" was originally published in a collection entitled *In the Kingdom of Kerry and other stories* (1896). Its narrator, Miss Janet MacTavish, tells the story of the noises she hears one night, as the coals are being raked in the kitchen. But what she sees once the match is struck does not correspond to what she hears; and she soon learns that these sounds have an ominous significance.

am an old maid, and am not the least ashamed of the circumstance. Pray, why should women not be allowed the benefit of the doubt like men, and be supposed to remain single from choice?

I can assure you that it is not from want of *offers* that I am Miss Janet MacTavish, spinster. I could tell—but no matter. It is not to set down a list of proposals that I have taken pen in hand, but to relate a very mysterious occurrence that happened in our house last spring.

My sister Matilda and I are a well-to-do couple of maiden ladies, having no poor relatives, and a comfortable private fortune. We keep four servants (all female), and occupy a large detached house in a fashionable part of Edinburgh, and the circle in which we move is most exclusive and genteel.

Matilda is a good deal older than I am (though we dress alike), and is somewhat of an invalid.

Our east winds are certainly trying, and last March she had a very sharp attack of bronchitis, brought on (between ourselves) by her own rash imprudence. Though I may not say this to her face, I may say it here.

She does not approve of fiction, though, goodness knows, what I am going to set down is not fiction, but fact; but any literary work in a gay paper cover (of course, I don't mean tracts), such as novels and magazines, is an abomination in her eyes, and "reading such-like trash" she considers sinful waste of time.

So, even if this falls into her hands by an odd chance, she will never read it, and I am quite safe in writing out everything that happened, as I dare not do if I thought that Mattie was coming after me and picking holes in every sentence.

Matilda is terribly particular about grammar and orthography, and reads over all my letters before I venture to close them.

Dear me, how I have wandered away from my point! I'm sure that no one will care to know that I am a little in awe of my elder, that she treats me sometimes as if I were still in my teens. But people may like to hear of the queer thing that happened to me, and I am really and truly coming to it at last.

Matilda was ill with bronchitis, very ill. Bella (that's our sewing-maid and general factotum, who has been with us twelve years this term) and I took it in turns to sit up with her at night. It happened to be my night, and I was sitting over the fire in a half-kind of doze, when Matilda woke up, and nothing would serve her but a cup of tea of all things, at two o'clock in the morning—the kitchen fire out, no hot water, and every one in the house in their beds, except myself.

I had some nice beef-tea in a little pan beside the hob, and I coaxed her hard to try some of that, but not a bit of it. Nothing would serve her but real tea, and I knew that once she had taken the notion in her head, I might just as well do her bidding first as last. So I opened the door and went out, thinking to take the small lamp, for, of course, all the gas was out, and turned off at the meter—as it ought to be in every decent house.

"You'll no do that!" she said, quite cross. Mattie speaks broad when she is vexed, and we had had a bit of argument about the tea. "You'll no do that, and leave me here without the light! Just go down and infuse me a cup of tea as quick as ever you can, for I know I'll be awfully the better of it!"

So there was just nothing else for it, and down I went in the pitch-black darkness, not liking the job at all.

It was not that I was afraid. Not I. But the notion of having to rake up and make the kitchen fire, and boil the kettle, was an errand that went rather against the grain, especially as I'm a terrible bad hand at lighting a fire.

I was thinking of this and wondering where were the wood and the matches to be found, when, just as I reached the head of the stairs, I was delighted to hear a great raking out of cinders below in the kitchen. Such a raking and poking and banging of coals and knocking about of the range I never did hear, and I said to myself—

"This is fine; it's washing morning" (we do our washing at home) "and later than I thought; and the servants are up, so it's all right;" and I ran down the kitchen stairs, quite inspirited like by the idea. As I passed the door of the servants' room (where cook and house-maid slept), Harris, that's the house-maid, called out—

"Who's that?"

I went to the door and said—

"It's I, Miss Janet. I want a cup of tea for Miss MacTavish."

In a moment Harris had thrown on some clothes and was out in the passage. She was always a quick, willing girl, and very obliging. She said (it was black dark, and I could not see her)—

"Never you mind, Miss Janet; I'll light the fire and boil up the kettle in no time."

"You need not do that," said I, "for there's some one at the fire already—cook, I suppose."

"Not me, ma'am" said a sleepy voice from the interior of the bedroom. "I'm in my bed."

"Then who can it be?" I asked, for the banging and raking had become still more tremendous, and the thunder of the poker was just awful!

"It must be Bella," said Harris, feeling her way to the kitchen door and pushing it open, followed by me.

We stood for full half a minute in the dark, whilst she felt about and groped for the matches, and still the noise continued.

"Bella," I said crossly, "what on earth—"

But at this instant the match was struck, and dimly lit up the kitchen. I strained my eyes into the darkness, whilst Harris composedly lit a candle. I looked, and looked, and looked again, but there was no one in the kitchen but ourselves.

I was just petrified, I can tell you, and I staggered against the dresser, and gaped at the now silent fireplace. The coals and cinders and ashes were exactly as they had gone out, not a bit disturbed; any one could see that they had never been stirred.

"In the name of goodness, Harris," I said in a whisper, "where is the person that was poking that fire? You heard them yourself!"

"I heard a noise, sure enough, Miss Janet," she said, not a bit daunted; "and if I was a body that believed in ghosts and such-like clavers, I'd say it was them," putting firewood in the grate as she spoke. "It's queer, certainly. Miss MacTavish will be wearying for her tea," she added. "I know well what it is to have a kind of longing for a good cup. Save us! what a cold air there is in this kitchen. I wonder where cook put the bellows."

Seeing that Harris was taking the matter so coolly, for very shame I was forced to do the like; so I did not say a word about my misgivings, nor the odd queer thrill I had felt as we stood in the pitch darkness and listened to the furious raking of the kitchen grate.

How icy cold the kitchen had been! just like a vault, and with the same damp, earthy smell!

I was in a mighty hurry to get back upstairs, believe me, and did all in my power to speed the fire and the kettle, and in due time we wended our way above, Harris bearing the tea on a tray, and walking last.

I left her to administer the refreshment, whilst I went into Bella's room, which was close by, candle in hand.

"You are awake, I see, Bella," I remarked, putting it down as I spoke (I felt that I must unbosom myself to some one, or never close an eye that night). "Tell me, did you hear a great raking of the kitchen fire just now?"

"Yes, miss, of course. Why, it woke me. I suppose you had occasion to go down for something, Miss Janet; but why did you not call me?"

"It was not I who woke you, Bella," I rejoined quickly. "I was on my way downstairs when I heard that noise below, and I thought it was cook or Harris, but when I got down Harris came out of the bedroom. Cook was in bed. Maggie, you know, is up above you, and we went into the kitchen, thinking it might be you or her, and lit a candle; but I give you my word of honour that, although the noise was really terrible till we struck a light, when we looked about us not a soul was to be seen!"

At this, Bella started up in bed, and became of a livid, chalky kind of colour.

"No one, Miss Janet?" she gasped out.

"Not a soul!" I replied solemnly.

"Then, oh!" she exclaimed, now jumping bodily out on the floor, and looking quite wild and distracted, "tell me, in Heaven's name, which of you went into the kitchen first, you or Harris?" She was so agitated, she seemed scarcely able to bring out the words, and her eyes rested upon mine with a strange, frightened look, that made me fancy she had taken temporary leave of her wits.

"Harris went first," I answered shortly.

"Thank Heaven for that!" she returned, now collapsing on the edge of her bed. "But poor Kate Harris is a dead woman!"

I stared hard at Bella, as well I might. Was she talking in her sleep? or was I dreaming?

"What do you mean, Bella Cameron?" I cried. "Are you gone crazy? Are you gone clean daft?"

"It was a warning," she replied, in a low and awe-struck voice. "We Highlanders understand the like well! It was a warning of death! Kate Harris's hour has come."

"If you are going to talk such wicked nonsense, Bella," I said, "I'm not going to stop to listen. Whatever you do, don't let Matilda hear you going on with such foolishness. The house would not hold her, and you know that well."

"All right, Miss Janet; you heard the commotion yourself—you will allow that; and you will see that the kitchen grate is never raked out for nothing. I only wish, from the bottom of my heart, that what I've told you may not come true; but, bad as it was, I'm thankful that you were not first in the kitchen."

A few more indignant expostulations on my part, and lamentations on Bella's, and then I went back to Matilda, and it being now near three o'clock, and she inclined to be drowsy, I lay down on the sofa, and got a couple of hours' sleep.

A day or two afterwards I was suddenly struck with a strange thrill of apprehension by noticing how very, very ill Kate Harris looked. I taxed her with not feeling well, and she admitted that she had not been herself, and could not say what ailed her. She had no actual pain, but she felt weak all over, and could scarcely drag herself about the house, "It would go off. She would not see a doctor—No, no, no!—It was only just a kind of cold feeling in her bones, and a sort of notion that a hand was gripping her throat. It was all fancy; and Dr. Henderson (our doctor) would make fine game of her if he saw her by way of being a patient. She would be all right in a day or two." Vain hope! In a day or two she was much worse. She was obliged to give in—to take to her bed. I sent for Dr. Henderson—indeed he called daily to visit Mattie—so I had only to pilot him down below to see Kate. He came out to me presently with a very grave face, and said—

"Has she any friends?"—pointing towards Kate's door with his thumb.

"Friends! To be sure," I answered. "She has a sister married to a tram conductor in Wickham Street."

"Send for her at once; and you had better have her moved. She can't last a week."

"Do you mean that she is going to die?" I gasped, clutching the balusters, for we were standing in the lower hall.

"I am sorry to say the case is hopeless. Nothing can save her, and the sooner she is with her own people the better."

I was, I need scarcely tell you, greatly shocked—terribly shocked—and presently, when I had recovered myself, I sent off, post-haste, for Kate's sister.

I went in to see her. She, poor creature, was all curiosity to know what the doctor had said.

"He would tell me nothing, miss," she observed smilingly. "Only felt my pulse, and tried my heart with a stethoscope, and my temperature with that queer little tube. I only feel a bit tired and out of breath; but you'll find I'll be all right in a day or two. I'm only sorry

I'm giving all this trouble, and Bella and Mary having to do my work. However, I'll be fit to clean the plate on Saturday."

Poor soul, little did she dream that her work in this world was done!

And I, as I sat beside the bed and looked at her always pale face, her now livid lips and hollow eyes, told myself that already I could see the hand of Death on her countenance. I was obliged to tell her sister what the doctor had said; and how she cried—and so did I—and who was to tell Kate? We wished to keep her with us undisturbed—Matilda and I—but her people would not hear of it, and so we had an ambulance from the hospital and sent her home.

She just lived a week, and, strange to say, she had always the greatest craving for me to be with her, for me to sit beside her, and read to her, and hold her hand. She showed far more anxiety for *my* company than for that of any of her own people.

Bella alone, of all the household, expressed no astonishment when she heard the doctor's startling verdict. Being in Mattie's room at the time, she merely looked over at me gravely, and significantly shook her head.

One evening Bella and I were with her; she had lain silent for a long time, and then she said to me quite suddenly—

"Miss Janet, you'll remember the morning you came downstairs looking for Miss MacTavish's tea?" (Did I not recollect it, only too well!) "Somehow, I got a queer kind of chill then; I felt it at the time, to the very marrow of my bones. I have never been warm since. It was just this day fortnight. I remember it well, because it was washing Monday."

That night Kate Harris died. She passed away, as it were, in her sleep, with her hand in mine. As she was with me on that mysterious night, so I was now with her.

Call me a superstitious old imbecile, or what you like, but I firmly believe that, had I entered that kitchen first, it would have been Janet MacTavish, and not Kate Harris, who was lying in her coffin!

Of course Matilda knows nothing of this, nor ever will. Perhaps—for she is one of your strong-minded folk—she would scout at the idea, and at me, for a daft, silly body, and try to explain it all away quite reasonable like. I only wish she could!

THE DAY OF MY DEATH

Elizabeth Stuart Phelps

The American essayist and writer Elizabeth Stuart Phelps (1844–1911) had many names during her lifetime. Born Mary Grey Phelps, she took her mother's name after losing her at the age of eight years old, and became known as Elizabeth Stuart Phelps in both her personal and her professional life. Most of her writings were published under this name, but she also used the pseudonym of Mary Adams, and signed some of her works as Elizabeth Stuart Phelps Ward after her marriage to the journalist and author Herbert Dickinson Ward in 1888. Phelps was an activist, and her writings often challenged women's traditional place in society, advocating financial independence and early feminist ideals through essays and fiction that focused on successful women outside of the home, in nonconventional professional careers. She was also known for her depiction of the afterlife in her so-called "spiritualist novels", which she wrote following the Civil War. Starting with *The Gates Ajar* (1868), the three works presented a positive vision of death, and a corporeal version of heaven as a welcoming and comforting place in which the deceased retained their physical shape and personality, and where families could be reunited, live together and participate in activities. In this, it departed from traditional Christian beliefs concerning the afterlife; and the novel proved extremely popular.

"The Day of my Death" was first published in *Harper's Magazine* in October 1868—that is to say, the same year as Phelps's first "spiritualist novel". It was then republished in her short story collection *Men, Women, and Ghosts* in 1869. In keeping with Phelps's interests, this tale engages with the afterlife and its connections to the living, and it features sceptical characters as well as a medium. They are confronted with possible messages from what the medium calls the "Influences" through the acoustic phenomenon of rapping, that is, audible blows struck on various surfaces of their home—which ultimately lead the protagonist to a ghostly rendezvous.

lison was sitting on a bandbox. She had generally been sitting on a bandbox for three weeks,—or on a bushel-basket, or a cupboard shelf, or a pile of old newspapers, or the baby's bath-tub. On one occasion it was the baby himself. She mistook him for the rag-bag.

If ever we had to move again,—which all the beneficence of the Penates forbid!—my wife should be locked into the parlour, and a cargo of Irishwomen turned loose about the premises to "attend to things." What it is that women find to do with themselves in this world I have never yet discovered. They are always "attending to things." Whatever that may mean, I have long ago received it as the only solution at my command of their superfluous wear and tear, and worry and flurry, and tears and nerves and headaches. A fellow may suggest Jane, and obtrude Bridget, and hire Peggy, and run in debt for Mehetable, and offer to take the baby on 'Change with him, but has he by a feather's weight lightened Madam's mysterious burden? My dear sir, don't presume to expect it. She has just as much to do as she ever had. In fact, she has a little more. "Strange, you don't appreciate it! Follow her about one day, and see for yourself!"

What I started to say, however, was that I thought it over often,—I mean about that invoice of Irishwomen,—coming home from the office at night, while we were moving out of Artichoke Street into Nemo's Avenue. It is not pleasant to find one's wife always sitting on a bandbox. I have seen her crawl to her feet when she heard me coming, and hold on by a chair, and try her poor little best to look as if she could stand twenty-four hours longer; she so disliked that I should find a "used-up looking house" under any circumstances. But I believe that was worse than the bandbox.

On this particular night she was too tired even to crawl. I found her all in a heap in the corner, two dusters and a wash-cloth in one blue-veined hand, and a broom in the other; an old corn-coloured silk handkerchief knotted over her hair,—her hair is black, and the effect was good,—and her little brown calico apron-string literally tied to the baby, who was shrieking at the end of his tether because he could just not reach the kitten and throw her into the fire. On Alison's lap, between a pile of shirts and two piles of magazines, lay a freshly opened letter. I noticed that she put it into her pocket before she dropped her dusters and stood up to lift her face for my kiss. She forgot about the apron-strings, and the baby tipped up the wrong way, and hung dangling in mid-air.

After we had taken tea,—that is to say, after we had drawn around the ironing-board put on two chairs in the front entry, made the cocoa in a tin dipper, stirred it with a fork, and cut the bread with a jack-knife,—after the baby was fairly off to bed in a champagne-basket, and Tip disposed of, his mother only knew where, we coaxed a consumptive fire into the parlour grate, and sat down before it in the carpetless, pictureless, curtainless, blank, bare, soapy room.

"Thank fortune, this is the last night of it!" I growled, putting my booted feet against the wall, (my slippers had gone over to the avenue in a water-pail that morning,) and tipping my chair back drearily,—my wife "*so* objects" to the habit!

Allis made no reply, but sat looking thoughtfully, and with a slightly perplexed and displeased air, into the sizzling wet wood that snapped and flared and smoked and hissed and blackened, and did everything but burn.

"I really don't know what to do about it," she broke silence at last.

"I'm inclined to think there's nothing better to do than to look at it."

"No; not the fire. O, I forgot,—I haven't shown it to you."

She drew from her pocket the letter which I had noticed in the afternoon, and laid it upon my knee. With my hands in my pockets—the room was too cold to take them out—I read:—

"DEAR COUSIN ALISON:—

"I have been so lonely since mother died, that my health, never of the strongest, as you know, has suffered seriously. My physician tells me that something is wrong with the periphrastic action, if you know what that is," [I suppose Miss Fellows meant the peristaltic action,] "and prophesies something dreadful, (I've forgotten whether it was to be in the head, or the heart, or the stomach,) if I cannot have change of air and scene this winter. I should dearly love to spend some time with you in your new home, (I fancy it will be drier than the old one,) if convenient to you. If inconvenient, don't hesitate to say so, of course. I hope to hear from you soon.

"In haste, your aff. cousin,
"GERTRUDE FELLOWS.

"P. S.—I shall of course insist upon being a boarder if I come.
"G. F."

"Hum-m. Insipid sort of letter."

"Exactly. That's Gertrude. No more flavour than a frozen pear. If she had one distinguishing peculiarity, good or bad, I believe I should like her better. But I'm sorry for the woman."

"Sorry enough to stand a winter of her?"

"If we hadn't just been through this moving! A new house and all,—nobody knows how the flues are yet, or whether we can heat a spare room. She hasn't had a home, though, since Cousin Dorothy died. But I was thinking about you, you see."

"O, she can't hurt me. She won't want the library, I suppose; nor my slippers, and the small bootjack. Let her come."

My wife sighed a small sigh of relief out from the depths of her hospitable heart, and the little matter was settled and dismissed as lightly as are most little matters out of which grow the great ones.

I had just begun to dream that night that Gertrude Fellows, in the shape of a large wilted pear, had walked in and sat down on a dessert plate, when Allis gave me a little pinch and woke me.

"My dear, Gertrude has *one* peculiarity. I never thought of it till this minute."

"Confound Gertrude's peculiarities! I want to go to sleep. Well, let's have it."

"Why, you see, she took up with some Spiritualistic notions after her mother's death; thought she held communications with her, and all that, Aunt Solomon says."

"Stuff and nonsense!"

"Of course. But, Fred, dear, I'm inclined to think she *must* have made her sewing-table walk into the front entry; and Aunt Solomon says the spirits rapped out the whole of Cousin Dorothy's history on the mantel-piece, behind those blue china vases,—you must have noticed them at the funeral,—and not a human hand within six feet."

"Alison Hotchkiss!" I said, waking thoroughly, and sitting up in bed to emphasise the opinion, "when I hear a spirit rap on *my* mantel-piece, and see *my* tables walk about the front entry, I'll believe that,—not before!"

"O, I know it! I'm not a Spiritualist, I'm sure, and nothing would tempt me to be. But still that sort of reasoning has a flaw in it, hasn't it, dear? The King of Siam, you know—"

I had heard of the King of Siam before, and I politely informed my wife that I did not care to hear of him again. Spiritualism was a system of refined jugglery. Just another phase of the same thing which brings the doves out of Mr. Hermann's empty hat. It might be entertaining if it had not become such an abominable imposition. There would always be nervous women and hypochondriac men enough for its dupes. I thanked Heaven that I was neither, and went to sleep.

Our new house was light and dry; the flues worked well, and the spare chamber heated admirably. The baby exchanged the champagne-basket for his dainty pink-curtained crib; Tip began to recover from the perpetual cold with which three weeks' sitting in draughts, and tumbling into water-pails, and playing in the sink, had sweetened his temper; Allis forsook her bandboxes for the crimson easy-chair (very becoming, that chair), or tripped about on her own rested feet; we returned to table-cloths, civilised life, and a fork apiece.

In short, nothing at all worth mentioning happened, till that one night,—I think it was our first Sunday,—when Allis waked me at twelve o'clock with the announcement that some one was knocking at the door. Supposing it to be Bridget with the baby,—croup, probably, or a fit,—I unlocked and unlatched it promptly. No one was there, however; and telling my wife, in no very gentle tone, if I remember correctly, that it would be a convenience, on such cold nights, if she could keep her dreams to herself, I shut the door distinctly and returned to my own.

In the morning I observed a little white circle about each of Allis's blue eyes, and after some urging she confessed to me that her sleep had been much broken by a singular disturbance in the room. I might laugh at her if I chose, and she had not meant to tell me, but somebody had rapped in that room all night long.

"On the door?"

"On the door, on the mantel, on the foot of the bed, on the head-board,—Fred, right on the head-board! I listened till I grew cold listening, but it rapped and it rapped, and by and by it was morning, and it stopped."

"Rats!" said I.

"Then rats have knuckles," said she.

"Mice!" said I, "wind! broken plaster! crickets! imagination! dreams! fancies! blind headache! nonsense! Next time wake me up, and fire pillows at me till I'm pleasant to you. Now I'll have a kiss and a cup of coffee. Any sugar in it?"

Tip fell down the cellar stairs that day, and the baby swallowed a needle and two gutta-percha buttons, which I had been waiting a week to have sewed on my vest, so that Alison had enough else to think about, and the little incident of the raps was forgotten. I believe it was not recalled by either of us till after Gertrude Fellows came.

It was on a Monday and in a drizzly storm that I brought her from the station. She was a thin, cold, phantom-like woman, shrouded in water-proofs and green *barège* veils. Why is it that homely women always wear green *barège* veils? She did not improve in appearance when her wraps were off, and she was seated by my parlour grate. Her large green eyes had no speculation in them. Her mouth—an honest mouth, that was one mercy—quivered and shrank when she was addressed suddenly, as if she felt herself to be a sort of foot-ball that the world was kicking about at pleasure,—your gentlest smile might prove a blow. She seldom spoke unless she were spoken to, and fell into long reveries, with her eyes on the window or the coals. She wore a horrible sort of ruff,—"illusion," I think Allis called it,—which, of all contrivances that she could have chosen to encircle her sallow neck, was exactly the most unbecoming. She was always knitting blue stockings,—I never discovered for what or whom; and she wore her lifeless hair in the shape of a small toy cartwheel, on the back of her head.

However, she brightened a little in the course of the first week, helped Alison about the baby, kept herself out of my way, read her Bible and the "Banner of Light" in about equal proportion, and became a mild, inoffensive, and, on the whole, not unpleasant addition to the family.

She had been in the house about ten days, I think, when Alison, with a disturbed face, confided to me that she had spent another wakeful night with those "rats" behind the head-board; I had been down with a sick-headache the day before, and she had not wakened me. I promised to set a trap and buy a cat before evening, and was closing the door upon the subject, being already rather late at the office, when the expression of Gertrude Fellows's face detained me.

"If I were you, I—wouldn't—really buy a very expensive trap, Mr. Hotchkiss. It will be a waste of money, I am afraid. I heard the noise that disturbed Cousin Alison"; and she sighed.

I shut the door with a snap, and begged her to be so good as to explain herself.

"It's of no use," she said, doggedly. "You know you won't believe me. But that makes no difference. They come all the same."

"*They?*" asked Allis, smiling. "Do you mean some of your spirits?"

The cold little woman flushed. "These are not *my* spirits. I know nothing about them. I did not mean to obtrude a subject so disagreeable to you while I was in your family; but I have seldom been in a house in which the Influences were so strong. I don't know what they mean, nor anything about them, but just that they're here. They wake me up, twitching my elbows, nearly every night."

"Wake you up *how?*"

"Twitching my elbows," she repeated, gravely.

I broke into a laugh, from which neither my politeness nor the woman's heightened colour could save me, bought the cat and ordered the rat-trap without delay.

That night, when Miss Fellows had "retired,"—she never "went to bed" in simple English like other people,—I stole softly out in my stockings and screwed a little brass button outside of her door. I had made a gimlet-hole for it in the morning when our guest was out shopping; it fitted into place without noise. Without noise I turned it, and went back to my own room.

"You suspect her, then?" said Alison.

"One is always justified in suspecting a Spiritualistic medium."

"I don't know about that," Allis said, decidedly. "It may have been mice that I heard last night, or the wind in a bottle, or any of the other proper and natural causes that explain away the ghost stories in the children's papers; but it was not Gertrude. Women know something about one another, my dear; and I tell you it was not Gertrude."

"I don't assert that it was; but with the bolt on Gertrude's door, the cat in the kitchen, and the rat-trap on the garret stairs, I am strongly inclined to anticipate a peaceful night. I will watch for a while, however, and you can go to sleep."

She went to sleep, and I watched. I lay till half past eleven with my eyes staring at the dark, wide awake and undisturbed and triumphant.

At half past eleven I must confess that I heard a singular sound.

Something whistled at the keyhole. It could not have been the wind, by the way, for there was no wind that night. Something else than the wind whistled in at the keyhole, sighed through into the room as much like a long-drawn breath as anything, and fell with a slight clink upon the floor.

I lighted my candle and got up. I searched the floor of the room, and opened the door and searched the entry. Nothing was visible or audible, and I went back to bed. For about ten minutes I heard no further disturbance, and was concluding myself to be in some undefined manner the victim of my own imagination, when there suddenly fell upon the head-board of my bed a blow so distinct and loud that I involuntarily sprang at the sound of it. It wakened Alison, and I had the satisfaction of hearing her sleepily inquire if I had caught that rat yet? By way of reply I relighted the candle, and gave the bed a shove which sent it rolling half across the room. I examined the wall; I examined the floor; I examined the head-board; I made Alison get up, so that I could shake the mattresses. Meantime the pounding had recommenced, in rapid, irregular blows, like the blows of a man's fist. The room adjoining ours was the nursery. I went in with my light. It was empty and silent. Bridget, with Tip and the baby, slept soundly in the large chamber across the hall. While I was searching the room my wife called loudly to me, and I ran back.

"It is on the mantel now," she said. "It struck the mantel just after you left; then the ceiling, three times, very loud; then the mantel again,—don't you hear?"

I heard distinctly; moreover, the mantel shook a little with the concussion. I took out the fire-board and looked up the chimney; I took out the register and looked down the furnace-pipe; I ransacked the garret and the halls; finally, I examined Miss Fellows's door,—it was locked as I had left it, upon the outside; and that locked door was the only means of egress from the room, unless the occupant fancied that of jumping from a two-story window upon a broad flight of stone steps.

I came thoughtfully back across the hall; an invisible trip-hammer appeared to hit the floor beside me at every step; I attempted to step aside from it, over it, away from it; but it followed me, pounding into my room.

"Wind?" suggested Allis. "Plaster cracking? Fancies? Dreams? Blind headaches?—I should like to know which you have decided upon?"

Quiet fell upon the house after that for an hour, and I was dropping into my first nap, when there came a light tap upon the door. Before I could reach it, it had grown into a thundering blow.

"Whatever it is I'll have it now!" I whispered, turned the latch without noise, and flung the door wide into the hall. It was silent, dark, and cold. A little glimmer of moonlight fell in and showed me the figures upon the carpet, outlined in a frosty bar. No hand or hammer, human or superhuman, was there.

Determined to investigate matters a little more thoroughly, I asked my wife to stand upon the inside of the doorway while I kept watch upon the outside. We took our position, and I closed the door between us. Instantly a series of furious blows struck the door; the sound was such as would be made by a stick of oaken wood. The solid door quivered under it.

"It's on your side!" said I.

"No, it's on yours!" said she.

"You're pounding yourself to fool me," cried I.

"You're pounding yourself to frighten me," sobbed she.

And we nearly had a quarrel. The sound continued with more or less intermission till daybreak. Allis fell asleep, but I spent the time in appropriate reflections.

Early in the morning I removed the button from Miss Fellows's door. She never knew anything about it.

I believe, however, that I had the fairness to exculpate her in my secret heart from any trickish connection with the disturbances of that night.

"Just keep quiet about this little affair," I said to my wife; "we shall come across an explanation in time, and may never have any more of it."

We kept quiet, and for five days so did "the spirits," as Miss Fellows was pleased to pronounce the trip-hammers.

The fifth day I came home early, as it chanced, from the office. Miss Fellows was writing letters in the parlour. Allis, upstairs, was sorting and putting away the weekly wash. I came into the room and sat down by the register to watch her. I always liked to watch her sitting there on the floor with the little heaps of linen and cotton stuff piled like blocks of snow about her, and her pink hands darting in and out of the uncertain sleeves that were just ready to give way in the gathers, trying the stockings' heels briskly, and testing the buttons with a little jerk.

She laid aside some under-clothing presently from the rest. "It will not be needed again this winter," she observed, "and had better go into the cedar closet." The garments, by the way, were marked and numbered in indelible ink. I heard her run over the figures in a busy, housekeeper's undertone, before carrying them into the closet. She locked the closet door, I think, for I remember the click of the key. If I remember accurately, I stepped into the hall after that to light a cigar, and Alison flitted to and fro with her clothes, dropping the baby's little white stockings every step or two, and anathematising them daintily—within orthodox bounds, of course. In about five minutes she called me; her voice was sharp and alarmed.

"Come quick! O Fred, look here! All those clothes that I locked into the cedar closet are out here on the bed!"

"My dear wife," I blandly observed, as I sauntered into the room, "too much of Gertrude Fellows hath made thee mad. Let *me* see the clothes!"

She pointed to the bed. Some white clothing lay upon it, folded in an ugly way, to represent a corpse, with crossed hands.

"Is it meant for a joke, Alison? You did it yourself, I suppose!"

"Fred! I have not touched it with the tip of my little finger!"

"Gertrude, then?"

"Gertrude is in the parlour writing."

So she was. I called her up. She looked surprised and troubled.

"It must have been Bridget," I proceeded, authoritatively, "or Tip."

"Bridget is out walking with Tip and the baby. Jane is in the kitchen making pies."

"At any rate these are not the clothes which you locked into the closet, however they came here."

"The very same, Fred. See, I noticed the numbers: 6 upon the stockings, 2 on the night-caps, and—"

"Give me the key," I interrupted.

She gave me the key. I went to the cedar closet and tried the door. It was locked. I unlocked it, and opened the drawer in which my wife assured me that the clothes had lain. Nothing was to be seen in it but the linen towel which neatly covered the bottom. I lifted it and shook it. The drawer was empty.

"Give me those clothes, if you please."

She brought them to me. I made in my diary a careful memorandum of their naming and numbering; placed the articles myself in the drawer,—an upper drawer, so that there could be no mistake in identifying it; locked the drawer, put the key in my pocket; locked the door of the closet, put the key in my pocket; locked the door of the room in which the closet was, and put that key in my pocket.

We sat down then in the hall, all of us; Allis and Gertrude to fill the mending-basket, I to smoke and consider. I saw Tip coming home with his nurse presently, and started to go down and let him in, when a faint scream from my wife arrested me. I ran past Miss Fellows, who was sitting on the stairs, and into my room. Allis, going in to put away Tip's little plaid aprons, had stopped, rather pale, upon the threshold. Upon the bed lay some clothing, folded, as before, in rude, hideous imitation of the dead.

I took each article in turn, and compared the name and number with the names and numbers in my diary. They were identical throughout. I took the clothes, took the three keys from my pocket, unlocked the "cedar-room" door, unlocked the closet door, unlocked the upper drawer, and looked in. The drawer was empty.

To say that from this time I failed to own—to myself, if not to other people—that some mysterious influence, inexplicable by common or scientific causes, was at work in my house, would be to accuse myself of more obstinacy than even I am capable of. I propounded theory after theory, and gave it up. I arrived at conclusion upon conclusion, and threw them aside. Finally, I held my peace, ceased to talk of "rats," kept my mind in a state of passive vacancy, and narrowly and quietly watched the progress of affairs.

From the date of that escapade with the underclothes confusion reigned in our corner of Nemo's Avenue. That night neither my wife nor myself closed an eye, the house so resounded and re-echoed with the blows of unseen hammers, fists, logs, and knuckles.

Miss Fellows, too, was pale with her vigils, looked troubled, and proposed going home. This I peremptorily vetoed, determined if the woman had any connection, honest or otherwise, with the mystery, to ferret it out.

The following day, just after dinner, I was writing in the library, when a child's cry of fright and pain startled me. It seemed to come from the little yard behind the house, and I hurried thither to behold a singular sight. There was one apple-tree in the yard,—an old, stunted, crooked thing; and in that tree I found my son and heir, Tip, tied fast with a small stout rope. "Tied" does not express it; he was gagged, manacled, twisted, contorted, wound about, crossed and recrossed, held without a chance of motion, scarcely of breath.

"You never tied yourself up here, child?" I asked, as I cut the knots.

The question certainly was unnecessary. No juggler could have bound himself in such a fashion; scarcely, then, a four-years' child. To my continued, clear, and gentle inquiries, the boy replied, persistently and consistently, that nobody tied him there,—"not Cousin Gertrude, nor Bridget, nor the baby, nor mamma, nor Jane, nor papa, nor the black kitty"; he was "just tooken up all at once into the tree, and that was all there was about it." He "s'posed it must have been God, or something like that, did it."

Poor Tip had a hard time of it. Two days after that, while his mother and I sat discussing the incident, and the child was at play upon the floor, he suddenly threw himself at full length, writhing with pain, and begging to "have them pulled out quick!"

"Have *what* pulled out?" exclaimed his terrified mother. She took the child into her lap, and found that he was stuck over from head to foot with large white pins.

"We haven't so many large pins in all the house," she said as soon as he was relieved.

As she spoke the words thirty or forty *small* pins pierced the boy. Where they came from no one could see. How they came there no one knew. We looked, and there they were, and Tip was crying and writhing as before.

For the remainder of that winter we had scarcely a day of quiet. The rumour that "the Hotchkisses had rented a haunted house" leaked out and spread abroad. The frightened servants gave warning, and other frightened servants took their place, to leave in turn. My wife was her own cook and nursery-maid a quarter of the time. The disturbances varied in character with every week, assuming, as time went on, an importunity which, had we not quietly settled it in our own minds "not to be beaten by a noise," would have driven us from the house.

Night after night the mysterious fingers rapped at the windows, the doors, the floors, the walls. Day after day uncomfortable tricks were sprung upon us by invisible agencies. We became used to the noises, so that we slept through them easily; but many of the phenomena were so strikingly unpleasant, and so singularly unsuited to the ordinary conditions of human happiness and housekeeping, that we scarcely became—as one of our excellent deacons had a cheerful habit of exhorting us to become—"resigned."

Upon one occasion we had invited a small and select number of friends to dine. It was to be rather a *recherché* affair for Nemo's Avenue, and my wife had spared no painstaking to suit herself with her table. We had had a comparatively quiet house the night before, so that our cook, who had been with us three days, consented to remain till our guests had been provided for. The soup was good, the pigeons better, the bread was *not* sour, and Allis looked hopeful, and inclined to trust Providence for the gravies and dessert.

It was just as I had begun to carve the beef that I observed my wife suddenly pale, and a telegram from her eyes turned mine in the direction of General Popgun, who sat at her right hand. My sensations "can better be imagined than described" when I saw General Popgun's fork, untouched by any human hand, dancing a jig on his plate. He grasped it and laid it firmly down. As soon as he released his hold it leaped from the table.

"Really—aw—very singular phenomena," began the General; "very singular! I was not prepared to credit the extraordinary accounts of spiritual manifestations in this house, but—aw—Well, I must say—"

Instantly it was Pandemonium at that dinner-table. Dr. Jump's knife, Mrs. M'Ready's plate, and Colonel Hope's tumbler sprang from their places. The pigeons flew from the platter, the caster rattled and rolled, the salt-cellars bounded to and fro, and the gravies, moved by some invisible disturber, spattered all over Mrs. Elias P. Critique's *moire antique*.

Mortified and angered beyond endurance, I for the first time addressed the spirits,—wrenched for the moment into a profound belief that they must be spirits indeed.

"Whatever you are, and wherever you are," I shouted, bringing my hand down hard upon the table, "go out of this room and let us alone!"

The only reply was a furious mazourka of all the dishes on the table. A gentleman present, who had, as he afterward told us, studied the subject of spiritualism somewhat, very sceptically and with unsatisfactory results, observed the performance keenly, and suggested that I should try a gentler method of appeal. Whatever the agent was,—and what it was he had not yet discovered,—he had noticed repeatedly that the quiet modes of meeting it were most effective.

Rather amused, I spoke more softly, addressing the caster, and intimating in my blandest manner that I and my guests would feel under obligations if we could have the room to ourselves till after we had dined. The disturbance gradually ceased, and we had no more of it that day.

A morning or two after Alison chanced to leave half a dozen tea-spoons upon the sideboard in the breakfast-room; they were of solid silver, and quite thick. She was going to rub them herself, I believe, and went into the china-closet, which opens from the room, for the silver-soap. The breakfast-room was left vacant, and it was vacant when she returned to it, and she insists, with a quiet conviction which it is hardly reasonable to doubt, that no human being did or could have entered the room without her knowledge. When she came back to the sideboard every one of those spoons lay there *bent double*. She showed them to me when I came home at noon. Had they been pewter toys they could not have been more completely twisted out of shape than they were. I took them without any remarks (I began to feel as if this mystery *were* assuming uncomfortable proportions), put them away, just as I found them, into a small cupboard in the wall of the breakfast-room, locked the cupboard door with the only key in the house which fitted it, put the key in my inner vest pocket, and meditatively ate my dinner.

About half an hour afterward a neighbour dropped in to groan over the weather and see the baby, and Allis chanced to mention the incident of the spoons.

"Really, Mrs. Hotchkiss!" said the lady, with a slight smile, and that indefinite, quickly smothered change of eye which signifies, "I don't believe a word of it!" "Are you sure that there is not a mistake somewhere, or a little mental hallucination? The story is very entertaining, but—I beg your pardon—I should be interested to see those spoons."

"Your curiosity shall be gratified, madam," I said, a little testily; and taking the key from my pocket, I led her to the cupboard and unlocked the door. I found those spoons as straight, smooth, and fair as ever spoons had been;—not a dent, not a wrinkle, not a bend nor untrue line could we discover anywhere upon them.

"*Oh!*" said our visitor, significantly.

That lady, be it recorded, then and thenceforward spared no pains to found and strengthen throughout Nemo's Avenue the theory that "the Hotchkisses were getting up all that spiritual nonsense to force their landlord into lower rents. And such respectable people too! It did seem a pity, didn't it?"

One night I was alone in the library. It was late; about half-past eleven, I think. The brightest gas jet was lighted, so that I could see to every portion of the small room. The door was shut. There was no furniture but the book-cases, my table, and chair; no sliding doors or concealed corners; no nook or cranny in which any human creature could lurk unseen by me; and I say that I was alone.

I had been writing to a confidential friend a somewhat minute account of the disturbances in my house, which were now of about six weeks' duration. I had begged him to come and observe them for himself, and help me out with a solution,—I myself was at a loss for a reasonable one. There certainly seemed to be evidence of superhuman agency; but I was hardly ready yet to commit myself thoroughly to that view of the matter, and—

In the middle of that sentence I laid down my pen. A consciousness, sudden and distinct, came to me that I was not alone in that bright little silent room. Yet to mortal eyes alone I was. I pushed away my writing and looked about. The warm air was empty of outline; the curtains were undisturbed; the little recess under the library table held nothing but my own feet; there was no sound but the ordinary rap-rapping on the floor, to which I had by this time become so accustomed that often it passed unnoticed. I rose and examined the room thoroughly, until quite satisfied that I was its only visible occupant; then sat down again. The rappings had meantime become loud and impatient.

I had learned that very week from Miss Fellows the spiritual alphabet with which she was in the habit of "communicating" with her dead mother. I had never asked her, nor had she proposed, to use it herself for my benefit. I had meant to try all other means of investigation before resorting to it. Now, however, being alone, and being perplexed and annoyed by my sense of having invisible company, I turned and spelled out upon the table, so many raps to a letter till the question was complete:—

"*What do you want of me?*"

Instantly the answer came rapping back:—

"*Stretch down your hand.*"

I put my fingers under the table, and I felt, as indubitably as I ever felt a touch in my life, the grasp of a *warm, human hand*.

I added to the broken paragraph in the letter to my friend a brief account of the occurrence, and reiterated my entreaties that he would come at his earliest convenience to my house. He was an Episcopal clergyman, by the way, and I considered that his testimony would uphold my fast-sinking character for veracity among my townspeople. I began to have an impression that this dilemma in which I found myself was a pretty serious one for a man of peaceable disposition and honest intentions to be in.

About this time I undertook to come to a little better understanding with Miss Fellows. I took her away alone, and having tried my best not to frighten the life out of her by my grave face, asked her seriously and kindly to tell me whether she supposed herself to have any connection with the phenomena in my house. To my surprise she answered promptly that she thought she had. I repressed a whistle, and "asked for information."

"The presence of a medium renders easy what would otherwise be impossible," she replied. "I offered to go away, Mr. Hotchkiss, in the beginning." I assured her that I had no desire to have her go away at present, and begged her to proceed.

"The Influences in the house are strong, as I have said before," she continued, looking through me and beyond me with her vacant eyes. "Something is wrong. They are never at rest. I hear them. I feel them. I see them. They go up and down the stairs with me. I find them in my room. I see them gliding about. I see them standing now, with their hands almost upon your shoulders."

I confess to a kind of chill that crept down my backbone at these words, and to having turned my head and stared hard at the bookcases behind me.

"But they—I mean something—rapped one night before you came," I suggested.

"Yes, and they might rap after I was gone. The simple noises are not uncommon in places where there are no better means of communication. The extreme methods of expression, such as you have witnessed this winter, are, I doubt not, practicable only when the system of a medium is accessible. They write all sorts of messages for you. You would ridicule them. I do not repeat them. You and Cousin Alison do not see, hear, feel as I do. We are differently made. There are lying spirits and true, good spirits and bad. Sometimes the bad deceive and distress me, but sometimes—sometimes my mother comes."

She lowered her voice reverently, and I was fain to hush the laugh upon my lips. Whatever the thing might prove to be to me, it was daily comfort to the nervous, unstrung, lonely woman, whom to suspect of trickery I began to think was worse than stupidity.

From the time of my midnight experience in the library I allowed myself to look a little further into the subject of "communications." Miss Fellows wrote them out at my request whenever they "came" to her. Writers on Spiritualism have described the process so frequently, that it is unnecessary for me to dwell upon it at length. The influences took her unawares in the usual manner. In the usual manner her arm—to all appearance the passive instrument of some unseen, powerful agency—jerked and glided over the paper, writing in curious, scrawly characters, never in her own neat little old-fashioned hand, messages of which, on coming out from the "trance" state, she would have no memory; of many of which at any time she could have had no comprehension. These messages assumed every variety of character from the tragic to the ridiculous, and a large portion of them had no point whatever.

One day Benjamin West desired to give me lessons in oil-painting. The next, my brother Joseph, dead now for ten years, asked forgiveness for his share in a little quarrel of ours which had embittered a portion of his last days,—of which, by the way, I am confident that Miss Fellows knew nothing. At one time I received a long discourse enlightening me on the arrangement of the "spheres" in the disembodied state of existence. At another, Alison's dead grandfather pathetically reminded her of a certain Sunday afternoon at "meetin'" long ago, when the child Allis hooked his wig off in the long prayer with a bent pin and a piece of fish-line.

One day we were saddened by the confused wail of a lost spirit, who represented his agonies as greater than soul could bear, and clamoured for relief. Moved to pity, I inquired:—

"What can we do for you?"

Unseen knuckles rapped back the touching answer:—

"Give me a piece of squash pie!"

I remarked to Miss Fellows that I supposed this to be a modern and improved version of the ancient drop of water which was to cool the tongue of Dives. She replied that it was the work of a mischievous spirit who had nothing better to do; they would not infrequently take in that way the reply from the lips of another. I am not sure whether we are to have lips in the spiritual world, but I think that was her expression.

Through all the nonsense and confusion of these daily messages, however, one restless, indefinite purpose ran; a struggle for expression that we could not grasp; a sense of something unperformed which was tormenting somebody.

One week we had been so much more than usually annoyed by the dancing of tables, shaking of doors, and breaking of crockery, that I lost all patience, and at length vehemently dared our unseen tormentors to show themselves.

"Who and what are you?" I cried, "destroying the peace of my family in this unendurable fashion. If you are mortal man, I will meet you as mortal man. Whatever you are, in the name of all fairness, let me see you!"

"If you see me it will be death to you," tapped the Invisible.

"Then let it be death to me! Come on! When shall I have the pleasure of an interview?"

"Tomorrow night at six o'clock."

"Tomorrow at six, then, be it."

And tomorrow at six it was. Allis had a headache, and was lying down upstairs. Miss Fellows and I were with her, busy with cologne and tea, and one thing and another. I had, in fact, forgotten all about my superhuman appointment, when, just as the clock struck six, a low cry from Miss Fellows arrested my attention.

"I see it!" she said.

"See what?"

"A tall man wrapped in a sheet."

"Your eyes are the only ones so favoured, it happens," I said, with a superior smile. But while I spoke Allis started from the pillows with a look of fear.

"*I* see it, Fred!" she exclaimed, under her breath.

"Women's imagination!" for I saw nothing.

I saw nothing for a moment; then I must depose and say that I *did* see a tall figure, covered from head to foot with a sheet, standing still in the middle of the room. I sprang upon it with raised arm; my wife states that I was within a foot of it when the sheet dropped. It dropped at my feet,—nothing but a sheet. I picked it up and shook it; only a sheet.

"It is one of those old linen ones of grandmother's," said Allis, examining it; there are only six, marked in pink with the boar's-head in the corner. It came from the blue chest up garret. They have not been taken out for years."

I took the sheet back to the blue chest myself,—having first observed the number, as I had done before with the underclothes; and locked it in. I came back to my room and sat down by Allis. In about three minutes we saw the figure standing still as before, in the middle of the room. As before, I sprang at it, and as before the drapery dropped, and there was nothing there. I picked up the sheet and turned to the numbered corner. It was the same that I had locked into the blue chest.

Miss Fellows was inclined to fear that I had really endangered my life by this ghostly rendezvous. I can testify, however, that it was by no means "death to me," nor did I experience any ill effects from the event.

My friend, the clergyman, made me the desired visit in January. For a week after his arrival, as if my tormentors were bent on convincing my almost only friend that I was a fool or a juggler, we had no disturbance at all beyond the ordinary rappings. These, the reverend gentleman confessed were of a singular nature, but expressed a polite desire to see some of the extraordinary manifestations of which I had written him.

But one day he had risen with some formality to usher a formal caller to the door, when, to his slight amazement and my secret delight, his chair—an easy-chair of good proportions—deliberately jumped up and hopped after him across the room. From this period the mystery "manifested" itself to his heart's content. Not only did the rocking-chairs, and the cane-seat chairs, and the round-backed chairs, and Tip's little chairs, and the affghans chase him about, and the heavy *tête-à-tête* in the corner evince symptoms of agitation at his approach, but the piano trundled a solemn minuet at him; the heavy walnut centre-table rose halfway to the ceiling under his eyes; the marble-topped stand, on which he sat to keep it still, lifted itself and him a foot from the ground; his coffee-cup spilled over when he tried to drink, shaken by an unseen elbow; his dressing-cases disappeared from his bureau and hid themselves, none knew how or when, in his closets and under his bed; mysterious uncanny figures, dressed in his best clothes and stuffed with straw, stood in his room when he came to it at night; his candlesticks walked, untouched by hands, from the mantel into space keys and chains fell from the air at his feet; and raw turnips dropped from the solid ceiling into his soup-plate.

"Well, Garth," said I one day, confidentially, "how are things? Begin to have a 'realising sense' of it, eh?"

"Let me think awhile," he answered.

I left him to his reflections, and devoted my attention for a day or two to Gertrude Fellows. She seemed to have been of late receiving less ridiculous, less indefinite, and more important messages from her spiritual acquaintances. The burden of them was directed at me. They were sometimes confused, but never contradictory, and the sum of them, as I cast it up, was this:—

A former occupant of the house, one Mr. Timothy Jabbers, had been in early life connected in the dry-goods business with my wife's father, and had, unknown to any but himself, defrauded his partner of a considerable sum for a young swindler,—some five hundred dollars, I think. This fact, kept in the knowledge only of God and the guilty man, had been his agony since his death. In the parlance of Spiritualism, he could never "purify" his soul and rise to a higher "sphere" till he had made restitution,—though to that part of the communications I paid little attention. This money my wife, as her father's sole living heir, was entitled to, and this money I was desired to claim for her from Mr. Jabbers's estate, then in the hands of some wealthy nephews.

I made some inquiries which led to the discovery that there had been a Mr. Timothy Jabbers once the occupant of our house, that he had at one period been in business with my wife's father, that he was now many years dead, and that his nephews in New York were his heirs. We never attempted to bring any claim upon them, for three reasons: in the first place, because we knew we shouldn't get the money; in the second, because such a procedure would give so palpable an "object" in people's eyes for the disturbances at the house that we should, in all probability, lose the entire confidence of the entire non-spiritualistic community; thirdly, because I thought it problematical whether any constable of ordinary size and courage could be found who would undertake to summon the witness to testify in the county court at Atkinsville.

I mention the matter only because, on the theories of Spiritualism, it appeared to give some point and occasion to the phenomena, and their infesting that particular house.

Whether poor Mr. Timothy Jabbers felt relieved by having unburdened himself of his confession, I cannot state; but after he found that I paid some attention to his messages, he gradually ceased to express himself through turnips and cold keys; the rappings grew less violent and frequent, and finally ceased altogether. Shortly after that Miss Fellows went home.

Garth and I talked matters over the day after she left. He had brought his "thinking" to a close, whittled his opinions to a point, and was quite ready to stick them into their places for my benefit, and leave them there, as George Garth left all his opinions, immovable as the everlasting hills.

"How much had she to do with it now,—the Fellows?"

"Precisely what she said she had, no more. She was a medium, but not a juggler."

"No trickery about the affair, then?"

"No trickery could have sent that turnip into my soup-plate, or that candlestick walking into the air. There *is* a great deal of trickery mixed with such phenomena. The next case you come across may be a regular cheat; but you will find it out,—you'll find it out. You've had three months to find this out, and you couldn't. Whatever may be the explanation of the mystery, the man who can witness what you and I have witnessed, and pronounce it the trick of that incapable, washed-out woman, is either a liar or a fool.

"You understand yourself and your wife, and you've tested your servants faithfully; so we're somewhat narrowed in our conclusions."

"Well, then, what's the matter?"

I was, I confess, a little startled by the vehemence with which my friend brought his clerical fist down upon the table, and exclaimed:—

"The Devil?"

"Dear me, Garth, don't swear; you in search of a pulpit just at this time, too!"

"I tell you I never spoke more solemnly. I cannot, in the face of facts, ascribe all these phenomena to human agency. Something that comes we know not whence, and goes we know not whither, is at work there in the dark. I am driven to grant to it an extra-human power. Yet when that flabby Miss Fellows, in the trance state, undertakes to bring me messages from my dead wife, and when she attempts to recall the most tender memories of our life together, I cannot,"—he paused and turned his face a little away,—"it would be pleasant to think I had a word from Mary, but I cannot think she is there. I don't believe good spirits concern themselves with this thing. It has in its fair developments too much nonsense and too much positive sin; read a few numbers of the 'Banner,' or attend a convention or two, if you want to be convinced of that. If they're not good spirits they're bad ones, that's all. I've dipped into the subject in various ways since I have been here; consulted the mediums, talked with the prophets; I'm convinced that there is no dependence to be placed on the thing. You never learn anything from it that it is worth while to learn; above all, you never can trust its *prophecies*. It is evil,—*evil* at the root; and except by physicians and scientific men it had better be let alone. They may yet throw light on it; you and I cannot. I propose for myself to drop it henceforth. In fact, it looks too much toward

95

putting one's self on terms of intimacy with the Prince of the Powers of the Air to please me."

"You're rather positive, considering the difficulty of the subject," I said.

The truth is, and it may be about time to own to it, that the three months' siege against the mystery, which I had held so pertinaciously that winter, had driven me to broad terms of capitulation. I assented to most of my friend's conclusions, but where he stopped I began a race for further light. I understood then, for the first time, the peculiar charm which I had often seen work so fatally with dabblers in Spiritualism. The fascination of the thing was upon me. I ransacked the papers for advertisements of mediums. I went from city to city at their mysterious calls. I held *séances* in my parlour, and frightened my wife with messages—some of them ghastly enough—from her dead relatives. I ran the usual gauntlet of strange seers in strange places, who told me my name, the names of all my friends, dead or alive, my secret aspirations and peculiar characteristics, my past history and future prospects.

For a long time they never made a failure. Absolute strangers told me facts about myself which not even my own wife knew: whether they spoke with the tongues of devils, or whether, by some unknown laws of magnetism, they simply *read my thoughts*, I am not even now prepared to say. I think if they had made a miss I should have been spared some suffering. Their communications had sometimes a ridiculous aimlessness, and occasionally a subtle deviltry coated about with religion, like a pill with sugar, but often a significant and fearful accuracy.

Once, I remember, they foretold an indefinite calamity to be brought upon me before sunset on the following Saturday. Before sunset on that Saturday I lost a thousand dollars in mining stock which had stood in all Eastern eyes as solid as its own gold. At another time I was warned by a medium in Philadelphia that my wife, then visiting in Boston, was taken suddenly ill. I had left her in perfect health; but feeling nevertheless uneasy, I took the night train and went directly to her. I found her in the agonies of a severe attack of pleurisy, just preparing to send a telegram to me.

"Their prophecies are unreliable, notwithstanding coincidences," wrote George Garth. "Let them alone, Fred, I beg of you. You will regret it if you don't."

"Once let me be fairly taken in and cheated to my face," I made reply, "and I may compress my views to your platform. Until then I must gang my own gait."

I now come to the remarkable portion of my story,—at least it seems to me the remarkable portion under my present conditions of vision.

In August of the summer following Miss Fellows's visit, and the manifestations in my house at Atkinsville, I was startled one pleasant morning, while sitting in the office of a medium in Washington Street in Boston, by a singularly unpleasant communication.

"The second day of next May," wrote the medium,—she wrote with the forefinger of one hand upon the palm of the other,—"the second of May, at one o'clock in the afternoon, you will be summoned into a spiritual state of existence."

"I suppose, in good English, that means I'm going to die," I replied, carelessly. "Would you be so good as to write it with a pen and ink, that there may be no mistake?"

She wrote it distinctly: "The second of May, at one o'clock in the afternoon."

I pocketed the slip of paper for further use, and sat reflecting.

"How do you know it?"

"*I* don't know it. I am told."

"Who tells you?"

"Jerusha Babcock and George Washington." Jerusha Babcock was the name of my maternal grandmother. What could the woman know of my maternal grandmother? It did not occur to me, I believe, to wonder what occasion George Washington could find to concern himself about my dying or my living. There stood the uncanny Jerusha as pledge that my informant knew what she was talking about. I left the office with an uneasy sinking at the heart. There was a coffin-store near by, and I remember the peculiar interest with which I studied the quilting of the satin lining, and the peculiar crawling sensation which crept to my fingers' ends.

Determined not to be unnecessarily alarmed, I spent the next three weeks in testing the communication. I visited one more medium in Boston, two in New York, one in New Haven, one in Philadelphia, and one in a little out-of-the-way Connecticut village, where I spent a night, and did not know a soul. None of these people, I am confident, had ever seen my face or heard my name before.

It was a circumstance calculated at least to arrest attention, that these seven people, each unknown to the others, and without concert with the others, repeated the ugly message which had sought me out through the happy summer morning in Washington Street. There was no hesitation, no doubt, no contradiction. I could not trip them or cross-question them out of it. Unerring, assured, and consistent, the fiat went forth:—

"On the second of May, at one o'clock in the afternoon, you will pass out of the body."

I would not have believed them if I could have helped myself. I sighed for the calm days when I had laughed at medium and prophet, and sneered at ghost and rapping. I took lodgings in Philadelphia, locked my doors, and paced my rooms all day and half the night, tortured by my thoughts, and consulting books of medicine to discover what evidence I could by any possibility give of unsuspected disease. I was at that time absolutely well and strong; absolutely well and strong I was forced to confess myself, after having waded through Latin adjectives and anatomical illustrations enough to make a ghost of Hercules. I devoted two days to researches in genealogical pathology, and was rewarded for my pains by discovering myself to be the possessor of one great-aunt who had died of heart disease at the advanced age of two months.

Heart disease, then, I settled upon. The alternative was accident. "Which will it be?" I asked in vain. Upon this point my friends the mediums held a delicate reserve. "The Influences were confusing, and they were not prepared to state with exactness."

"Why *don't* you come home?" my wife wrote in distress and perplexity. "You promised to come ten days ago, and they need you at the office, and I need you more than anybody."

"I need you more than anybody!" When the little clinging needs of three weeks grew into the great want of a lifetime,—O, how could I tell *her* what was coming?

I did not tell her. When I had hurried home, when she came bounding through the hall to meet me, when she held up her face, half laughing, half crying, and flushing and paling, to mine,—the poor little face that by and by would never watch and glow at my coming,—I could not tell her.

When the children were in bed and we were alone after tea, she climbed gravely up into my lap from the little cricket on which she had been sitting, and put her hands upon my shoulders.

"You're sober, Fred, and pale. Something ails you, you know, and you are going to tell me all about it."

Her pretty, mischievous face swam suddenly before my eyes. I kissed it, put her gently down as I would a child, and went away alone till I felt more like myself.

The winter set in gloomily enough. It may have been the snow-storms, of which we had an average of one every other day, or it may have been the storm in my own heart which I was weathering alone.

Whether to believe those people, or whether to laugh at their predictions; whether to tell my wife, or whether to continue silent,— these questions tormented me through many wakeful nights and dreary days. My fears were in nowise allayed by a letter which I received one day in January from Gertrude Fellows.

"Why don't you read it aloud? What's the news?" asked Alison. But at one glance over the opening page I folded the sheet, and did not read it till I could lock myself into the library alone. The letter ran:—

"I have been much disturbed lately on your behalf. My mother and your brother Joseph appear to me nearly every day, and charge me with some message to you which I cannot distinctly grasp. It seems to be clear, however, as far as this: that some calamity is to befall you in the spring,—in May, I should say. It seems to me to be of the nature of death. I do not learn that you can avoid it, but that they desire you to be prepared for it."

After receiving this last warning, certain uncomfortable words filed through my brain for days together:—

"Set thine house in order, for thou shalt surely die."

"Never knew you read your Bible so much in all your life," said Alison, with a pretty pout. "You'll grow so good that I can't begin to keep up with you. When I try to read my polyglot, the baby comes and bites the corners, and squeals till I put it away and take him up."

As the winter wore away I arrived at this conclusion: If I were in fact destined to death in the spring, my wife could not help herself or me by the knowledge of it. If events proved that I was deluded in the dread, and I had shared it with her, she would have had all her pain and anxiety to no purpose. In either case I would insure her happiness for these few months; they might be her last happy months. At any rate happiness was a good thing, and she could not have too much of it. To say that I myself felt no uneasiness as to the event would be affectation. The old sword of Damocles hung over me. The hair might hold, but it was a hair.

As the winter passed,—it seemed to me as if winter had never passed so rapidly before,—I found it natural to watch my health with the most careful scrutiny; to avoid improper food and undue excitement; to refrain from long and perilous journeys; to consider whether each new cook who entered the family might have occasion to poison me. It was an anomaly which I did not observe at the time, that while in my heart of hearts I expected to breathe my last upon the second of May, I yet cherished a distinct plan of fighting, cheating, persuading, or overmatching death.

I closed a large speculation on which I had been inclined, in the summer, to "fly"; Alison could never manage petroleum ventures. I wound up my business in a safe and systematic manner. "Hotchkiss must mean to retire," people said. I revised my will, and held one long and necessary conversation with my wife about her future, should "anything happen" to me. She listened and planned without tears or exclamations; but after we had finished the talk, she crept up to me with a quiet, puzzled sadness that I could not bear.

"You are growing so blue lately, Fred! Why, what can 'happen' to you? I don't believe God can mean to leave me here after you are gone; I don't believe he *can* mean to!"

All through the sweet spring days we were much together. I went late to the office. I came home early. I spent the beautiful twilights at home. I followed her about the house. I made her read to me, sing to me, sit by me, touch me with her little, soft hand. I watched her face till the sight choked me. How soon before she would know? How soon?

"I feel as if we'd just been married over again," she said one day, pinching my cheek with a low laugh. "You are so good! I'd no idea you cared so much about me. By and by, when you get over this lazy fit and go about as you used to, I shall feel so deserted,—you've no idea! I believe I will order a little widow's cap, and put it on, and wear it about,—now, what do you mean by getting up and stalking off to look out of the window? Fine prospect you must have, with the curtain down!"

It is, to say the least, an uncomfortable state of affairs when you find yourself drawing within a fortnight of the day on which seven people have assured you that, you are going to shuffle off this mortal coil. It is not agreeable to have no more idea than the dead (probably not as much) of the manner in which your demise is to be effected. It is not in all respects a cheerful mode of existence to dress yourself in the morning with the reflection that you are never to half wear out your new mottled coat, and that this striped neck-tie will be laid away by and by in a little box, and cried over by your wife; to hear your immediate acquaintances all wondering why you *don't* get yourself some new boots; to know that your partner has been heard to say that you are growing dull at trade; to find the children complaining that you have engaged no rooms yet at the beach; to look into their upturned eyes and wonder how long it is going to take for them to forget you; to go out after breakfast and wonder how many more times you will shut that front door; to come home in the perfumed dusk and see the faces pressed against the window to watch for you, and feel warm arms about your neck, and wonder how soon they will shrink from the chill of you; to feel the glow of the budding world, and think how blossom and fruit will crimson and drop without you, and wonder how the blossom and fruit of life can slip from you in the time of violet smells and orioles.

April, spattered with showers and dripped upon a little with ineffectual suns, slid restlessly away from me, and I locked my office door one night, reflecting that it was the night of the first of May, and that tomorrow was the second.

I spent the evening alone with my wife. I have spent more agreeable evenings. She came and nestled at my feet, and the fire-light painted her cheeks and hair, and her eyes followed me, and her hand was in mine; but I have spent more agreeable evenings.

The morning of the second broke without a cloud. Blue jays flashed past my window; a bed of royal pansies opened to the sun, and the smell of the fresh, moist earth came up where Tip was digging in his little garden.

"Not feeling exactly like work today," as I told my wife, I did not go to the office. I asked her to come into the library and sit with me. I remember that she had a pudding to bake, and refused at first; then yielded, laughing, and said that I must go without my dessert. I thought it highly probable that I *should* go without my dessert.

I remember precisely how pretty she was that morning. She wore a bright dress,—blue, I think,—and a white crocus in her hair; she had a dainty white apron tied on, "to cook in," she said, and her pink nails were powdered with flour. Her eyes laughed and twinkled at me. I remember thinking how young she looked, and how unready for suffering. I remember that she brought the baby in after a while, and that Tip came all muddy from the garden, dragging his tiny hoe over the carpet; that the window was open, and that, while we all sat there together, a little brown bird brought some twine and built a nest on an apple-bough just in sight.

I find it difficult to explain the anxiety which I felt, as the morning wore on, that dinner should be punctually upon the table at half past twelve. But I now understand perfectly, as I did not once, the old philosophy: "Let us eat and drink, for tomorrow we die."

It was ironing-day, and our dinners were apt to be late upon ironing-days. I concluded that, if the soup were punctual, and not too hot, I could leave myself ten or perhaps fifteen unoccupied minutes before one o'clock. It strikes me as curious now, the gravity with which this thought underran the fever and pain and dread of the morning.

I fell to reading my hymn-book about twelve o'clock, and when Alison called me to dinner I did not remember to consult my watch.

The soup was good, though hot. A grim Epicurean stolidity crept over me as I sat down before it. A man had better make the most of his last chance at mock-turtle. Fifteen minutes were enough to die in.

I am confident that I ate more rapidly than is consistent with con-summate elegance. I remember that Tip imitated me, and that Allis opened her eyes at me. I recall distinctly the fact that I had passed my plate a second time.

I had passed my plate a second time, I say, and had just raised the spoon to my lips, when it fell from my palsied hand; for the little bronze clock upon the mantel struck one.

I sat with drawn breath and glared at it; at the relentless silver hands; at the fierce, and, as it seemed to me, *living* face of the Time on its top, who stooped and swung his scythe at me.

"I would like a very *big* white potato," said Tip, breaking the solemn silence.

You may or may not believe me, but it is a fact that that is all which happened.

I slowly turned my head. I resumed my spoon.

"The kitchen clock is nearly half an hour too slow," observed Alison. "I told Jane that you would have it fixed this week."

I finished my soup in silence.

It may interest the reader to learn that up to the date of this article "I still live."

II.

"I had heard the words with painful distinctness":
Perceiving ghostly voices

THE SPIRIT'S WHISPER

Unknown

"The Spirit's Whisper" was first published in the Christmas issue of *Tinsleys' Magazine* in 1868, which bore the title "A Stable for Nightmares" and contained several tales. Its authorship is uncertain: originally published anonymously, it was then reprinted in a collection entitled *A Stable for Nightmares, or Weird Tales* in 1896. The title page of the latter announces "by J. Sheridan Le Fanu" (whose name features too on the front boards) but also enigmatically lists "Sir Charles Young, Bart., and others", and the individual stories of the collection are not credited more precisely. Consequently, "The Spirit's Whisper" has often been attributed to Sheridan Le Fanu, for several reasons. Sir Charles Lawrence Young, 7th Baronet (1839–1887) was primarily known as a dramatist writing comedic plays; and the mention of "others" without precise names rather suggests uncertainty on the part of the editor of the collection. But Joseph Thomas Sheridan Le Fanu (1814–1873), an Irish writer of Gothic and horror tales, seemed a more suitable candidate. Best known for *Uncle Silas* (1864), a locked-room mystery novel, and *Carmilla* (1872), a defining work of vampire fiction, Le Fanu was also a prolific and admired writer of ghost stories. His first ghost tale, "The Ghost and the Bone-Setter", was published in 1838 in the *Dublin University Magazine*, of which he later became editor and proprietor. His writing relied on subtlety and tone, with an often-implicit supernatural presence; and the tone of the story "The Spirit's Whisper" has been argued as consistent with much of Le Fanu's work. Considering all these factors, it is little wonder, then, to find that "The Spirit's Whisper" has often been attributed to him. However, there is no concrete evidence to prove Le Fanu's authorship, and many other stories in *Spectral Sounds* and other Tales of the Weird volumes have proven that writers of other genres often wrote ghost tales and terrifying tales, too. For now, the mystery remains.

This story is perfectly suited to open the second section of this anthology, dedicated to ghostly voices. The narrator, John, begins his story by dramatically exclaiming "Yes, I have been haunted!"—and leaves it up to whoever hears his tale to decide whether he suffered from delusions when he heard and followed the eponymous spirit's whispers.

es, I have been haunted!—haunted so fearfully that for some little time I thought myself insane. I was no raving maniac; I mixed in society as heretofore, although perhaps a trifle more grave and taciturn than usual; I pursued my daily avocations; I employed myself even on literary work. To all appearance I was one of the sanest of the sane; and yet all the while I considered myself the victim of such strange delusions that, in my own mind, I fancied my senses—and one sense in particular—so far erratic and beyond my own control that I was, in real truth, a madman. How far I was then insane it must be for others, who hear my story, to decide. My hallucinations have long since left me, and, at all events, I am now as sane as I suppose most men are.

My first attack came on one afternoon when, being in a listless and an idle mood, I had risen from my work and was amusing myself with speculating at my window on the different personages who were passing before me. At that time I occupied apartments in the Brompton Road. Perhaps, there is no thoroughfare in London where the ordinary passengers are of so varied a description or high life and low life mingle in so perpetual a medley. South-Kensington carriages there jostle costermongers' carts; the clerk in the public office, returning to his suburban dwelling, brushes the labourer coming from his work on the never-ending modern constructions in the new district; and the ladies of some of the surrounding squares flaunt the most gigantic of *chignons*, and the most exuberant of motley dresses, before the envying eyes of the ragged girls with their vegetable-baskets.

There was, as usual, plenty of material for observation and conjecture in the passengers, and their characters or destinations, from my window on that day. Yet I was not in the right cue for the thorough enjoyment of my favourite amusement. I was in a rather melancholy mood. Somehow or other, I don't know why, my memory had reverted to a pretty woman whom I had not seen for many years. She had been my first love, and I had loved her with a boyish passion as genuine as it was intense. I thought my heart would have broken, and I certainly talked seriously of dying, when she formed an attachment to an ill-conditioned, handsome young adventurer, and, on her family objecting to such an alliance, eloped with him. I had never seen the fellow, against whom, however, I cherished a hatred almost as intense as my passion for the infatuated girl who had flown from her home for his sake. We had heard of her being on the Continent with her husband, and learned that the man's shifty life had eventually taken him to the East. For some years nothing more had been heard of the poor girl. It was a melancholy history, and its memory ill-disposed me for amusement.

A sigh was probably just escaping my lips with the half-articulated words, "Poor Julia!" when my eyes fell on a man passing before my window. There was nothing particularly striking about him. He was tall, with fine features, and a long, fair beard, contrasting somewhat with his bronzed complexion. I had seen many of our officers on their return from the Crimea look much the same. Still, the man's aspect gave me a shuddering feeling, I didn't know why. At the same moment, a whispering, low voice uttered aloud in my ear the words, "It is he!" I turned, startled; there was no one near me, no one in the room. There was no fancy in the sound; I had heard the words with painful distinctness. I ran to the door, opened it—not a sound on the staircase, not a sound in the whole house—nothing but the hum from the street. I came back and sat down. It was no use reasoning with myself; I had the ineffaceable conviction that I had heard the voice. Then first the idea crossed my mind that I might be the victim of hallucinations. Yes, it must have been so, for now I recalled to mind that the voice had been that of my poor lost Julia; and at the moment I heard it I had been dreaming of her. I questioned my own state of health. I was well; at least I had been so, I felt fully assured, up to that moment. Now a feeling of chilliness and numbness and faintness had crept over me, a cold sweat was on my forehead. I tried to shake off this feeling by bringing back my thoughts to some other subject. But, involuntarily as it were, I again uttered the words, "Poor Julia!" aloud. At the same time a deep and heavy sigh, almost a groan, was distinctly audible close by me. I sprang up; I was alone—quite alone. It was, once more, an hallucination.

By degrees the first painful impression wore away. Some days had passed, and I had begun to forget my singular delusion. When my thoughts did revert to it, the recollection was dismissed as that of a ridiculous fancy. One afternoon I was in the Strand, coming from Charing Cross, when I was once more overcome by that peculiar feeling of cold and numbness which I had before experienced. The day was warm and bright and genial, and yet I positively shivered. I had scarce time to interrogate my own strange sensations when a man went by me rapidly. How was it that I recognised him at once as the individual who had only passed my window so casually on that morning of the hallucination? I don't know, and yet I was aware that this man was the tall, fair passer-by of the Brompton Road. At the same moment the voice I had previously heard whispered distinctly in my ear the words, "Follow him!" I stood stupefied. The usual throngs of indifferent persons were hurrying past me in that crowded thoroughfare, but I felt convinced that not one of these had spoken to me. I remained transfixed for a moment. I was bent on a matter of business in the contrary direction to the individual I had remarked, and so, although with unsteady step, I endeavoured to proceed on my way. Again that voice said, still more emphatically, in my ear, "Follow him!" I stopped involuntarily. And a third time, "Follow him!" I told myself that the sound was a delusion, a cheat of my senses, and yet I could not resist the spell. I turned to follow. Quickening my pace, I soon came up with the tall, fair man, and, unremarked by him, I followed him. Whither was this foolish pursuit to lead me? It was useless to ask myself the question—I was impelled to follow.

I was not destined to go very far, however. Before long the object of my absurd chase entered a well-known insurance-office. I stopped at the door of the establishment. I had no business within, why should I continue to follow? Had I not already been making a sad fool of myself by my ridiculous conduct? These were my thoughts as I stood heated by my quick walk. Yes, heated; and yet, once more, came the sudden chill. Once more that same low but now awful voice spoke in my ear: "Go in!" it said. I endeavoured to resist the spell, and yet I felt that resistance was in vain. Fortunately, as it seemed to me, the thought crossed my mind that an old acquaintance was a clerk in that same insurance-office. I had not seen the fellow for a great length of time, and I never had been very intimate with him. But here was a pretext; and so I went in and inquired for Clement Stanley. My acquaintance came forward. He was very busy, he said. I invented, on the spur of the moment, some excuse of the most frivolous and absurd nature, as far as I can recollect, for my intrusion.

"By the way," I said, as I turned to take my leave, although my question was "by the way" of nothing at all, "who was that tall, fair man who just now entered the office?"

"Oh, that fellow?" was the indifferent reply; "a Captain Campbell, or Canton, or some such name; I forget what. He is gone in before the board—insured his wife's life—and she is dead; comes for a settlement, I suppose."

There was nothing more to be gained, and so I left the office. As soon as I came without into the scorching sunlight, again the same feeling of cold, again the same voice—"Wait!" Was I going mad? More and more the conviction forced itself upon me that I was decidedly a monomaniac already. I felt my pulse. It was agitated and yet not feverish. I was determined not to give way to this absurd hallucination; and yet, so far was I out of my senses, that my will was no longer my own. Resolved as I was to go, I listened to the dictates of that voice and waited. What was it to me that this Campbell or Canton had insured his wife's life, that she was dead, and that he wanted a settlement of his claim? Obviously nothing; and I yet waited.

So strong was the spell on me that I had no longer any count of time. I had no consciousness whether the period was long or short that I stood there near the door, heedless of all the throng that passed, gazing on vacancy. The fiercest of policemen might have told me to "move on," and I should not have stirred, spite of all the terrors of the "station." The individual came forth. He paid no heed to me. Why should he? What was I to him? This time I needed no warning voice to bid me follow. I was a madman, and I could not resist the impulses of my madness. It was thus, at least I reasoned with myself. I followed into Regent Street. The object of my insensate observation lingered, and looked around as if in expectation. Presently a fine-looking woman, somewhat extravagantly dressed, and obviously not a lady, advanced toward him on the pavement. At the sight of her he quickened his step, and joined her rapidly. I shuddered again, but this time a sort of dread was mingled with that strange shivering. I knew what was coming, and it came. Again that voice in my ear. "Look and remember!" it said. I passed the man and woman as they stopped at their first meeting.

"Is all right, George?" said the female.

"All right, my girl," was the reply.

I looked. An evil smile, as if of wicked triumph, was on the man's face, I thought. And on the woman's? I looked at her, and I remembered. I could not be mistaken. Spite of her change in manner, dress, and appearance, it was Mary Simms. This woman some years before, when she was still very young, had been a sort of humble companion to my mother. A simple-minded, honest girl, we thought her. Sometimes I had fancied that she had paid me, in a sly way, a marked attention. I had been foolish enough to be flattered by her stealthy glances and her sighs. But I had treated these little demonstrations of partiality as due only to a silly girlish fancy. Mary Simms, however, had come to grief in our household. She had been detected in the abstraction of sundry jewels and petty ornaments. The morning after discovery she had left the house, and we had heard of her no more. As these recollections passed rapidly through my mind I looked behind me. The couple had turned back. I turned to follow again; and spite of carriages and cabs, and shouts and oaths of drivers, I took the middle of the street in order to pass the man and woman at a little distance unobserved. No; I was not mistaken. The woman was Mary Simms, though without any trace of all her former simple-minded airs; Mary Simms, no longer in her humble attire, but flaunting in all the finery of overdone fashion. She wore an air of reckless joyousness in her face; and yet, spite of that, I pitied her. It was clear she had fallen on the evil ways of bettered fortune—bettered, alas! for the worse.

I had an excuse now, in my own mind, for my continued pursuit, without deeming myself an utter madman—the excuse of curiosity to know the destiny of one with whom I had been formerly familiar, and in whom I had taken an interest. Presently the game I was hunting down stopped at the door of the Grand Café. After a little discussion they entered. It was a public place of entertainment; there was no reason why I should not enter also. I found my way to the first floor. They were already seated at a table, Mary holding the *carte* in her hand. They were about to dine. Why should not I dine there too? There was but one little objection,—I had an engagement to dinner. But the strange impulse which overpowered me, and seemed leading me on step by step, spite of myself, quickly overruled all the dictates of propriety toward my intended hosts. Could I not send a prettily devised apology? I glided past the couple, with my head averted, seeking a table, and I was unobserved by my old acquaintance. I was too agitated to eat, but I made a semblance, and little heeded the air of surprise and almost disgust on the bewildered face of the waiter as he bore away the barely touched dishes. I was in a very fever of impatience and doubt what next to do. They still sat on, in evident enjoyment of their meal and their constant draughts of sparkling wine. My impatience was becoming almost unbearable when the man at last rose. The woman seemed to have uttered some expostulation, for he turned at the door and said somewhat harshly aloud, "Nonsense; only one game and I shall be back. The waiter will give you a paper—a magazine—something to while away the time." And he left the room for the billiard-table, as I surmised.

Now was my opportunity. After a little hesitation, I rose, and planted myself abruptly on the vacant seat before the woman.

"Mary," I said.

She started, with a little exclamation of alarm, and dropped the paper she had held. She knew me at once.

"Master John!" she exclaimed, using the familiar term still given me when I was long past boyhood; and then, after a lengthened gaze, she turned away her head. I was embarrassed at first how to address her.

"Mary," I said at last, "I am grieved to see you thus."

"Why should you be grieved for me?" she retorted, looking at me sharply, and speaking in a tone of impatient anger. "I am happy as I am."

"I don't believe you," I replied.

She again turned away her head.

"Mary," I pursued, "can you doubt, that, spite of all, I have still a strong interest in the companion of my youth?"

She looked at me almost mournfully, but did not speak. At that moment I probably grew pale; for suddenly that chilly fit seized me again, and my forehead became clammy. That voice sounded again in my ear: "Speak of him!" were the words it uttered. Mary gazed on me with surprise, and yet I was assured that *she* had not heard that voice, so plain to me. She evidently mistook the nature of my visible emotion.

"O Master John!" she stammered, with tears gathering in her eyes, reverting again to that name of bygone times, "if you had loved me then—if you had consoled my true affection with one word of hope, one look of loving-kindness—if you had not spurned and crushed me, I should not have been what I am now."

I was about to make some answer to this burst of unforgotten passion, when the voice came again: "Speak of him!"

"You have loved others since," I remarked, with a coldness which seemed cruel to myself. "You love *him* now." And I nodded my head toward the door by which the man had disappeared.

"Do I?" she said, with a bitter smile. "Perhaps; who knows?"

"And yet no good can come to you from a connection with that man," I pursued.

"Why not? He adores me, and he is free," was her answer, given with a little triumphant air.

"Yes," I said, "I know he is free: he has lately lost his wife. He has made good his claim to the sum for which he insured her life."

Mary grew deadly pale. "How did you learn this? what do you know of him?" she stammered.

I had no reply to give. She scanned my face anxiously for some time; then in a low voice she added, "What do you suspect?"

I was still silent, and only looked at her fixedly.

"You do not speak," she pursued nervously. "Why do you not speak? Ah, you know more than you would say! Master John, Master John, you might set my tortured mind at rest, and clear or confirm those doubts which *will* come into my poor head, spite of myself. Speak out—O, do speak out!"

"Not here; it is impossible," I replied, looking around. The room as the hour advanced, was becoming more thronged with guests, and the full tables gave a pretext for my reticence, when in truth I had nothing to say.

"Will you come and see me—will you?" she asked with earnest entreaty.

I nodded my head.

"Have you a pocketbook? I will write you my address; and you will come—yes, I am sure you will come!" she said in an agitated way.

I handed her my pocketbook and pencil; she wrote rapidly.

"Between the hours of three and five," she whispered, looking uneasily at the door; "*he* is sure not to be at home."

I rose; Mary held out her hand to me, then withdrew it hastily with an air of shame, and the tears sprang into her eyes again. I left the room hurriedly, and met her companion on the stairs.

That same evening, in the solitude of my own room, I pondered over the little event of the day. I had calmed down from my state of excitement. The living apparition of Mary Simms occupied my mind almost to the exclusion of the terrors of the ghostly voice which had haunted me, and my own fears of coming insanity. In truth, what was that man to me? Nothing. What did his doings matter to such a perfect stranger as myself? Nothing. His connection with Mary Simms was our only link; and in what should that affect me? Nothing again. I debated with myself whether it were not foolish of me to comply with my youthful companion's request to visit her; whether it were not imprudent in me to take any further interest in the lost woman; whether there were not even danger in seeking to penetrate mysteries which were no concern of mine. The resolution to which I came pleased me, and I said aloud, "No, I will not go!"

At the same moment came again the voice like an awful echo to my words—"Go!" It came so suddenly and so imperatively, almost without any previous warning of the usual shudder, that the shock was more than I could bear. I believe I fainted; I know I found myself, when I came to consciousness, in my arm-chair, cold and numb, and my candles had almost burned down into their sockets.

The next morning I was really ill. A sort of low fever seemed to have prostrated me, and I would have willingly seized so valid a reason for disobeying, at least for that day—for some days, perhaps—the injunction of that ghostly voice. But all that morning it never left me. My fearful chilly fit was of constant recurrence, and the words "Go! go! go!" were murmured so perpetually in my ears—the sound was one of such urgent entreaty—that all force of will gave way completely. Had I remained in that lone room, I should have gone wholly mad. As yet, to my own feelings, I was but partially out of my senses.

I dressed hastily; and, I scarce know how—by no effort of my own will, it seemed to me—I was in the open air. The address of Mary Simms was in a street not far from my own suburb. Without any power of reasoning, I found myself before the door of the house. I knocked, and asked a slipshod girl who opened the door to me for "Miss Simms." She knew no such person, held a brief shrill colloquy with some female in the back-parlour, and, on coming back, was about to shut the door in my face, when a voice from above—the voice of her I sought—called down the stairs, "Let the gentleman come up!"

I was allowed to pass. In the front drawing-room I found Mary Simms.

"They do not know me under that name," she said with a mournful smile, and again extended, then withdrew, her hand.

"Sit down," she went on to say, after a nervous pause. "I am alone now; and I adjure you, if you have still one latent feeling of old kindness for me, explain your words of yesterday to me."

I muttered something to the effect that I had no explanation to give. No words could be truer; I had not the slightest conception what to say.

"Yes, I am sure you have; you must, you will," pursued Mary excitedly; "you have some knowledge of that matter."

"What matter?" I asked.

"Why, the insurance," she replied impatiently. "You know well what I mean. My mind has been distracted about it. Spite of myself, terrible suspicions have forced themselves on me. No; I don't mean that," she cried, suddenly checking herself and changing her tone;

"don't heed what I said; it was madness in me to say what I did. But do, do, do tell me all you know."

The request was a difficult one to comply with, for I knew nothing. It is impossible to say what might have been the end of this strange interview, in which I began to feel myself an unwilling impostor; but suddenly Mary started.

"The noise of the latchkey in the lock!" she cried, alarmed; "He has returned; he must not see you; you must come another time. Here, here, be quick! I'll manage him."

And before I could utter another word she had pushed me into the back drawing-room and closed the door. A man's step on the stairs; then voices. The man was begging Mary to come out with him, as the day was so fine. She excused herself; he would hear no refusal. At last she appeared to consent, on condition that the man would assist at her toilet. There was a little laughter, almost hysterical on the part of Mary, whose voice evidently quivered with trepidation.

Presently both mounted the upper stairs. Then the thought stuck me that I had left my hat in the front room—a sufficient cause for the woman's alarm. I opened the door cautiously, seized my hat, and was about to steal down the stairs, when I was again spellbound by that numb cold.

"Stay!" said the voice. I staggered back to the other room with my hat, and closed the door.

Presently the couple came down. Mary was probably relieved by discovering that my hat was no longer there, and surmised that I had departed; for I heard her laughing as they went down the lower flight. Then I heard them leave the house.

I was alone in that back drawing-room. Why? what did I want there? I was soon to learn. I felt the chill invisible presence near me; and the voice said, "Search!"

The room belonged to the common representative class of back drawing-rooms in "apartments" of the better kind. The only one unfamiliar piece of furniture was an old Indian cabinet; and my eye naturally fell on that. As I stood and looked at it with a strange unaccountable feeling of fascination, again came the voice—"Search!"

I shuddered and obeyed. The cabinet was firmly locked; there was no power of opening it except by burglarious infraction; but still the voice said, "Search!"

A thought suddenly struck me, and I turned the cabinet from its position against the wall. Behind, the woodwork had rotted, and in many portions fallen away, so that the inner drawers were visible. What could my ghostly monitor mean—that I should open those drawers? I would not do such a deed of petty treachery. I turned defiantly, and addressing myself to the invisible as if it were a living creature by my side, I cried, "I must not, will not, do such an act of baseness."

The voice replied, "Search!"

I might have known that, in my state of what I deemed insanity, resistance was in vain. I grasped the most accessible drawer from behind, and pulled it toward me. Uppermost within it lay letters: they were addressed to "Captain Cameron,"—"Captain George Cameron." That name!—the name of Julia's husband, the man with whom she had eloped; for it was he who was the object of my pursuit.

My shuddering fit became so strong that I could scarce hold the papers; and "Search!" was repeated in my ear.

Below the letters lay a small book in a limp black cover. I opened this book with trembling hand; it was filled with manuscript—Julia's well-known handwriting.

"Read!" muttered the voice. I read. There were long entries by poor Julia of her daily life; complaints of her husband's unkindness, neglect, then cruelty. I turned to the last pages: her hand had grown very feeble now, and she was very ill. "George seems kinder now," she wrote; "he brings me all my medicines with his own hand." Later on: "I am dying; I know I am dying: he has poisoned me. I saw him last night through the curtains pour something in my cup; I saw it in his evil eye. I would not drink; I will drink no more; but I feel that I must die."

These were the last words. Below were written, in a man's bold hand, the words "Poor fool!"

This sudden revelation of poor Julia's death and dying thoughts unnerved me quite. I grew colder in my whole frame than ever.

"Take it!" said her voice. I took the book, pushed back the cabinet into its place against the wall, and, leaving that fearful room, stole down the stairs with trembling limbs, and left the house with all the feelings of a guilty thief.

For some days I perused my poor lost Julia's diary again and again. The whole revelation of her sad life and sudden death led but to one conclusion,—she had died of poison by the hands of her unworthy husband. He had insured her life, and then—

It seemed evident to me that Mary Simms had vaguely shared suspicions of the same foul deed. On my own mind came conviction. But what could I do next? how bring this evil man to justice? what proof would be deemed to exist in those writings? I was bewildered, weak, irresolute. Like Hamlet, I shrank back and temporised. But I was not feigning madness; my madness seemed but all too real for me. During all this period the wailing of that wretched voice in my ear was almost incessant. O, I must have been mad!

I wandered about restlessly, like the haunted thing I had become. One day I had come unconsciously and without purpose into Oxford Street. My troubled thoughts were suddenly broken in upon by the solicitations of a beggar. With a heart hardened against begging impostors, and under the influence of the shock rudely given to my absorbing dreams, I answered more hardly than was my wont. The man heaved a heavy sigh, and sobbed forth, "Then Heaven help me!" I caught sight of him before he turned away. He was a ghastly object, with fever in his hollow eyes and sunken cheeks, and fever on his dry, chapped lips. But I knew, or fancied I knew, the tricks of the trade, and I was obdurate. Why, I asked myself, should the cold shudder come over me at such a moment? But it was so strong on me as to make me shake all over. It came—that maddening voice. "Succour!" it said now. I had become so accustomed already to address the ghostly voice that I cried aloud, "Why, Julia, why?" I saw people laughing in my face at this strange cry, and I turned in the direction in which the beggar had gone. I just caught sight of him as he was tottering down a street toward Soho. I determined to have pity for this once, and followed the poor man. He led me on through I know not what streets. His steps was hurried now. In one street I lost sight of him; but I felt convinced he must have turned into a dingy court. I made inquiries, but for a time received only rude jeering answers from the rough men and women whom I questioned. At last a little girl informed me that I must mean the strange man who lodged in the garret of a house she pointed out to me. It was an old dilapidated building, and I had much repugnance on entering it. But again I was no master of my will. I mounted some creaking stairs to the top of the house, until I could go no further. A shattered door was open; I entered a wretched garret; the object of my search lay now on a bundle of rags on the bare floor. He opened his wild eyes as I approached.

"I have come to succour," I said, using unconsciously the word of the voice; "what ails you?"

"Ails me?" gasped the man; "hunger, starvation, fever."

I was horrified. Hurrying to the top of the stairs, I shouted till I had roused the attention of an old woman. I gave her money to bring me food and brandy, promising her a recompense for her trouble.

"Have you no friends?" I asked the wretched man as I returned.

"None," he said feebly. Then as the fever rose in his eyes and even flushed his pallid face, he said excitedly, "I had a master once—one I perilled my soul for. He knows I am dying; but, spite of all my letters, he will not come. He wants me dead, he wants me dead—and his wish is coming to pass now."

"Cannot I find him—bring him here?" I asked.

The man stared at me, shook his head, and at last, as if collecting his faculties with much exertion, muttered, "Yes; it is a last hope; perhaps you may, and I can be revenged on him at least. Yes revenged. I have threatened him already." And the fellow laughed a wild laugh.

"Control yourself," I urged, kneeling by his side; "give me his name—his address."

"Captain George Cameron," he gasped, and then fell back.

"Captain George Cameron!" I cried. "Speak! what of him?"

But the man's senses seemed gone; he only muttered incoherently. The old woman returned with the food and spirits. I had found one honest creature in that foul region. I gave her money—provide her more if she would bring a doctor. She departed on her new errand. I raised the man's head, moistened his lips with the brandy, and then poured some of the spirit down his throat. He gulped at it eagerly, and opened his eyes; but he still raved incoherently, "I did not do it, it was he. He made me buy the poison; he dared not risk the danger himself, the coward! I knew what he meant to do with it, and yet I did not speak; I was her murderer too. Poor Mrs. Cameron! poor Mrs. Cameron! do you forgive?—can you forgive?"

And the man screamed aloud and stretched out his arms as if to fright away a phantom.

I had drunk in every word, and knew the meaning of those broken accents well. Could I have found at last the means of bringing justice on the murderer's head? But the man was raving in a delirium, and I was obliged to hold him with all my strength. A step on the stairs. Could it be the medical man I had sent for? That would be indeed a blessing. A man entered—it was Cameron!

He came in jauntily, with the words, "How now, Saunders, you rascal! What more do you want to get out of me?"

He started at the sight of a stranger.

I rose from my kneeling posture like an accusing spirit. I struggled for calm; but passion beyond my control mastered me, and was I not a madman? I seized him by the throat, with the words, "Murderer! poisoner! where is Julia?" He shook me off violently.

"And who the devil are you, sir?" he cried.

"That murdered woman's cousin!" I rushed at him again.

"Lying hound!" he shouted, and grappled me. His strength was far beyond mine. He had his hand on my throat; a crimson darkness was in my eyes; I could not see, I could not hear; there was a torrent of sound pouring in my ears. Suddenly his grasp relaxed. When I recovered my sight, I saw the murderer struggling with the fever-stricken man, who had risen from the floor, and seized him from behind. This unexpected diversion saved my life; but the ex-groom was soon thrown back on the ground.

"Captain George Cameron," I cried, "kill me, but you will only heap another murder on your head!"

He advanced on me with something glittering in his hand. Without a word he came and stabbed at me; but at the same moment I darted at him a heavy blow. What followed was too confused for clear remembrance. I saw—no, I will say I fancied that I saw—the dim form of Julia Staunton standing between me and her vile husband. Did he see the vision too? I cannot say. He reeled back, and fell heavily to the floor. Maybe it was only my blow that felled him. Then came confusion—a dream of a crowd of people—policemen—muttered accusations. I had fainted from the wound in my arm.

Captain George Cameron was arrested. Saunders recovered, and lived long enough to be the principal witness on his trial. The murderer was found guilty. Poor Julia's diary, too, which I had abstracted, told fearfully against him. But he contrived to escape the gallows; he had managed to conceal poison on his person, and he was found dead in his cell. Mary Simms I never saw again. I once received a little scrawl, "I am at peace now, Master John. God bless you!"

I have had no more hallucinations since that time; the voice has never come again. I found out poor Julia's grave, and, as I stood and wept by its side, the cold shudder came over me for the last time. Who shall tell me whether I was once really mad, or whether I was not?

A CASE OF EAVESDROPPING

Algernon Blackwood

Algernon Henry Blackwood (1869–1951) is a pillar of the ghost story genre. Raised in a strict religious family, Blackwood rapidly turned away from Evangelicalism as he developed an interest for mystical philosophies and occultism. He was a member of The Ghost Club, which is believed to be the oldest paranormal investigation organisation in the world; and of the Hermetic Order of the Golden Dawn, a secret society devoted to the occult. Blackwood was a man of paradoxes: known as cheerful, but also versed into horror, he loved the outdoors and would go mountain-climbing or skiing, when he wasn't engrossed in books. Amidst a very varied professional life (he was a dairy farmer, a model, a businessman, and a bartender, among other things), Blackwood was a prolific writer, from journal articles and essays to children's books and plays. His short stories dealt with the supernatural, horror, the occult, the weird, and ghosts; and he is thought to have written at least ten short story collections. Underscoring once again the aural potential of ghost stories, Blackwood also told his stories on television or on the radio. His work has been anthologised many times since his death, including by British Library Publishing as *The Whisperers and Other Stories: A Lifetime of the Supernatural* (2022).

"A Case of Eavesdropping" comes from Blackwood's first short story collection, *The Empty House and Other Ghost Stories* (1906). In this tale, the ghostly nature of the voices is not straightforward:

as hinted at by the title, they are only heard through a wall as the protagonist eavesdrops. This prevents any visual contact and thus strengthens the story's reliance on aurality, but it also simultaneously distorts the acoustic qualities of the scene; and both character and reader are left to wonder, as the voices continue to speak to each other.

im Shorthouse was the sort of fellow who always made a mess of things. Everything with which his hands or mind came into contact issued from such contact in an unqualified and irremediable state of mess. His college days were a mess: he was twice rusticated. His schooldays were a mess: he went to half a dozen, each passing him on to the next with a worse character and in a more developed state of mess. His early boyhood was the sort of mess that copy-books and dictionaries spell with a big "M," and his babyhood—ugh! was the embodiment of howling, yowling, screaming mess.

At the age of forty, however, there came a change in his troubled life, when he met a girl with half a million in her own right, who consented to marry him, and who very soon succeeded in reducing his most messy existence into a state of comparative order and system.

Certain incidents, important and otherwise, of Jim's life would never have come to be told here but for the fact that in getting into his "messes" and out of them again he succeeded in drawing himself into the atmosphere of peculiar circumstances and strange happenings. He attracted to his path the curious adventures of life as unfailingly as meat attracts flies, and jam wasps. It is to the meat and jam of his life, so to speak, that he owes his experiences; his afterlife was all pudding, which attracts nothing but greedy children. With marriage the interest of his life ceased for all but one person, and his path became regular as the sun's instead of erratic as a comet's.

The first experience in order of time that he related to me shows that somewhere latent behind his disarranged nervous system there lay psychic perceptions of an uncommon order. About the age of twenty-two—I think after his second rustication—his father's purse and patience had equally given out, and Jim found himself stranded high and dry in a large American city. High and dry! And the only clothes that had no holes in them safely in the keeping of his uncle's wardrobe.

Careful reflection on a bench in one of the city parks led him to the conclusion that the only thing to do was to persuade the city editor of one of the daily journals that he possessed an observant mind and a ready pen, and that he could "do good work for your paper, sir, as a reporter." This, then, he did, standing at a most unnatural angle between the editor and the window to conceal the whereabouts of the holes.

"Guess we'll have to give you a week's trial," said the editor, who, ever on the lookout for good chance material, took on shoals of men in that way and retained on the average one man per shoal. Anyhow it gave Jim Shorthouse the wherewithal to sew up the holes and relieve his uncle's wardrobe of its burden.

Then he went to find living quarters; and in this proceeding his unique characteristics already referred to—what theosophists would call his Karma—began unmistakably to assert themselves, for it was in the house he eventually selected that this sad tale took place.

There are no "diggings" in American cities. The alternatives for small incomes are grim enough—rooms in a boarding-house where meals are served, or in a room-house where no meals are served—not even breakfast. Rich people live in palaces, of course, but Jim had nothing to do with "sich-like." His horizon was bounded by boarding-houses and room-houses; and, owing to the necessary irregularity of his meals and hours, he took the latter.

It was a large, gaunt-looking place in a side street, with dirty windows and a creaking iron gate, but the rooms were large, and the one he selected and paid for in advance was on the top floor. The landlady looked gaunt and dusty as the house, and quite as old. Her eyes were green and faded, and her features large.

"Waal," she twanged, with her electrifying Western drawl, "that's the room, if you like it, and that's the price I said. Now, if you want it, why, just say so; and if you don't, why, it don't hurt me any."

Jim wanted to shake her, but he feared the clouds of long-accumulated dust in her clothes, and as the price and size of the room suited him, he decided to take it.

"Anyone else on this floor?" he asked.

She looked at him queerly out of her faded eyes before she answered.

"None of my guests ever put such questions to me before," she said; "but I guess you're different. Why, there's no one at all but an old gent that's stayed here every bit of five years. He's over thar," pointing to the end of the passage.

"Ah! I see," said Shorthouse feebly. "So I'm alone up here?"

"Reckon you are, pretty near," she twanged out, ending the conversation abruptly by turning her back on her new "guest," and going slowly and deliberately downstairs.

The newspaper work kept Shorthouse out most of the night. Three times a week he got home at 1 a.m., and three times at 3 a.m. The room proved comfortable enough, and he paid for a second week. His unusual hours had so far prevented his meeting any inmates of the house, and not a sound had been heard from the "old gent" who shared the floor with him. It seemed a very quiet house.

One night, about the middle of the second week, he came home tired after a long day's work. The lamp that usually stood all night in the hall had burned itself out, and he had to stumble upstairs in the dark. He made considerable noise in doing so, but nobody seemed to be disturbed. The whole house was utterly quiet, and probably everybody was asleep. There were no lights under any of the doors. All was in darkness. It was after two o'clock.

After reading some English letters that had come during the day, and dipping for a few minutes into a book, he became drowsy and got ready for bed. Just as he was about to get in between the sheets, he stopped for a moment and listened. There rose in the night, as he did so, the sound of steps somewhere in the house below. Listening attentively, he heard that it was somebody coming upstairs—a heavy tread, and the owner taking no pains to step quietly. On it came up the stairs, tramp, tramp, tramp—evidently the tread of a big man, and one in something of a hurry.

At once thoughts connected somehow with fire and police flashed through Jim's brain, but there were no sounds of voices with the steps, and he reflected in the same moment that it could only be the old gentleman keeping late hours and tumbling upstairs in the darkness. He was in the act of turning out the gas and stepping into bed, when the house resumed its former stillness by the footsteps suddenly coming to a dead stop immediately outside his own room.

With his hand on the gas, Shorthouse paused a moment before turning it out to see if the steps would go on again, when he was startled by a loud knocking on his door. Instantly, in obedience to a curious and unexplained instinct, he turned out the light, leaving himself and the room in total darkness.

He had scarcely taken a step across the room to open the door, when a voice from the other side of the wall, so close it almost sounded in his ear, exclaimed in German, "Is that you, father? Come in."

The speaker was a man in the next room, and the knocking, after all, had not been on his own door, but on that of the adjoining chamber, which he had supposed to be vacant.

Almost before the man in the passage had time to answer in German, "Let me in at once," Jim heard someone cross the floor and unlock the door. Then it was slammed to with a bang, and there was audible the sound of footsteps about the room, and of chairs being drawn up to a table and knocking against furniture on the way. The men seemed wholly regardless of their neighbour's comfort, for they made noise enough to waken the dead.

"Serves me right for taking a room in such a cheap hole," reflected Jim in the darkness. "I wonder whom she's let the room to!"

The two rooms, the landlady had told him, were originally one. She had put up a thin partition—just a row of boards—to increase her income. The doors were adjacent, and only separated by the massive upright beam between them. When one was opened or shut the other rattled.

With utter indifference to the comfort of the other sleepers in the house, the two Germans had meanwhile commenced to talk both at once and at the top of their voices. They talked emphatically, even angrily. The words "Father" and "Otto" were freely used. Shorthouse understood German, but as he stood listening for the first minute or two, an eavesdropper in spite of himself, it was difficult to make head or tail of the talk, for neither would give way to the other, and the jumble of guttural sounds and unfinished sentences was wholly unintelligible. Then, very suddenly, both voices dropped together; and, after a moment's pause, the deep tones of one of them, who seemed to be the "father," said, with the utmost distinctness—

"You mean, Otto, that you refuse to get it?"

There was a sound of someone shuffling in the chair before the answer came. "I mean that I don't know how to get it. It is so much, father. It is *too* much. A part of it—"

"A part of it!" cried the other, with an angry oath, "a part of it, when ruin and disgrace are already in the house, is worse than useless. If you can get half you can get all, you wretched fool. Half-measures only damn all concerned."

"You told me last time—" began the other firmly, but was not allowed to finish. A succession of horrible oaths drowned his sentence, and the father went on, in a voice vibrating with anger—

"You know she will give you anything. You have only been married a few months. If you ask and give a plausible reason you can get all we want and more. You can ask it temporarily. All will be paid back. It will re-establish the firm, and she will never know what was done with it. With that amount, Otto, you know I can recoup all these terrible losses, and in less than a year all will be repaid. But without it... You must get it, Otto. Hear me, you must. Am I to be arrested for the misuse of trust moneys? Is our honoured name to be cursed and spat on?" The old man choked and stammered in his anger and desperation.

Shorthouse stood shivering in the darkness and listening in spite of himself. The conversation had carried him along with it, and he had been for some reason afraid to let his neighbourhood be known. But at this point he realised that he had listened too long and that he must inform the two men that they could be overheard to every single syllable. So he coughed loudly, and at the same time rattled the handle of his door. It seemed to have no effect, for the voices continued just as loudly as before, the son protesting and the father growing more and more angry. He coughed again persistently, and also contrived purposely in the darkness to tumble against the partition, feeling the thin boards yield easily under his weight, and making a considerable noise in so doing. But the voices went on unconcernedly, and louder than ever. Could it be possible they had not heard?

By this time Jim was more concerned about his own sleep than the morality of overhearing the private scandals of his neighbours, and he went out into the passage and knocked smartly at their door. Instantly, as if by magic, the sounds ceased. Everything dropped into utter silence. There was no light under the door and not a whisper could be heard within. He knocked again, but received no answer.

"Gentlemen," he began at length, with his lips close to the key-hole and in German, "please do not talk so loud. I can overhear all you say in the next room. Besides, it is very late, and I wish to sleep."

He paused and listened, but no answer was forthcoming. He turned the handle and found the door was locked. Not a sound broke the stillness of the night except the faint swish of the wind over the skylight and the creaking of a board here and there in the house below. The cold air of a very early morning crept down the passage, and made him shiver. The silence of the house began to impress him disagreeably. He looked behind him and about him, hoping, and yet fearing, that something would break the stillness. The voices still seemed to ring on in his ears; but that sudden silence, when he knocked at the door, affected him far more unpleasantly than the voices, and put strange thoughts in his brain—thoughts he did not like or approve.

Moving stealthily from the door, he peered over the banisters into the space below. It was like a deep vault that might conceal in its shadows anything that was not good. It was not difficult to fancy he saw an indistinct moving to-and-fro below him. Was that a figure sitting on the stairs peering up obliquely at him out of hideous eyes? Was that a sound of whispering and shuffling down there in the dark halls and forsaken landings? Was it something more than the inarticulate murmur of the night?

The wind made an effort overhead, singing over the skylight, and the door behind him rattled and made him start. He turned to go back to his room, and the draught closed the door slowly in his face as if there were someone pressing against it from the other side. When he pushed it open and went in, a hundred shadowy forms seemed to dart swiftly and silently back to their corners and hiding-places. But in the adjoining room the sounds had entirely ceased, and Shorthouse soon crept into bed, and left the house with its inmates, waking or sleeping, to take care of themselves, while he entered the region of dreams and silence.

Next day, strong in the common sense that the sunlight brings, he determined to lodge a complaint against the noisy occupants of the next room and make the landlady request them to modify their voices at such late hours of the night and morning. But it so happened that she was not to be seen that day, and when he returned from the office at midnight it was, of course, too late.

Looking under the door as he came up to bed he noticed that there was no light, and concluded that the Germans were not in. So much the better. He went to sleep about one o'clock, fully decided that if they came up later and woke him with their horrible noises he would not rest till he had roused the landlady and made her reprove them with that authoritative twang, in which every word was like the lash of a metallic whip.

However, there proved to be no need for such drastic measures, for Shorthouse slumbered peacefully all night, and his dreams—chiefly of the fields of grain and flocks of sheep on the far-away farms of his father's estate—were permitted to run their fanciful course unbroken.

Two nights later, however, when he came home tired out, after a difficult day, and wet and blown about by one of the wickedest storms he had ever seen, his dreams—always of the fields and sheep—were not destined to be so undisturbed.

He had already dozed off in that delicious glow that follows the removal of wet clothes and the immediate snuggling under warm blankets, when his consciousness, hovering on the borderland between sleep and waking, was vaguely troubled by a sound that rose indistinctly from the depths of the house, and, between the gusts of wind and rain, reached his ears with an accompanying sense of uneasiness and discomfort. It rose on the night air with some pretence of regularity, dying away again in the roar of the wind to reassert itself distantly in the deep, brief hushes of the storm.

For a few minutes Jim's dreams were coloured only—tinged, as it were, by this impression of fear approaching from somewhere insensibly upon him. His consciousness, at first, refused to be drawn back from that enchanted region where it had wandered, and he did not immediately awaken. But the nature of his dreams changed unpleasantly. He saw the sheep suddenly run huddled together, as though frightened by the neighbourhood of an enemy, while the fields of waving corn became agitated as though some monster were moving uncouthly among the crowded stalks. The sky grew dark, and in his dream an awful sound came somewhere from the clouds. It was in reality the sound downstairs growing more distinct.

Shorthouse shifted uneasily across the bed with something like a groan of distress. The next minute he awoke, and found himself sitting straight up in bed—listening. Was it a nightmare? Had he been dreaming evil dreams, that his flesh crawled and the hair stirred on his head?

The room was dark and silent, but outside the wind howled dismally and drove the rain with repeated assaults against the rattling windows. How nice it would be—the thought flashed through his mind—if all winds, like the west wind, went down with the sun! They made such fiendish noises at night, like the crying of angry voices. In the daytime they had such a different sound. If only—

Hark! It was no dream after all, for the sound was momentarily growing louder, and its *cause* was coming up the stairs. He found himself speculating feebly what this cause might be, but the sound was still too indistinct to enable him to arrive at any definite conclusion.

The voice of a church clock striking two made itself heard above the wind. It was just about the hour when the Germans had commenced their performance three nights before. Shorthouse made up his mind that if they began it again he would not put up with it for very long. Yet he was already horribly conscious of the difficulty he would have of getting out of bed. The clothes were so warm and comforting against his back. The sound, still steadily coming nearer, had by this time become differentiated from the confused clamour of the elements, and had resolved itself into the footsteps of one or more persons.

"The Germans, hang 'em!" thought Jim. "But what on earth is the matter with me? I never felt so queer in all my life."

He was trembling all over, and felt as cold as though he were in a freezing atmosphere. His nerves were steady enough, and he felt no diminution of physical courage, but he was conscious of a curious sense of malaise and trepidation, such as even the most vigorous men have been known to experience when in the first grip of some horrible and deadly disease. As the footsteps approached this feeling of weakness increased. He felt a strange lassitude creeping over him, a sort of exhaustion, accompanied by a growing numbness in the extremities, and a sensation of dreaminess in the head, as if perhaps the consciousness were leaving its accustomed seat in the brain and preparing to act on another plane. Yet, strange to say, as the vitality was slowly withdrawn from his body, his senses seemed to grow more acute.

Meanwhile the steps were already on the landing at the top of the stairs, and Shorthouse, still sitting upright in bed, heard a heavy body brush past his door and along the wall outside, almost immediately afterwards the loud knocking of someone's knuckles on the door of the adjoining room.

Instantly, though so far not a sound had proceeded from within, he heard, through the thin partition, a chair pushed back and a man quickly cross the floor and open the door.

"Ah! it's you," he heard in the son's voice. Had the fellow, then, been sitting silently in there all this time, waiting for his father's arrival? To Shorthouse it came not as a pleasant reflection by any means.

There was no answer to this dubious greeting, but the door was closed quickly, and then there was a sound as if a bag or parcel had been thrown on a wooden table and had slid some distance across it before stopping.

"What's that?" asked the son, with anxiety in his tone.

"You may know before I go," returned the other gruffly. Indeed his voice was more than gruff: it betrayed ill-suppressed passion.

Shorthouse was conscious of a strong desire to stop the conversation before it proceeded any further, but somehow or other his will was not equal to the task, and he could not get out of bed. The conversation went on, every tone and inflexion distinctly audible above the noise of the storm.

In a low voice the father continued. Jim missed some of the words at the beginning of the sentence. It ended with: "... but now they've all left, and I've managed to get up to you. You know what I've come for." There was distinct menace in his tone.

"Yes," returned the other; "I have been waiting."

"And the money?" asked the father impatiently.

No answer.

"You've had three days to get it in, and I've contrived to stave off the worst so far—but tomorrow is the end."

No answer.

"Speak, Otto! What have you got for me? Speak, my son; for God's sake, tell me."

There was a moment's silence, during which the old man's vibrating accents seemed to echo through the rooms. Then came in a low voice the answer—

"I have nothing."

"Otto!" cried the other with passion, "nothing!"

"I can get nothing," came almost in a whisper.

"You lie!" cried the other, in a half-stifled voice. "I swear you lie. Give me the money."

A chair was heard scraping along the floor. Evidently the men had been sitting over the table, and one of them had risen. Shorthouse heard the bag or parcel drawn across the table, and then a step as if one of the men was crossing to the door.

"Father, what's in that? I must know," said Otto, with the first signs of determination in his voice. There must have been an effort on the son's part to gain possession of the parcel in question, and on the father's to retain it, for between them it fell to the ground. A curious rattle followed its contact with the floor. Instantly there were sounds of a scuffle. The men were struggling for the possession of the box. The elder man with oaths, and blasphemous imprecations, the other with short gasps that betokened the strength of his efforts. It was of short duration, and the younger man had evidently won, for a minute later was heard his angry exclamation.

"I knew it. Her jewels! You scoundrel, you shall never have them. It is a crime."

The elder man uttered a short, guttural laugh, which froze Jim's blood and made his skin creep. No word was spoken, and for the space of ten seconds there was a living silence. Then the air trembled with the sound of a thud, followed immediately by a groan and the crash of a heavy body falling over on to the table. A second later there was a lurching from the table on to the floor and against the partition that separated the rooms. The bed quivered an instant at the shock, but the unholy spell was lifted from his soul and Jim Shorthouse sprang out of bed and across the floor in a single bound. He knew that ghastly murder had been done—the murder by a father of his son.

With shaking fingers but a determined heart he lit the gas, and the first thing in which his eyes corroborated the evidence of his ears was the horrifying detail that the lower portion of the partition bulged unnaturally into his own room. The glaring paper with which it was covered had cracked under the tension and the boards beneath it bent inwards towards him. What hideous load was behind them, he shuddered to think.

All this he saw in less than a second. Since the final lurch against the wall not a sound had proceeded from the room, not even a groan or a footstep. All was still but the howl of the wind, which to his ears had in it a note of triumphant horror.

Shorthouse was in the act of leaving the room to rouse the house and send for the police—in fact his hand was already on the door-knob—when something in the room arrested his attention. Out of the corner of his eyes he thought he caught sight of something moving. He was sure of it, and turning his eyes in the direction, he found he was not mistaken.

Something was creeping slowly towards him along the floor. It was something dark and serpentine in shape, and it came from the place where the partition bulged. He stooped down to examine it with feelings of intense horror and repugnance, and he discovered that it was moving toward him from the *other side* of the wall. His eyes were fascinated, and for the moment he was unable to move. Silently, slowly, from side to side like a thick worm, it crawled forward into the room beneath his frightened eyes, until at length he could stand it no longer and stretched out his arm to touch it. But at the instant of contact he withdrew his hand with a suppressed scream. It was sluggish—and it was warm! and he saw that his fingers were stained with living crimson.

A second more, and Shorthouse was out in the passage with his hand on the door of the next room. It was locked. He plunged forward with all his weight against it, and, the lock giving way, he fell headlong into a room that was pitch dark and very cold. In a moment he was on his feet again and trying to penetrate the blackness. Not a sound, not a movement. Not even the sense of a presence. It was empty, miserably empty!

Across the room he could trace the outline of a window with rain streaming down the outside, and the blurred lights of the city beyond. But the room was empty, appallingly empty; and so still. He stood there, cold as ice, staring, shivering listening. Suddenly there was a step behind him and a light flashed into the room, and when he turned quickly with his arm up as if to ward off a terrific blow he found himself face to face with the landlady. Instantly the reaction began to set in.

It was nearly three o'clock in the morning, and he was standing there with bare feet and striped pyjamas in a small room, which in the merciful light he perceived to be absolutely empty, carpetless, and without a stick of furniture, or even a window-blind. There he stood staring at the disagreeable landlady. And there she stood too, staring and silent, in a black wrapper, her head almost bald, her face white as chalk, shading a sputtering candle with one bony hand and peering over it at him with her blinking green eyes. She looked positively hideous.

"Waal?" she drawled at length, "I heard yer right enough. Guess you couldn't sleep! Or just prowlin' round a bit—is that it?"

The empty room, the absence of all traces of the recent tragedy, the silence, the hour, his striped pyjamas and bare feet—everything together combined to deprive him momentarily of speech. He stared at her blankly without a word.

"Waal?" clanked the awful voice.

"My dear woman," he burst out finally, "there's been something awful—" So far his desperation took him, but no farther. He positively stuck at the substantive.

"Oh! there hasn't been nothin'," she said slowly still peering at him. "I reckon you've only seen and heard what the others did. I never can keep folks on this floor long. Most of 'em catch on sooner or later—that is, the ones that's kind of quick and sensitive. Only you being an Englishman I thought you wouldn't mind. Nothin' really happens; it's only thinkin' like."

Shorthouse was beside himself. He felt ready to pick her up and drop her over the banisters, candle and all.

"Look there," he said, pointing at her within an inch of her blinking eyes with the fingers that had touched the oozing blood; "look there, my good woman. Is that only thinking?"

She stared a minute, as if not knowing what he meant.

"I guess so," she said at length.

He followed her eyes, and to his amazement saw that his fingers were as white as usual, and quite free from the awful stain that had been there ten minutes before. There was no sign of blood. No amount of staring could bring it back. Had he gone out of his mind? Had his eyes and ears played such tricks with him? Had his senses become false and perverted? He dashed past the landlady, out into the passage, and gained his own room in a couple of strides. Whew!... the partition no longer bulged. The paper was not torn. There was no creeping, crawling thing on the faded old carpet.

"It's all over now," drawled the metallic voice behind him. "I'm going to bed again."

He turned and saw the landlady slowly going downstairs again, still shading the candle with her hand and peering up at him from time to time as she moved. A black, ugly, unwholesome object, he thought, as she disappeared into the darkness below, and the last flicker of her candle threw a queer-shaped shadow along the wall and over the ceiling.

Without hesitating a moment, Shorthouse threw himself into his clothes and went out of the house. He preferred the storm to the horrors of that top floor, and he walked the streets till daylight. In the evening he told the landlady he would leave next day, in spite of her assurances that nothing more would happen.

"It never comes back," she said—"that is, not after he's killed."

Shorthouse gasped.

"You gave me a lot for my money," he growled.

"Waal, it aren't my show," she drawled. "I'm no spirit medium. You take chances. Some'll sleep right along and never hear nothin'. Others, like yourself, are different and get the whole thing."

"Who's the old gentleman?—does he hear it?" asked Jim.

"There's no old gentleman at all," she answered coolly. "I just told you that to make you feel easy like in case you did hear anythin'. You were all alone on the floor."

"Say now," she went on, after a pause in which Shorthouse could think of nothing to say but unpublishable things, "say now, do tell, did you feel sort of cold when the show was on, sort of tired and weak, I mean, as if you might be going to die?"

"How can I say?" he answered savagely; "what I felt God only knows."

"Waal, but He won't tell," she drawled out. "Only I was wonderin' how you really did feel, because the man who had that room last was found one morning in bed—"

"In bed?"

"He was dead. He was the one before you. Oh! You don't need to get rattled so. You're all right. And it all really happened, they do say. This house used to be a private residence some twenty-five years ago, and a German family of the name of Steinhardt lived here. They had a big business in Wall Street, and stood 'way up in things."

"Ah!" said her listener.

"Oh yes, they did, right at the top, till one fine day it all bust and the old man skipped with the boodle—"

"Skipped with the boodle?"

"That's so," she said; "got clear away with all the money, and the son was found dead in his house, committed soocide it was thought. Though there was some as said he couldn't have stabbed himself and fallen in that position. They said he was murdered. The father died in prison. They tried to fasten the murder on him, but there was no motive, or no evidence, or no somethin'. I forget now."

"Very pretty," said Shorthouse.

"I'll show you somethin' mighty queer anyways," she drawled, "if you'll come upstairs a minute. I've heard the steps and voices lots of times; they don't pheaze me any. I'd just as lief hear so many dogs barkin'. You'll find the whole story in the newspapers if you look it up—not what goes on here, but the story of the Germans. My house would be ruined if they told all, and I'd sue for damages."

They reached the bedroom, and the woman went in and pulled up the edge of the carpet where Shorthouse had seen the blood soaking in the previous night.

"Look thar, if you feel like it," said the old hag. Stooping down, he saw a dark, dull stain in the boards that corresponded exactly to the shape and position of the blood as he had seen it.

That night he slept in a hotel, and the following day sought new quarters. In the newspapers on file in his office after a long search he found twenty years back the detailed story, substantially as the woman had said, of Steinhardt & Co.'s failure, the absconding and subsequent arrest of the senior partner, and the suicide, or murder, of his son Otto. The landlady's room-house had formerly been their private residence.

A SPEAKIN' GHOST

Annie Trumbull Slosson

Anna Trumbull Slosson (1838–1926), known as Annie, was an American
author and renowned entomologist. Slosson had no formal scientific
education, but developed her skills through extensive field work and
relationships with other entomologists. She collected rare entomological specimens and identified previously unknown species; and in
1892, she became a founding member and the first female member
of the New York Entomological Society. As a fiction writer, Slosson
mostly wrote short stories and is a significant author in the American
literary regionalism movement of the late nineteenth century. Her
fiction tended to include detailed descriptions of the natural world,
and sometimes entomological themes. After her death, her literary
output was largely overlooked in favour of her scientific contributions.

"A Speakin' Ghost" is the last tale in the short story collection
Seven Dreamers (1890). The story is connected to aurality in different ways. Its epigraph is a quotation from the first scene of William
Shakespeare's *Hamlet* (first performed in 1602), in which the two
grave-diggers see a ghost and exhort it to speak, directly echoing the
title of the short story. In terms of writing technique, the oral style
and the transcription of the accent of the narrator, Mary Ann, bring
the tale to life, as if the reader was entering into a conversation with
her. "A Speakin' Ghost" combines the theme of ghostly children with
that of the acoustic, as the ghost of an ordinary young boy appears
to Mary Ann, and speaks to her.

es, I do bleeve in 'em—in one of 'em, tennerate. An' I know why you ask me if I do. Somebody's put you up to it, so's you can make me tell my ghost story. Well, you're welcome to that if you want it. It's no great of a story, but it's true; an' arter all, that's the main p'int in a story—ghost or no ghost.

Well, I s'pose I'll s'prise you when I say it all happened in New York city. Seein' me here in Kitt'ry, an' knowin' my name's Jenness—a real Kitt'ry an' Portsmouth an' Rye name—why, o' course you'd take it for granted I'd allers lived round here, an' all my happenin's had been in this local'ty. Well, you're right one way. I was born about here, an' come of good old Scataqua River stock. My father was Andronicus Jenness, born an' raised in Rye, an' the fust thing I rec'lect we was livin' in Portsmouth, on the old Odiorne's P'int road.

There was father 'n' mother, three boys—Amos, Ezry, an' Peleg—an' me, Mary Ann, the oldest o' the family an' the only girl. It's the ghost story you want to hear, so I ain't goin' to bother you with anything else.

But that time I lived there in the old red house, with my own folks round me—'pears to me now the only time I did ever reely live. We was pretty well to do, we had a good home, an' we was all together. Father was a good man, mother the very best o' women, an' I was dreffle fond on 'em. An' the boys, they was just rugged, noisy, good-natur'd chaps, that kep' the house lively enough, I can tell you. But when I was nigh on to twenty-five, an' the boys was twenty an' seventeen an' fifteen, it all ended, that life in the old red house. Father an' my three laughin', high-sperrited, pleasant-spoken boys, was all drownded at once, one day in September. They went out in a sail-boat, a storm come up—'twas the beginnin' of the line gale—an' their boat capsized, an' them that went out rugged an' big an' healthy, laughin' back at ma an' me as we stood at the door to see 'em off, was fetched back stiff an' wet an' cold, an' so dreffle still I never'd seen the boys still afore in all their lives.

Mother never held up her head arter that day, an' afore the new year come in she'd follered pa an' the boys. It left me dreffle lonesome. You couldn't 'a' broke up a fam'ly in all that section that'd 'a' took it harder. For we'd allers set so much by each other, an' done ary thing we could to keep together an' not be sep'rated, an' there we was, all broke up at once, an' the old house nothin' now but a dry holler shell. I didn't want, o' course, to rattle round in it longer'n I could help. I got red on it's fast as I could, an' went over to Rye. I knowed how to work an' wa'n't afraid of it, an', o' course, the more I had to do jest then the better for me. For I was stupid an' scared an' sore with the dreffle trouble that come on me so quick an' suddin, an' I was so terr'ble lonesome.

Well, I s'pose 'twas because I'd allers liked boys, an' was used to havin' 'em round, an' because, too, o' my missin' my own boys so bad, that I got a place at fust in Mr. Sheaf's school. 'Twas a boys' school, an' they took me for a kind of housekeeper—to see to things generally. 'Twas a sort of comfort—as much as anything in this world could be a comfort—to see the boys an' do for 'em. I had a little place to myself right off the school-room, an' there I used to do my mendin' an' everything I could contrive to do for an excuse to stay right there, where I could see an' hear them boys. 'Twas a kind of eddication jest to hear 'em go over their lessons—their jography an' rethmetic an' grammar—an' partikly their readin' an' sayin' pieces.

Ev'ry speakin' day—Friday 'twas—I was allers on hand, never losin' a word, an' sometimes I'd practise the boys 'forehand till they knowed their pieces perfect. I stayed there about six months, an' I hoped I could stay there the rest o' my days. But even that poor comfort had to be took away; for Mr. Sheaf's health broke down; he give up the school an' moved away. So I lost even them borrered boys, who'd been in a sort o' way helpin' to fill up the places o' my own. An' so agin I was left terr'ble lonesome. I didn't know what to do, nor care much. So, when I had an opp'tunity to go to New York I took it.

'Twas a lady who'd had a boy at the school, an' had been there herself an' seen me. Mis' Davis she was, an' she writ to know if I'd come on to stay in her house through the summer, an' do for her pa, while she an' her children was off to the country. As I said afore, I didn't much care what I done, I was so lonesome an' mis'rable; so I said I'd go.

But if I'd been lonesome afore, I was a hunderd times lonesomer there. I never'd been in a big city afore, an' I'd kind o' thought 'twould be folksy an' 'livenin' an' cheerful. But 'twa'n't a mite like that. The house was mostly shet up an' dark. Mr. Rice—Mis' Davis's pa—was off all day long, took his dinner an' supper to a tavern somewheres, an' was only to home to sleep an' eat his breakfast. I didn't have much of anything to do. I had a big downstairs room they called the front basement to set in. It had two windows on the street, but 'twas so low down that you couldn't see much out of 'em without screwin' your neck an' peekin' up. There was lots o' folks passin' by all the time, but you couldn't scasly see anything but their feet an' legs. An' oh, the noise o' the wagons an' cars! It made me 'most crazy at fust, but bimeby I got a little used to it. But I thought I should jest die o' homesickness. How I'd think an' think an' think o' the old days an' the old house on the Odiorne's P'int road! How diff'rent it was from this city one! The old home was so quiet an' still outside, an' so noisy an' lively indoors; an' the city house was so noisy an' lively outdoors, an' so dreffle still an' quiet inside.

An' 'twas right there in the front basement o' that city house that I see the ghost. 'Twa'n't like ary other ghost I ever heerd on. Them I've read about mostly wore white sheets, an' looked dreffle skully an' bony, an' kind o' awful. One o' that sort would 'a' scaret me, I know; but this one—why, I never felt a mite scaret from the very fust. Fact is, I never knowed 'twas a ghost for a spell, for it looked like a boy, jest a common, ord'nary boy; an' 'twas a speakin' one. I don't mean one that talked, but a speakin' one that spoke pieces.

I don't think I smelt pepp'mint the fust time it come. I don't rec'lect it anyway, but allers arter that I did. I was settin' in the front basement when it come. 'Twas between five an' six in the arternoon, light enough still outdoors, but kind o' dusky in my downstairs room. I wasn't doin' anythin' jest then but settin' in my chair an' thinkin'. I don't know what 'twas exackly that made me look up an' across the room, but I done it; an' there, standin' right near the table an' lookin' at me, was the ghost; though, 's I said afore, I didn't know it for a ghost then; it looked like a boy. But he wasn't a city boy, nor like any one I'd seen for a long spell. He was about fourteen or fifteen, I should think, an' he wa'n't no way pretty to look at, but I liked him from the fust minute. He was real freckled, but that never was a great drawback to me; an' he had kind o' light, reddish-yellow hair, not very slick, but mussy an' rough like. His eyes was whity-blue, an' he hadn't much in the way o' eye-winkers or eyebrows. An' his nose was kind o' wide, an' jest a mask o' freckles, like a turkey egg. So, you see, he wa'n't much to look at for beauty, but I took to him right off. I knowed he was from the country's soon as I see him. Any one could tell that. His hands was red an' rough an' scratched, an' he had warts. Then his clothes showed it too. You could see in a jiffy they was home-made, an' cut over an' down from his pa's. There was a sort o' New Hampshire look about him too, an' I felt a real drawin' to him right off. I was jest a mite s'prised to see him standin' there, for I hadn't heerd a knock or anything, but afore I could speak an' ask him what he wanted, he stepped up in front o' me, an' says, sort o' quick an' excited like,

"Don't you want to hear me speak my piece?"

An' afore I had time to say that yes, bless his little heart, I jest would, he begun:

> "My name is Norvle; on the crampin' hills
> My father feeds his flock."

an' a lot more about his folks, an' all so pretty spoken an' nice. When he'd done he drawed one foot up to t'other an' made a bow, real polite, an' then he stood stock-still agin. O' course I praised him up, said he'd spoke his piece beautiful, an' asked him if he wouldn't like a cooky. I got up an' went to the pantry to get some, but when I turned round to ask him if he liked sugar or m'lasses best, he'd gone. I thought 'twas pretty suddin, but then I s'posed he was bashful, an' had took that way o' leavin' to save talk an' fuss. I looked out o' the winder to see if he was round, but there wa'n't a sign on him, an' I give him up. An' 'twas jest then I begun to smell pepp'mint. But I didn't put the two things—the boy an' the pepp'mint—together then; not till some time arterwards.

Well, you don't know how it chirked me up, that little visit. To be sure, it had been real short an' unsat'sfact'ry. He hadn't never told me one word about hisself—where he come from, who he was, nor anything. But that didn't seem to make no diff'rence to me. I felt 's if I knowed him real well, an' his folks afore him; an' somehow, too, I had a feelin' that he'd come agin, an' I'd find out all I wanted to about him an' his belongin's. But thinkin' about him an' his call an' all made the time pass real quick, an' 'twas bedtime afore I knowed it—the fust evenin' sence I come there that I hadn't jest longed for nine, an' looked at the clock twenty times an hour.

The next day slipped by in the same slippety way, for I was goin' over in my mind what he'd done an' said, an' s'posin' an' s'posin' who his folks was, an' all that.

About the same time o' day, towards six o'clock or so, I set down in the same place by the winder an' begun to watch for him. He hadn't said he'd come, but I had a strong feelin' inside that he was goin' to. An' he did. But 'twa'n't out o' the winder I see him. For I begun to smell a strong pepp'minty kind o' smell agin, an' I turned to look up at the shelf where I kept my med'cines to see if the bottle was broke or the stopple out, an'—there stood the ghost. Though even then I never dreamed 'twas a ghost. I thought 'twas jest a boy. He was standin' across the room, jest where I fust see him, by the table, an' lookin' straight at me. An' afore I could say a word he started right for me, an' says, lookin' real bright an' int'rested, "Don't you want to hear me speak my piece?" An' off he went as glib as could be. I can't, for the life o' me, rec'lect what 'twas he spoke that time. I get the pieces mixed somehow them days, afore the time come when they meant somethin', an' I begun to take in their meanin's. Mebbe 'twas

"At midnight when the sun was low,"

or it might be

"On Linden in his gardin tent,"

156

for I know he spoke them some time. Tennerate he said off something. An' when he'd done he drawed up his foot an' bowed real
nice. I clapped my hands an' praised him up, an' then I begun to
ask questions. I wanted to know what his name was, where he come
from, who his folks was, how he knowed about me, why he come,
an' lots o' things. He stayed quite a long spell, an' I did jest enjoy
that talk. Bimeby I went into the closet to get something to show
him, an' when I come back, he was gone agin. 'Twa'n't till some time
arter he'd left that I rec'lected that though it seemed 's if I'd had a
good talk with him, I'd done it all my own self, an' he never 'd said
one single word—nothin', I mean, but that one thing he allers said,
"Don't you want to hear me speak my piece?"

An' yet somehow I knowed lots more about him than afore. In
the fust place, I'd come to feel cert'n sure his name was Norvle, an'
that he wa'n't only speakin' a piece about that, but meant it for gospel
truth. An' arter that I never thought o' him by any other name. An' I
did think o' him lots. For even in them two little visits, when I'd done
most o' the talk myself, I'd got dreffle fond on him. You know I allers
liked boys, partikerly boys raised in the country deestricks. An' up to
this time an' quite a spell arterwards I never guessed he was anything
but a boy, jest a common, ord'nary boy. Well, he kept comin'. Every
single arternoon, jest about six o'clock, or a speck earlier or later,
I begun to smell a sort o' pepp'minty smell, an' in come that boy,
walked up to me, with his eyes all shinin', lookin' pleased an' sort
o' excited, an' says, "Don't you want to hear me speak my piece?"

Then he'd speak. They was diff'rent kinds o' pieces; some was
verses an' some wasn't. But they was all nice, pretty pieces. There was
one I remember about a boy standin' on the deck of a ship afire, an'
how he stood an' stood an' stood, an' wouldn't set down a minute.
Another r'lated to the breakin' waves, an' how they dashed up real

high. An' there was a long one that didn't rhyme, about Romans an' countrymen an' lovers; he did speak that jest beautiful.

Then he'd hold out one arm straight an' tell how nobody never heerd a drum nor a fun'ral note the time they buried somebody in a awful hurry. Agin he'd start off speechifyin' about its bein' a real question arter all whether you hadn't better be, or hadn't better not be. That one seemed to be a kind o' riddle; not much sense to it. An' there was a loud one where he jest insisted that our chains is forged. "Their clankin'," he says, "may be heerd on the plains o' Boston." I b'lieve 'twas in that one he kep' a-sayin', "Let it come; I repeat it, sir, let it come. Gentlemen may cry peace, peace, but there ain't no peace," an' so on. Real el'quent 'twas, I hold.

An' I growed so proud o' that boy. By this time I knowed a good deal about him, for I'd have long talks with him 'most every day. That is, I thought I was havin' long talks with him; but allers, arter he'd gone, I'd rec'lect he hadn't really said anything. But tennerate, strange as it seems, I did know lots more about him every time. As I said afore, his name was Norvle. His folks was plain farmin' people. You know he spoke of his pa's keepin' sheep the fust time he come. An' 'twas up in the mountins they lived; prob'ly somewheres in the White Mountins, this State. I know once he spoke o' Conway's if he lived round there. That was in a piece about there bein' 'jest seven children in their fam'ly. He was real partikler about the quantity, an' kep' callin' attention to the fact that there was exackly seven; no more, no less. He says,

> "Two of us at Conway dwells,
> An' two has gone to sea";

an' he went on to say,

"Two of us in the church-yard lays,"

(that was him an' another, I s'pose now), but still says he,

"Seven boys an' girls is we."

I was sorry he hadn't been brought up near the water as my boys had, with the great big sea to look at an' sail on. No wonder he spoke o' the crampin' hills. It allers seemed to me dreffle crampin' to be shut up amongst the hills an' away from the salt-water.

An' now he was off from home an' real lonesome, so 'twas a comfort to him to come over an' see me, a plain, self-respectin' countrywoman, like his ma an' his aunts. So I about made up my mind to take charge on him, do for him, an'—if his folks would let me—sort o' adopt him, in the place o' my own boys layin' in Portsmouth graveyard.

I never 's long 's I live shall forget the day I found out he wa'n't a boy, a common, ord'nary boy, but a ghost. He'd jest come in, an' was sayin' his piece, when the grocer come to the door with some things.

"Wait a minute, Norvle," I says, for I didn't like to lose a word of his speeches, I liked 'em all so, an' I went to the door. But as I opened it an' let the man in, I heerd the boy goin' right on speakin'. So I says to the grocer man, in a kind o' whisper, beck'nin' as I spoke, "Jest come in an' hear this boy!" For I was real proud of him, an' glad of a chance to show him off.

The man looked rather s'prised, but he follered me in, an' we both stood there by the door, list'nin' to the little feller. That is, I was list'nin' with all my ears, for 'twas one o' his very best, about England may 's well 'tempt a dam up the waters o' the Nile with bulrushes. But when I looked round at the man, smilin' at him an' noddin' my head, 's if to say, "Ain't he smart?" I see he wa'n't 'pearin' to hear anything 'tall. He was lookin' at me, an' then round, an' seemin' so dumfoundered.

"What's the matter o' you?" he says. "What's up?"

Norvle was jest closin' then, an' I waited till he'd made his bow, an' then I says agin, "Wait a minute, Norvle, an' then we'll have our talk." Then I turned round to the grocer, an' I says, "Don't he speak fust-rate?"

"What you talkin' about?" says he. "Got a sunstroke?"

Somehow I knowed all at once that he wa'n't foolin', an' that he didn't see nor hear what I see an' hear so plain, so plain. An' I knowed more'n that, for that one little thing opened my eyes that I jest wouldn't open till then, 'an I couldn't shet 'em agin. I felt queer an' dizzy, my head swum, an' I put out my hands to keep from fallin'. The man stiddied me, helped me into my chair, fetched me some water, an' I was well enough arter a little to speak. I told him I felt better, an' he could go; so he went away. I looked for Norvle, but he wasn't there. There was jest a little smell o' pepp'mint in the air, but the boy'd gone. I was glad he had, for I wanted to be all alone for a spell.

Well, you can't understand anything about what I went through then; nobody can. To folks I'm jest a queer old woman who tells a com'cal ghost story out of her stupid old head. It wa'n't very com'cal to me that day. For I'd got so fond o' that boy. I allers liked 'em; an' I'd lost all I ever had. An' now this one had come to me when I was so lonesome an' low in my mind, an' I'd gone an took him right into my heart. An' he wa'n't a boy at all, but a ghost! That meant so much. Queer 's it seems, the fust thought that struck me was this: he wa'n't *be* or *him*, but jest *it*. Then I remembered how I'd planned some new clothes for him. But ghosts don't wear out their clothes.

An' I'd meant—if his folks would let me—to adopt him; bring him up like my own. How ever could I adopt a ghost? Wa'n't it impossible? Come to think o' it, could I have dealin's in any way with a ghost? We'd allers been a respect'ble family; none more so in all New Hampshire; a religious fam'ly too, orth'dox, every single one. Never, 's fur 's I'd heerd, was there a ghost of any kind mixed up with ary branch o' the Jennesses for gen'rations. To be sure, there was a story of one that appeared to one o' the Fosses, connected by marriage with the Jennesses, 'way back fifty years or more. But that one never showed itself; 'twas only a sort o' weepin' an' groanin' an' complainin' noise goin' through the house at night. An' they never encouraged it a mite, but sent for old Parson Williams an' had him pray at it till it cleared out. Then they aired the house thoroughly, an' never had a sign of it agin. But here was I talkin' with one, 'sociatin' with it, gettin' fond on it, an' really talkin' of adoptin' it. What was I goin' to do? What was I goin' not to do? Over an' over in my mind I went at that, an' little sleep I got that night, I tell you. As I said afore, we was brought up in a pious fam'ly, an' my religion, small 's it was to what it oughter been, had brought me through all my troubles so fur, as nothin' else could 'a' done. So I prayed a good deal that night, an' read my Bible lots. An' bimeby—'most mornin' 'twas—I begun to get red o' that whirlin', scaret kind o' thinkin', an' to look at things stiddier an' easier. Mebbe 'twas the prayin'; anyway I got all o' a suddin so 's to see the matter reasonable an' cipher it out plain for myself. 'Twas about this way I went at it. Fust place I says to myself: "What's a ghost, anyway? Why, it's a sperrit. An' what's a sperrit? Why, it's a soul. Well, there ain't no harm in a soul; we've all got 'em. But then," thinks I to myself, "what's this soul doin' here? Where's it been sence the boy died?" Well, you see, I knowed too much about heaven, from Scripter an' sermons an' all, to think that a soul that once got there would leave it to traipse round here agin an' speak pieces. So I had to feel cert'in it hadn't ever got to heaven 'tall. An' as for the other place—why, you never, never in the world, could 'a' made me bleeve that Norvle had been there. He wa'n't that kind, I knowed. 'Twasn't jest because I'd got so fond o' him, but I felt sure, sure, sure that he'd never been there, in that awful suff'rin' an' sin. He'd a showed it if he had. Now you see I was orth'dox, an' my folks afore me, an' I'd never even heerd that any one thought there might be another place besides them two local'ties. Sence then I've read somewheres that there is sexes who bleeve that, but I'd never heerd a hint of it then. But seein' that he hadn't been to ary o' them two places, then where had he been, an' why did he come to me? When I got to that p'int I had to stop short agin, an havin' nothin' better to do, I went to prayin'. An' jest's the mornin' light shone into my window, there come a light shinin' right into my heart, an' I see it all. 'Twas this way. Norvle hadn't been fetched up by religious folks. For, strange 's it may seem, there's people like that, even in a Christian land. He'd been a well-meanin' boy, an' if he'd ever been learnt he'd 'a' took right hold o' religion, an' glad enough too. But he lived 'way off in the mountins, there wa'n't no meetin'-house within miles, an' his folks was like heathen. Even the deestrick school was too fur off for him to go, or else his pa wouldn't spare him to 'tend. So he'd growed up ign'runt of all he'd oughter know, never seein' a Bible, hearin' a sermon, or touchin' a cat'chism in all his life. He'd learnt how to read somehow, an' up in the garret he'd come acrost a book o' pieces sech as boys speak to school. An' he'd took to 'em, studied 'em, an' got so he could say 'em all. But he had to do it all by hisself. Nobody ever heerd him say 'em. Nobody would listen when he tried to show off. That's terr'ble hard on a boy. They like so to be praised up an' noticed when they've done anything. Why Peleg, the

youngest o' my three boys, you know, allers set so by my lookin' at
his whittlin', or hearin' him sing, or praisin' the pictur's he drawed
on his slate. But bimeby Norvle died; I don't know how. I never was
able to find that out; whether 'twas o' sickness or an accident. But he
died without ever havin' been grounded in the right things. An'—oh,
don't you see it now? Don't you know what come to me that early
mornin', as I laid cryin' an' prayin' in my bed there? He—I mean *it*,
Norvle's poor little ign'runt soul—had been let to come to me; me
that loved boys an' had lost 'em all. An' I was to be the one to learn
it what he hadn't never had a chance to pick up afore he died. So
I see I needn't stop bein' fond o' it, but go on lovin' it harder an'
harder, till I'd loved it right straight up into heaven, where it would
'a' been now but for lack o' information.

I tell you that was a solemn day to me. I was happy one way, sorry
another, an' I felt such a awful responsibility. I tell you 'tain't many
that has sech a heft put on 'em as that. Jest think of it! the hull religious trainin' of a ghost! I was busy all day preparin' for it. I looked
up all my books, the ones I used when I learnt the boys, an' the
Sabbath-school ones. An' I made a kind o' plan how I was to begin,
an' how long 'twould take to go through all the doctrines an' beliefs.
Our folks was Congregationals, an' though I wa'n't as set in my ways
about my own Church as some be, still, as Norvle didn't seem to
have any partikler leanin' to ary other belief, I meant to bring him
up as I'd been brought. So o' course I had to begin with the fall, an'
I studied on that 'most all day. As the time drawed nigh for the visit
I was dreffle worked up. Seemed 's if I couldn't scasly bear it, to see
the boy I'd got so attached to an' built so much on, an' know that
he wa'n't a boy at all, but a ghost. I was settin' there, in my old seat
by the window, an' for quite a spell arter the pepp'mint scent come
into the room I wouldn't turn my head. Fact is, I was cryin' so 't I

could hardly see out of my eyes. But bimeby I looked round, an', jest 's I thought, there it stood. My eyes was pretty wet, but I winked out the water 's well 's I could. An' 's soon 's I could see its face plain, I knowed that it knowed I knowed. It didn't have that pleased, shinin' look in its eyes, but was sort o' doubtful an' scary. It stepped slow an' softly, as if it was goin' to stop every step, an' when 'twas in front o' me, it said, almost in a whisper, an' so mournful, "Don't you want to hear me speak my piece?"

I brushed the water out o' my eyes an' says, real hearty an' cordial, "Yes, deary, course I do."

He begun in sech a low, shaky voice:

> "Here rests his head upon the lap of airth,
> A youth to fortin an' to fame unknown."

Poor little feller! I jest ached for him, an' my throat felt all swelled up 's if I had the quinsy. I made up my mind that minute to give up the rest o' my days, if it took that long, to savin' that little soul o' Norvle's. An' he shouldn't never feel, if I could help it, that I didn't exackly approve o' ghosts, or thought a mite less o' him for bein' one. Then I begun my religious teachin'. As I said afore, my startin'-p'int was the fall. But o' course I had to allude to the creation fust, Adam an' Eve, an' all that. Then I larnt him the verse out o' the New England Primer about "In Adam's fall," an' that led right up, you see, to 'riginal sin, nat'ral depravity, an' all that relates to them doctrines. I had to begin jest as you would with a baby, you see, right at the el'mentary things. Then I took the Westminster Shorter, an' learnt him from "man's chief end" to the decrees. 'Twas a short lesson, but I didn't want to tire him the fust time. He seemed real int'rested, an' I forgot for a minute he was a ghost, an' I says, "Norvle, s'pose you take this cat'chism home, an'—" I stopped right off short, for I rec'lected he hadn't got any home, but was jest a wand'rin', ramblin', uneasy ghost. An' oh, where did he sleep nights? Thinkin' o' that made the tears come agin, an' I turned away to sop 'em up. When I looked round, it was gone.

You see I say "it" sometimes, an' then agin I say "him." I know I'd oughter say "it" all the time; but—well, 'way down in my old heart it's "him" an' "he" allers, an' he's no diff'nt from my other three boys.

I was a mite nervous next time. I wasn't quite certin I'd gone to work right with my lessons. I'd had some exper'ence teachin', what with my own boys an' a Sabbath-school class. But how did I know but a ghost's mind was all diff'ent, an' couldn't take in the same things in the same way? Then he didn't have no books, an' couldn't look over the lesson at home. So mebbe—I kep' sayin' to myself—he don't remember a single word about Adam, or his sin, an' the terr'ble consequences. But I needn't 'a' worried; for I hadn't hardly time to answer that same old question, "Don't you want to hear me speak my piece?" afore he started off:

> "Oh, what a fall was there, my countrymen!
> Then me an' you an' all on us fell down."

Could a perfessor in the the'logical sem'nary 'a' put it better? The real cat'chism doctrine, you see, "all mankind by the fall," an' so on. So I begun to feel encouraged. This time I took foreord'nation an' election, an' easy things like that. Eternal punishment goes along o' that lesson by rights, but 'twas sech a pers'nal subjeck for that poor soul that I skipped it that once. So it went on day arter day. I didn't allers keep to the doctrines. I made 'lowances for Norvle's bringin' up, an' had more int'restin' things now an' agin, like who was the fust man, the strongest man, the meekest man, an' them. An' seein' he was so fond o' pieces, I learnt him pretty verses out o' the New England Primer, like

> "Vashti for pride
> Was set aside,"

or

> "Elijah hid,
> By ravens fed."

He was so tickled with that piece about

> "Good children must
> Fear God all day,
> Parents obey,
> No false thing say,"

an' so on. An' he liked about John Rogers, an' Agur's prayer, an' took right off to that advice at the very eend o' the Primer, by the late rev'rent an' ven'rable Mr. Nathan'el Clap, o' Newport, on Rhode Island.

But the days was slippin' by, an' I begun to worry. 'Twas September now, an' my time was up early in October, for the fam'ly was comin' home then. An' go 's fast 's I could I hadn't been able to git beyond "the mis'ry o' that estate whereinto man fell" in the cat'chism, an' the buildin' o' the temple in the Bible. All about sin an' punishment an' the old dispensation, you see, an' never a speck o' light an' hope for that poor sperrit. For o' course I had to go reg'lar an' take subjecks as they come, an' didn't dast skip over into the New Test'ment comfort till its turn come. I was in a heap o' trouble about it, when all of a suddin another chance was give me. Old Mr. Rice come to me with a letter in his hand, an' asked me if I couldn't be induced to stay on an' take care o' the house through the winter. Seems that one o' the children—Mis' Davis's, I mean—had took cold, an' its throat or lungs or something was weak. So the doctor had ordered them to take her 'crost the water, an' they was goin' right off, without comin' home at all. Wasn't it wonderful? A int'position o' Providence, cert'in sure, an' I thanked the Lord on my bended knees. I kep' on now in the reg'lar way, not havin' to hurry, givin' all the time I wanted to the doctrines. For there's nothin' like bein' well grounded in them. Norvle never said much, but he showed plain enough that he took 'em all in, by the appropit pieces he spoke arter each lesson. I wish I could rec'lect 'em all; they was wonderful. I know one time we had free-will, an' 'twas the most excitin' occasion. I got so worked up over it, showin' how 'twas consistent with election an' foreord'nation, an' argifyin' that we was jest as free to pick an' choose as—as—anybody. An' next time he up an' speaks, "Hard, hard indeed was the contest for freedom an' the struggle for independence."

Oh, 'twas good as a sermon! An' agin, arter a course o' lessons on the power o' the devil an' how to resist him, he spoke that powerful piece, "They tell us, sir, that we are weak, unable to scope with so form'dable a adversary; but when shall we be stronger?" An' how he did go on about "Shall we 'quire the means o' effectooal resistance by lyin' s'pinely on our backs an' huggin' the d'lusive phantom o' hope?" an' all that. One day I talked very strong about the Cath'lics, warned him ag'inst the Pope o' Rome, an' forbid him ever to go near popish folks. Next time he come he up an' spoke a piece about

> "Banished from Rome? What's banished but set free
> From daily contracts?"

That showed his views about the Pope plain enough, I think.

Oh, I never see a boy—let alone a ghost—take in truths like him. An' it done me good too. I'd got a little rusty on them doctrinal b'liefs myself, an' it rubbed up my knowledge wonderful. I studied up days, an' could hardly wait for class-time to come; an' jest 's soon 's I had the fust sniff o' pepp'mint arternoons, I'd be ready to start off. But I'd allers give him his chance fust, an' I growed to love that one thing he said every time, the only thing I ever heerd him reely say, "Don't you want to hear me speak my piece?" It seemed to mean more an' more each day, an' bimeby was 'most like a whole conversation. Jest from that one remark I begun to know all about his past life an' doin's, his folks, his home, an' all. A poor, empty, neglected, lonesome life 'twas, an' my heart ached over it as it come out day by day in our talks. To think o' his never havin' had what my boys had so much on, all their days: meetin's, Sabbath-schools, cat'chisms, preparat'ry lectur's, monthly concerts, prayer-meetin's; he never'd had one o' them blessed priv'leges in his hull narrer little life. Well, as I said, I enjoyed the doctrinal teachin', the Old Test'ment an' all; but I was awful glad when with a clear conscience I could turn over the leaf an' show him t'other side. He'd been gettin' rather low in his mind lately, an' no wonder. For I hadn't felt to tell him anything yet but about our dreffle state o' sin, the punishment we deserved, an' the justice o' Him who could give it to us. To be sure, I got him to the p'int where he knowed 'twould be all perfectly right, consid'rin' the circumstances, if he should be sent right down to the place, as the hymn says,

"Where crooked ways o' sinners lead."

He was resigned to it, but he wa'n't exackly glad, an' he looked rather
solemn. So I was pleased enough when I begun to let in a mite o'
sunshinin' an' told him the gospel story. An' I declare it never'd meant
so much to me myself, church member as I'd been for more'n a dozen
years, as when I begun to tell it to that poor little ghost. I begun way
at the very beginnin', an' it was quite a spell afore he see what was
comin'. He thought I was jest givin' an account of a common, ord'nary
boy. I see that was the way to int'rest him, so I told about Him as a
little feller, with his mother, an' in the carpenter's shop, an' round
the water an' the shore with the fishermen an' sailors. I was thinkin'
o' my own boys on the salt-water at Portsmouth an' Kitt'ry when I
dwelt so on that part. But pretty soon I rec'lected how Norvle was
fetched up on risin' ground, so I told about His bein' so fond o' the
hills, goin' up "into a mountin apart," as the Bible says, to pray an'
to preach, or to set there alone. An' how Norvle's face did light up
then, an' his whity-blue eyes shine! I don't doubt he was thinkin'
o' the New Hampshire hills. For crampin' 's they be, folks that lives
among 'em do learn to love 'em lots. So it went on, till it come nigh
the last part o' the narr'tive. No need for me to remind you o' that.
I'd knowed it allers, learnt it to my Sabbath-school scholars, heerd
it talked an' preached an' sung all my born days, but 'twas like a
bran'-new thing 's I told it to Norvle, an' the tears jest ran down my
face like rain. He didn't cry. I guess ghosts never does. But oh, how
mournful an' sorry he looked, with his eyes opened wide an' lookin'
straight into my face, an' his lips kind o' tremblin'! For quite a spell
now he'd been speakin' diff'ent sort o' pieces—hymns an' sech. An'
now he begun to say sech beautiful ones, hymns an' psalms I hadn't
even thought on for years. Some o' 'em I learnt afore I could read,

from hearin' mother say 'em over 'n' over to me as I set on the little cricket at her feet. How I felt as he'd say, soft an' gentle like, "Don't you want to hear me speak my piece?" an' then foller it right up with one o' them sweet old hymns I always rec'lected in mother's voice! Oh, I loved him harder 'n' harder every day! He was jest 's homely 's ever, jest 's freckled, his hair jest 's reddish-yeller an' mussy, but he looked diff'ent, somehow. There was a kind o' rested, quiet, satisfied look come on his face by spells that made him prettier to look at. An' bimeby that look come to stay. I couldn't make you understand 'f I tried—an' I ain't goin' to try—how I see what was happenin' in that soul. But I did see. I knowed the very hour—the minute 'most—when he see the hull truth an' give up to it. There didn't seem to be any powerful conviction o' sin. Mebbe ghosts don't need to go through that. P'r'aps it's their bodies that makes that work so strong in folks, an' ghosts 'ain't got any bodies. So 'twas a easy, smooth specie o' conversion, an' Norvle hisself didn't seem to know when it happened. He kep' comin' jest the same, allers askin' his little question, an' speakin' his piece. An' allers there come with him that pepp'minty scent. To this day that common, ev'ry-day, physicky smell brings more things back to me than even cinnamon-roses or day-lilies like them in the old garden on the Odiorne's P'int road. I went on all the time with my teachin'. I knowed Norvle was all right now, an' safe for ever 'n' ever. But there's plenty o' things even perfessors need to know, an' I did so like to learn him.

'Twas gettin' past the middle o' December now. One day I walked a little ways down street for exercise an' fresh air, an' all to once there come over me sech a strong rec'lection o' Portsmouth woods. I didn't know why 'twas for a minute, but then I begun to smell a piny, woodsy smell, an' I see right on the side-walk a lot o' evergreens—pine an' hemlock an' spruce. Then I remembered that

Christmas was comin'. You see, pa an' ma had allers made a good deal o' Christmas. Congregational in old times never done so. I know pa said that one time old Parson Pickerin', o' Greenland, sent back a turkey that gran'f'ther Jenness give him Christmas, sayin' he'd ruther have it some other time than on a popish hollerday. But we was fetched up to keep the day. Why, up to the very last Christmas o' their lives my three boys hung their blue yarn stockin's up by the fireplace, though Amos was past nineteen then, an' Ezry goin' on seventeen. So 'twas a time full o' rec'lectin' for me. The year afore I'd jest put it all out o' my head an' tried to forget what day 'twas. But I couldn't forget it here. 'Twas in the air; 'twas ev'rywhere you went The stores was full o' playthings, folks was traipsin' through the streets with their hands an' arms full o' bundles, ev'rybody that passed you was talkin' about it, an' 'twas no use tryin' to git red on it. It made me choky an' wat'ry-eyed all the time, an' I couldn't see nothin' ary blessed minute but the old wood fire at home, with the big yarn stockin's hangin' there. But one day arter Norvle had left, an' the pepp'mint scent hadn't quite gone out o' the room, I begun to think why I couldn't make a Christmas for him. Now don't laugh at me. I wa'n't a fool. I knowed 's well 's you do that ghosts don't want presents or keep days. But I was so lonesome, an' jest hungry for a stockin' to fill—a boy's stockin'. "So why," I says to myself, "shouldn't I make bleeve—'play' 's the children says—that Norvle wants a real old-fashioned Christmas, an' I can give him one?" The next time he come I led up to the subject an' found out, 's I suspicioned, that he'd never heerd o' Christmas or Santy Claus in all his born days. So I told him all about it, an' he was so int'rested.

Fust I told him whose birthday 'twas, o' course, an' why folks kep' it. Then I told him all about fam'lies all gettin' together at that time, an' comin' home from everywheres, to be with their own folks. An'

I went on about hangin' up stockin's an' fillin' 'em with presents. "An' now, Norvle," I says, "I'm goin' to make a real old-fashioned Christmas for you this year, sech as we used to have in the old house; sech as we made for Amos an' Ezry an' Peleg. For," I says, "you've been a real good boy this winter, an' I set as much by you 'most— p'r'aps jest as much—as I done by my own boys." He looked dreffle tickled, an' so 'twas settled. How I did enjoy gettin' ready! 'Twa'n't so easy as it seems. For I'd set my heart on havin' the same kind o' presents as we used to give the boys, an' they wa'n't plenty in New York city. The stockin' was easy enough, for I had one o' Peleg's. You see, I kind o' liked to have some o' the boys' things about, an' I had some o' the old blue feetin' layin' on my stockin' basket 's if they was waitin' to be darned. They looked nat'ral an' good, you see. Peleg was nigh about Norvle's size. Then I wanted a partikler specie o' apple, big an' red an' shiny; we called 'em the Boardman reds. I found some to the market at last. They didn't exackly look like the old kind; but the man said they was, he'd jest fetched 'em from Portsmouth hisself. The hick'ry-nuts I got easy enough, an' the maple-sugar. I was goin' to get some pepp'mint lozengers, for my boys all thought so much o' them, but it seemed too pers'nal, an' I give 'em up. I got a big stick o' ball lick'rish, though—boys allers like that—an' some B'gundy pitch to chew. Then o' course there must be a jack-knife. I found jest the right kind, big, with a black horn handle an' two blades. I set up late nights an' riz early to knit a pair o' red yarn mittens, like Peleg's; they're so good for snowbal-lin', you know. An' I wound a yarn ball, an' covered it with leather. I had a diff'cult time findin' the fishhooks an' sinkers, for I hadn't been round no great in New York, an' there ain't no general store there. But I found 'em at last. Right on top I was goin' to put Pely's little chunky, leather cover Bible. Mother give it to him the day he jined the Church, an' writ his name in her straight up an' down, prim handwritin'. I knowed she an' him both would be willin' it should go to this poor little soul the Scripters meant so much to, an' had done so much for.

The New York greens didn't satisfy me. There was some stuff with sicky green leaves an' white, tallery-lookin' berries, an' some all shinin' an' pricky, with red fruit. But they didn't look nat'ral. Bimeby I come acrost some ground-pine, sech as growed all through the wood lot behind the old house, spranglin' over the ground, an' some juniper, like what spread amongst the rocks there, with its little black berries an' sharp, scratchy needles. I couldn't get any black alder nor bittersweet berries, an' had to do without 'em. Oh, you don't know what it was to me, an' my poor empty heart that had ached till 'twas 'most numb, to get that stockin' ready. Ev'ry day I talked Christmas to Norvle, never lettin' him know, o' course, what I was goin' to give him, but tellin' all about diff'ent Christmases I'd knowed. I went on about how the fam'ly was allers together, an' father wore his best clothes an' set to the head o' the table, an' mother t'other end, an' me an' the boys all there. 'Twas nat'ral I s'pose, consid'rin', that I dwelt on that part of it, folks all bein' together that day, lovin' an' doin' for their very own. Then I told him how Christmas Eve we all used to stand together, the boys an' me, an' sing pa's favrit piece, "Home, sweet Home." I carried the toon, Peleg sung a real sweet second, Ezry had the high part, an' Amos the low. How it fetched it all back to tell it over to him!

The last night but one come—the twenty-third 'twas. Norvle had looked real mournful-like lately. Ev'ry time I spoke o' father's house, or fam'lies gettin' together or goin' home for Christmas, I see he looked kind o' sorry an' 's if he wanted somethin'. But I wouldn't see what it meant. That arternoon, though, when he'd ast, in a shaky, still voice, "Don't you want to hear me speak my piece?" he follered it up with the dear old hymn mother whispered part of, the very last day of her life—

> "Airth has engrossed my love too long,
> 'Tis time to lift my eyes."

He went on with all the verses, an' when he come to

> "O let me mount to join their song,"

he said it's if he was prayin' to me, an' sech a longin' sound come into his voice, an' sech a longin' look into his eyes, that I was all goose-flesh, an' so choky. When he'd finished, I turned away to get my handk'chief, an' when I looked back agin he was gone.

Well, I s'pose you see now what I'd got to do, an' what my plain duty was. I really had knowed it all along, but I'd shet my eyes to it a purpose till now; but I couldn't no longer. That poor soul o' Norvle's was regen'rated, saved cert'in sure, an' what business had I to keep it down here any longer? You see it plain enough, but no one but me—an' One other—knows how much it meant to me that night. "Couldn't I," says I to myself—"couldn't I keep him only one day longer, jest over that seas'n o' Christmas, so hard, so ter'ble hard to bear without him? Anyway, couldn't I have him till mornin', an' let him have his stockin'? When he was goin' to have sech a long, long time up there, would jest one day more down here make any great diff'rence?" The answer come quick enough. Yes, 'twould! He b'longed somewhere's else, an' I must send him there, an' right straight off, too, even if it broke my heart all to pieces doin' it.

All the next day I went about my work very softly. It seemed like the day o' the boys' fun'ral. I'd filled the stockin' two days afore—I couldn't wait—an' there it laid in my room, never, never to be hung up, all bulgy an' onreg'lar an' knobby. I knowed what ary bulge meant. That one by the ankle was the jack-knife, an' that queer place nigh the knee was where the stick o' lick'rish had got crosswise an' poked 'way out each side. There was one Boardman red apple roundin' out the toe like a darnin' ball, an' right in the top was Pely's chunky little Bible jest showin' above the ribbed part. I didn't empty it. Folks will keep sech things, you know, an' it's up in my bedroom somewher's now, I bleeve.

Well, Christmas-eve come, an' come quick—too quick for me that time. I'd made up my mind 'twouldn't never do to let Norvle see how I felt. I had a good deal o' Jenness grit, an' I called it all up now. So, when he come in, I was jest as usual, an' smiled at him real pleasant; but I felt 'twouldn't do to wait a single minute, for fear I'd break down, so afore he could make his one little remark, for the fust time sence I knowed him, I begun fust, an' he stood still an' listened.

"Norvle," I says, speakin' 's I used to to the boys' playfellers that used to come an' see 'em an' want to stay on an' on—"Norvle, I've had a real nice visit with you. I've enjoyed your comp'ny lots, an' I wish I could ask you to stay longer. But it's Christmas-eve, you know, an', 's I've often told you, people 'd oughter be with their own folks tonight. You know now where your folks is, least-ways your Father an' your Elder Brother. So, I'm dreffle sorry to seem imperlite an' send you off, but—why, this bein' Christmas Eve, 's I said afore, I really think—the best thing for you to do—is—to go—Home!" I got it out somehow; I don't see how I done it.

Norvle looked right at me, kind o' mournfle. He stood stock-still, an' I thought he was goin' to make his one little remark, but he didn't. Jest 's true 's I live, that boy opened his mouth an' begun to sing. An' oh! what do you suppose he sung? "Home, sweet Home!" He'd never sung afore; I didn't know 's he could; but his voice was like a wood-robin now. An' in a minute, though there wa'n't anybody but him an' me in the room, seemed 's if I heerd some other voices. Norvle carried the toon, but I heerd a real sweet second, an' then a high part an' a low. 'Twas jest like four boys singin' together. An' while I looked at him the music sounded further 'n' further off, till when he got to the last "sweet—sweet—home," I had to lean 'way forward to ketch a sound. An' when it stopped—why, he stopped. He didn't go; he jest wasn't there.

Well, I've got along somehow. You do get along through most things, hard 's they be. It's more'n forty year now sence my ghost story happened, an' I'm an old woman. I'm failin' lately pretty fast, an' it makes me think a good deal about goin' home myself to jine pa 'n' ma 'n' the boys. I might 's well tell you that when I say the boys, I mean *four* on 'em. For, b'sides my three, I'm cert'in there's goin' to be another one, a little chap with rough, reddish-yeller hair, an' lots o' freckles. Course I know it's all diff'ent up there, an' things ain't a speck like what they be here; but somehow it won't seem exackly nat'ral if that little feller don't somewher's in the course o' conv'sation bring in that favrit remark o' his'n,

"Don't you want to hear me speak my piece?"

THE END.

THE WHISPERING WALL

H. D. Everett

Henrietta Dorothy Everett (1851–1923) was a British writer, long published under the pseudonym of Theo Douglas. Though her works were rather popular and her identity was revealed during her lifetime (in 1910), relatively little is known about her life, and her works were long overlooked—until recent efforts to recover the work of forgotten women writers. Everett published over twenty books: from resurrected mummies to spiritual possession, a large number of her novels engaged with the supernatural, though she also wrote three historical novels. Two short story collections were published during her lifetime: *More Uncanny Stories* (1918) and *The Death-Mask, and Other Ghosts* (1920), which she published under her own name. I have chosen to include two short stories by Everett in this anthology, because they engage with sounds and voices in beautifully different ways.

"The Whispering Wall" was not published within one of Everett's two short story collections, but in *Novel Magazine* in February 1916, under the name of Theo Douglas. The fact that it was published during World War One is a very particular context, which is reflected in the story. The "acoustic peculiarity" that the sceptical characters investigate is, as the title suggests, a whispering heard along the walls in the oldest wing of a house. This story is short, but particularly touching, as it turns out that the whispers were not so unintelligible after all.

y story begins before the war, though not long before. We were a party of light-hearted undergraduates in Jack Lovell's rooms at Cambridge, and we had been laughing uproariously over some story of psychical marvels. Jack was the only one of us who took the matter seriously.

After the others had gone, I said to him:

"Surely you didn't believe that farrago of nonsense Smith was telling, did you? I was surprised to hear you argue that it might be true."

"Only that it might be true, not that it was. I saw no impossibility; that was all."

"Why, old man, you do surprise me! You are the last fellow I should have thought likely to give in to spooks."

Jack was smoking; he knocked out his pipe before he answered, and began to fill it with deliberation.

"And you would have been right, when the evidence was hearsay. But the position alters to one who has heard and seen."

"Why, you don't mean to say that you—"

Jack had his pipe between his teeth again, so he merely nodded. But the nod was enough.

"My dear old Jack! But you haven't reflected what cheats these mediums are. They are past-masters as conjurers—have to be, and all their spooks are faked. I know a fellow who is a Psychical Researcher, and he says—"

"I have not been to mediums. My people live in a house up in the north which has a queer reputation. The old wing is practically shut up, because of what you call spooks; a ghost that is heard rather frequently, and sometimes seen."

"And you do not suspect any one of playing tricks?"

"What, for a hundred and fifty years on end?" Jack seemed to consider the question, and then he shook his head. "There is no trick about it. No."

"Before I believed, I should have to hear and see for myself, and investigate a lot to make sure. I would rather like to try."

"Then come to Marchmore with me next week. We go down then, as you know. You will be very welcome. You are not fixed anywhere else?"

I had no fixtures, and I accepted the invitation then and there. I received the welcome he promised me, and Jack did not proclaim me a ghost-hunter, or give me away.

Marchmore was a larger house than I expected: Jack was not one who said much about his family. It was built on three sides of a quadrangle, of which the iron gates supplied the fourth, and surrounded by a stretch of park-land. The centre was the family dwelling, with an older wing on your left as you faced the entrance, and a quite modern one on the right, which contained the servants' quarters. The guest-chamber allotted to me was in the centre building, but Jack's rooms, bedroom and sitting-room together, were on the first floor of the old wing, which was supposed to be the habitat of the ghost.

I went off to smoke with Jack when we retired for the night, and found him pleasantly established, with cheerful light and fire, lounge chairs, and every comfort. I suppose I was impatient, for I said as soon as we were alone:

"When is the entertainment going to begin, and where is it held?"

I do not think Jack quite liked his spooks taken in that spirit.

"I told you I could not answer for it, and you might be disappointed," he returned with some sharpness in his voice. "It may happen at any moment, or you may have to wait for it—days, or even weeks. But as to where it happens, I can show you now. Come upstairs with me."

He took up the lamp, and led the way out on to the landing, where he unlocked a door which shut in an inclosed staircase leading to the attic floor.

"Come up here whenever you like," he said; "you will have a better chance alone."

The stairs were uncarpeted, with a window behind them at the top, which lighted a narrow passage under the pitch of the high tiled roof. A closed door faced us at the end, and there were also doors to right and left.

"You can look into all these rooms," Jack said. "You will find them empty, as we do not use them, even for lumber. But it is here in the passage that you must listen for the voice."

The place was grim enough. I confess I did not care for it, but I was not going to show the white feather.

"You haven't told me yet what I should hear."

"It is a sort of whispering which travels along the wall on the left, beginning quite away at the end; and as it draws near and passes you it gets distinct." He touched the side wall of the passage as he spoke.

"Hum—some acoustic peculiarity?" I suggested.

"Very likely! I have often thought that, but the sound shapes itself into words, and sometimes—not always—they have meaning. Probably they differ to each hearer. I cannot say how they would come to you."

We stood in silence for a while, and nothing happened; the place was close and oppressive with its one window closed—indeed, there seemed to be an unnatural deadness about the air. Jack moved first.

"It will not come tonight, so we had better go down"; and he led the way with his lamp. At the foot of the staircase he locked the inclosing door, but left the key standing; and I confess to a certain relief when we were back in his pleasant sitting-room, and the ghost hunt was over for the night.

Marchmore had other attractions, but I tore myself away from them next morning on the pretext of letters to write in Jack's room. I did write one or two, that there might be some correspondence of mine in the letter-bag as a result; but these epistles were of the briefest. Then I sought the attic staircase, closing the door after me to prevent surprise from below. The narrow passage, with its blank surroundings of shut doors, lighted only from the window behind me, was hardly more cheerful on a daylight view. I did not believe in the thing; I was determined not to believe in it; but, despite my scepticism, I experienced a creeping thrill about the spine, and an odd sensation in my ears, which were strained to listen.

The silence, however, was absolute. Of course, I said to myself, this happened to be a still day, and no doubt the phenomenon depended upon wind whistling round the eaves and crannies of the old house. Then I turned my attention to the five shut doors.

Those on the right and left opened into four narrow garrets, empty as described to me; two of them lighted with small dormer windows, the other two by oblongs of thick glass let into the slope of the roof; dismal chambers, which, apart from the ill reputation of this upper floor, would hardly be chosen for occupation.

The fifth door at the end of the passage opened into a much larger and more cheerful room, which had the advantage of a broad, low window, nearly the width of the front gable, and also of a rusty fireplace at the side. Probably at some distant date children had used it for a play-room; it was empty of furniture, but in one corner was a dilapidated rocking-horse, and a lidless box half-full of broken toys.

I wondered whose were the children who once had played here unafraid; and then as I turned away from the toy-box, as if caused by its suggestion, I had the brief illusion that one of them stood beside me: a little fair-haired lad in a belted pinafore. Of course, it was a trick of the imagination, and I quickly saw how it was caused. This room also had a glazed pane let into the roof, and sunshine through the parting clouds had thrown down, on to the floor below, a shaft of light.

After that I went away downstairs, but I resolved not to mention that odd fancy of mine to Jack, as he might attach to it some psychical meaning. He had described to me no visible ghost; he had spoken only of the whispers, and these I had not heard.

I was in Jack's room the third evening of my stay, and we had been discussing quite other matters. I had not even the ghost in mind, when there was a patter of footsteps overhead, quick small footsteps, like a child's. They seemed to run across the large attic and along the passage, and presently back again over the uncarpeted floors.

"What is that?" I exclaimed.

Jack did not give a direct answer. "It often comes before the whispers," he said. "If you come upstairs now, I believe that you will hear."

He took up the lamp and led the way. I noticed that he needed to unlock the door shutting in the staircase. His light showed the passage empty and doors shut, and the pattering footsteps had ceased.

We stood as before, facing the wall on the left; and presently, at the far end, the whispering began. However caused, it was undistinguishable from a human voice, and, as the whisperer approached, the vague sounds formed themselves into spoken words, but words without meaning. "*Ah Mont*," and again "*Ah—Mont*" and then, with a sort of sighing gasp, it added "*Year*."

The voice died away to our left, above the hollow of the stairs; and then, after the interval of a couple of minutes, began again by the shut door. The same words were repeated as it approached us the second time, and after that the stillness was unbroken. Jack, still holding up his lamp, one after another opened the five doors, and showed the rooms empty.

Then we went down into the smoking-room, locking in the ghost as before. "Well," he said, "can you account for it?"

"No," I answered.

After we had settled back in our respective chairs and relit our pipes, Jack asked: "Did you distinguish words?"

"Yes," I replied, and told him what I had heard. "Is it always the same?"

"I heard it just as you did, and the phrase was new. I have no idea what it means. The words sometimes are: 'Come and play'—as if a child spoke them."

The impression was too recent and vivid to allow of jesting, as I might have jested once. I inquired if there were any legend which explained the haunting.

"No legend. But there is a saying that if one of us Lovells sees the child, he will not live to have children of his own."

I heard no more while I was at Marchmore, and, the day but one after, my visit came to an end.

That fateful summer of 1914 brought many changes. Jack Lovell and I ceased to be students at the University. We both joined the Army, and went out immediately after the retreat, so we were in the November fighting, half-forgotten now amidst all that has come after, but it was mentioned in the dispatches as "heavy."

A village was held by our regiment against stubborn assaults, repulsed with the bayonet. Jack Lovell was wounded, how severely we others did not know, for there was much confusion. He was sent down to the base hospital; and two days after I got a shrapnel tear on the shoulder—a surface affair, but it began to look angry, and so I too was ordered down. I asked at once for Jack, and was deeply distressed to be told his hurt was serious, and he was not expected to live.

I was allowed to see him, and presently was at his bedside, with his hand in mine. His face looked grey and pinched; it was hardly the face I knew.

"You'll be going back to England, Eccles, lucky fellow!" he said presently, and he smiled—such a wan smile it was. He would come too, I answered; he mustn't lose heart about himself; you know the sort of thing one says, even when it is a lie.

"Yes, but not the way you will," he answered. "The child at Marchmore wants me; he was always whispering to me to come and play. And you know what you heard at the wall: what we both heard there. I've been thinking about it tonight. You know the place where we were fighting? Tell me the name of it—Eccles—tell me!"

Was he wandering? I thought so. But, of course, I answered him. "It was near Armentières."

"Wasn't that what the voice whispered? You heard it, too. *Ah-mont-year*. Why, of course it was! I know what he was driving at, though I did not understand it then. It's all as it should be."

And then again he smiled, and, turning his face from me, appeared to fall asleep.

I went home for my wound to heal, but he remained behind. That is, what was mortal of him; for I left the best pal I ever had in a soldier's grave in France.

NO LIVING VOICE

Thomas Street Millington

Not much is known about Thomas Street Millington (1821–1906). Born in London, he was a clergyman and, from curate, became the vicar of Woodhouse Eaves, a small village in the Charnwood Forest area of Leicestershire. Married and with two children, Millington's output included theology works, but also so-called boys' fiction (that is, adventure stories serialised in periodicals such as *Boys' Own Paper*) between the 1870s and the 1890s. A few examples are *Boy and Man: A Story for Young and Old* (1877), *Through Fire and Through Water: A Story of Peril and Adventure* (1888) and *No Choice: A Story of the Unforeseen* (1890).

"No Living Voice" was first published anonymously in April 1872, in the London magazine *Temple Bar*. The tale uses the narrative technique of the *mise en abyme*, that is to say, of a story within a story, to captivate its readers: it is presented as an after-dinner retelling of a ghost story. The "matter of fact" narrator's encounter with a voice whose groaning makes his blood run cold underscores the inherent horror attached to hearing a ghostly voice; but at the same time, it also outlines the potentially transformative power of listening.

"ow do you account for it?"

"I don't account for it at all. I don't pretend to understand it."

"You think, then, that it was really supernatural?"

"We know so little what Nature comprehends—what are its powers and limits—that we can scarcely speak of anything that happens as beyond it or above it."

"And you are certain that this did happen?"

"Quite certain; of that I have no doubt whatever."

These sentences passed between two gentlemen in the drawing-room of a country house, where a small family party was assembled after dinner; and in consequence of a lull in the conversation occurring at the moment they were distinctly heard by nearly everybody present. Curiosity was excited, and enquiries were eagerly pressed as to the nature or super nature of the event under discussion. "A ghost story!" cried one; "oh! delightful! we must and will hear it." "Oh! please, no," said another; "I should not sleep all night—and yet I am dying with curiosity."

Others seemed inclined to treat the question rather from a rational or psychological point of view, and would have started a discussion upon ghosts in general, each giving his own experience; but these were brought back by the voice of the hostess, crying, "Question, question!" and the first speakers were warmly urged to explain what particular event had formed the subject of their conversation.

"It was you, Mr. Browne, who said you could not account for it; and you are such a very matter-of-fact person that we feel doubly anxious to hear what wonderful occurrence could have made you look so grave and earnest."

"Thank you," said Mr. Browne. "I am a matter-of-fact person, I confess; and I was speaking of a fact; though I must beg to be excused saying any more about it. It is an old story; but I never even think of it without a feeling of distress; and I should not like to stir up such keen and haunting memories merely for the sake of gratifying curiosity. I was relating to Mr. Smith, in few words, an adventure which befell me in Italy many years ago, giving him the naked facts of the case, in refutation of a theory which he had been propounding."

"Now we don't want theories, and we won't have naked facts; they are hardly proper at any time, and at this period of the year, with snow upon the ground," they would be most unseasonable; but we must have that story fully and feelingly related to us, and we promise to give it a respectful hearing, implicit belief, and unbounded sympathy. So draw round the fire, all of you, and let Mr. Browne begin."

Poor Mr. Browne turned pale and red, his lips quivered, his entreaties to be excused became quite plaintive; but his good nature and perhaps, also, the consciousness that he could really interest his hearers, led him to overcome his reluctance; and after exacting a solemn promise that there should be no jesting or levity in regard to what he had to tell, he cleared his throat twice or thrice, and in a hesitating nervous tone began as follows:

"It was in the spring of 18—. I had been at Rome during the Holy Week, and had taken a place in the diligence for Naples. There were two routes: one by way of Terracina and the other by the Via Latina, more inland. The diligence, which made the journey only twice a week, followed these routes alternately, so that each road was traversed only once in seven days. I chose the inland route, and after a long day's journey arrived at Ceprano, where we halted for the night.

"The next morning we started again very early, and it was scarcely yet daylight when we reached the Neapolitan frontier, at a short distance from the town. There our passports were examined, and to my great dismay I was informed that mine was not en règle. It was covered, indeed, with stamps and signatures, not one of which had been procured without some cost and trouble; but one "visa" yet was wanting, and that the all-important one, without which none could enter the kingdom of Naples. I was obliged therefore to alight, and to send my wretched passport back to Rome, my wretched self being doomed to remain under police surveillance at Ceprano, until the diligence should bring it back to me on that day week, at soonest.

"I took up my abode at the hotel where I had passed the previous night, and there I presently received a visit from the Capo di Polizia, who told me very civilly that I must present myself, every morning and evening at his bureau, but that I might have liberty to 'circulate' in the neighbourhood during the day. I grew so weary of this dull place, that after I had explored the immediate vicinity of the town I began to extend my walks to a greater distance, and as I always reported myself to the police before night I met with no objection on their part.

"One day, however, when I had been as far as Alatri and was returning on foot, night overtook me. I had lost my way, and could not tell how far I might be from my destination. I was very tired and had a heavy knapsack on my shoulders, packed with stones and relics from the ruins of the old Pelasgic fortress which I had been exploring, besides a number of old coins and a lamp or two which I had purchased there. I could discern no signs of any human habitation, and the hills, covered with wood, seemed to shut me in on every side. I was beginning to think seriously of looking out for some sheltered spot under a thicket in which to pass the night, when the welcome sound of a footstep behind me fell upon my ears. Presently a man dressed in the usual long shaggy coat of a shepherd overtook me, and hearing of my difficulty offered to conduct me to a house at a short distance from the road, where I might obtain a lodging; before we reached the spot he told me that the house in question was an inn and that he was the landlord of it. He had not much custom, he said, so he employed himself in shepherding during the day; but he could make me comfortable, and give me a good supper also, better than I should expect, to look at him; but he had been in different circumstances once, and had lived in service in good families, and knew how things ought to be, and what a signore like myself was used to.

"The house to which he took me seemed like its owner to have seen better days. It was a large rambling place and much dilapidated, but it was tolerably comfortable within; and my landlord, after he had thrown off his sheepskin coat, prepared me a good and savoury meal, and sat down to look at and converse with me while I ate it. I did not much like the look of the fellow; but he seemed anxious to be sociable and told me a great deal about his former life when he was in service, expecting to receive similar confidences from me. I did not gratify him much, but one must talk of something, and he seemed to think it only proper to express an interest in his guests and to learn as much of their concerns as they would tell him.

"I went to bed early, intending to resume my journey as soon as it should be light. My landlord took up my knapsack, and carried it to my room, observing as he did so that it was a great weight for me to travel with. I answered jokingly that it contained great treasures, referring to my coins and relics; of course he did not understand me, and before I could explain he wished me a most happy little night, and left me.

"The room in which I found myself was situated at the end of a long passage; there were two rooms on the right side of this passage, and a window on the left, which looked out upon a yard or garden. Having taken a survey of the outside of the house while smoking my cigar after dinner, when the moon was up, I understood exactly the position of my chamber—the end room of a long narrow wing, projecting at right angles from the main building, with which it was connected only by the passage and the two side rooms already mentioned. Please to bear this description carefully in mind while I proceed.

"Before getting into bed, I drove into the floor close to the door a small gimlet which formed part of a complicated pocket-knife which I always carried with me, so that it would be impossible for any one to enter the room without my knowledge; there was a lock to the door, but the key would not turn in it; there was also a bolt, but it would not enter the hole intended for it, the door having sunk apparently from its proper level. I satisfied myself, however, that the door was securely fastened by my gimlet, and soon fell asleep.

"How can I describe the strange and horrible sensation which oppressed me as I woke out of my first slumber? I had been sleeping soundly, and before I quite recovered consciousness I had instinctively risen from my pillow, and was crouching forward, my knees drawn up, my hands clasped before my face, and my whole frame quivering with horror. I saw nothing, felt nothing; but a sound was ringing in my ears which seemed to make my blood run cold. I could not have supposed it possible that any mere sound, whatever might be its nature, could have produced such a revulsion of feeling or inspired such intense horror as I then experienced. It was not a cry of terror that I heard—that would have roused me to action—nor the moaning of one in pain—that would have distressed me, and called forth sympathy rather than aversion. True, it was like the groaning of one in anguish and despair, but not like any mortal voice: it seemed too dreadful, too intense, for human utterance. The sound had begun while I was fast asleep—close in the head of my bed—close to my very pillow; it continued after I was wide awake—a long, loud, hollow, protracted groan, making the midnight air reverberate, and then dying gradually away until it ceased entirely. It was some minutes before I could at all recover from the terrible impression which seemed to stop my breath and paralyse my limbs. At length I began to look about me, for the night was not entirely dark, and I could discern the outlines of the room and the several pieces of furniture in it. I then got out of bed, and called aloud, 'Who is there? What is the matter? Is anyone ill?' I repeated these enquiries in Italian and in French, but there was none that answered. Fortunately I had some matches in my pocket and was able to light my candle. I then examined every pan of the room carefully, and especially the wall at the head of my bed, sounding it with my knuckles; it was firm and solid there, as in all other places. I unfastened my door, and explored the passage and the two adjoining rooms, which were unoccupied and almost destitute of furniture; they had evidently not been used for some time. Search as I would I could gain no clue to the mystery. Returning to my room I sat down upon the bed in great perplexity, and began to turn over in my mind whether it was possible I could have been deceived—whether the sounds which caused me such distress might be the offspring of some dream or nightmare; but to that conclusion I could not bring myself at all, much as I wished it, for the groaning had continued ringing in my ears long after I was wide awake and conscious. While I was thus reflecting, having neglected to close the door which was opposite to the side of my bed where I was sitting, I heard a soft footstep at a distance, and presently a light appeared at the further end of the passage. Then I saw the shadow of a man cast upon the opposite wall; it moved very slowly, and presently stopped. I saw the hand raised, as if making a sign to someone, and I knew from the fact of the shadow being thrown in advance that there must be a second person in the rear by whom the light was earned. After a short pause they seemed to retrace their steps, without my having had a glimpse of either of them, but only of the shadow which had come before and which followed them as they withdrew. It was then a little after one o'clock, and I concluded they were retiring late to rest, and anxious to avoid disturbing me, though I have since thought that it was the light from my room which caused their retreat. I felt half inclined to call to them, but I shrank, without knowing why, from making known what had disturbed me, and while I hesitated they were gone; so I fastened my door again, and resolved to sit up and watch a little longer by myself. But now my candle was beginning to burn low, and I found myself in this dilemma: either I must extinguish it at once, or I should be left without the means of procuring a light in case I should be again disturbed. I regretted that I had not called for another candle while there were people yet moving in the house, but I could not do so now without making explanations; so I grasped my box of matches, put out my light, and lay down, not without a shudder, in the bed.

"For an hour or more I lay awake thinking over what had occurred, and by that time I had almost persuaded myself that I had nothing but my own morbid imagination to thank for the alarm which I had suffered. 'It is an outer wall,' I said to myself; 'they are all outer walls, and the house is built of stone; it is impossible that any sound could be heard through such a thickness. Besides, it seemed to be in my room, close to my ear. What an idiot I must be, to be excited and alarmed about nothing; I'll think no more about it.' So I turned on my side, with a smile (rather a forced one) at my own foolishness, and composed myself to sleep.

"At that instant I heard, with more distinctness than I ever heard any other sound in my life, a gasp, a voiceless gasp, as if someone were in agony for breath, biting at the air, or trying with desperate efforts to cry out or speak. It was repeated a second and a third time; then there was a pause; then again that horrible gasping; and then a long-drawn breath, an audible drawing up of the air into the throat, such as one would make in heaving a deep sigh. Such sounds as these could not possibly have been heard unless they had been close to my ear; they seemed to come from the wall at my head, or to rise up out of my pillow. That fearful gasping, and that drawing in of the breath, in the darkness and silence of the night, seemed to make every nerve in my body thrill with dreadful expectation. Unconsciously I shrank away from it, crouching down as before, with my face upon my knees. It ceased, and immediately a moaning sound began, which lengthened out into an awful, protracted groan, waxing louder and louder, as if under an increasing agony, and then dying away slowly and gradually into silence; yet painfully and distinctly audible even to the last.

"As soon as I could rouse myself from the freezing horror which seemed to penetrate even to my joints and marrow, I crept away from the bed, and in the furthest corner of the room lighted with shaking hand my candle, looking anxiously about me as I did so, expecting some dreadful revelation as the light flashed up. Yet, if you will believe me, I did not feel alarmed or frightened; but rather oppressed, and penetrated with an unnatural, overpowering, sentiment of awe. I seemed to be in the presence of some great and horrible mystery, some bottomless depth of woe, or misery, or crime. I shrank from it with a sensation of intolerable loathing and suspense. It was a feeling akin to this which prevented me from calling to my landlord. I could not bring myself to speak to him of what had passed; not knowing how nearly he might be himself involved in the mystery. I was only anxious to escape as quietly as possible from the room and from the house. The candle was now beginning to flicker in its socket, but the stars were shining outside, and there was space and air to breathe there, which seemed to be wanting in my room; so I hastily opened my window, tied the bedclothes together for a rope, and lowered myself silently and safely to the ground.

"There was a light still burning in the lower part of the house; but I crept noiselessly along, feeling my way carefully among the trees, and in due time came upon a beaten track which led me to a road, the same which I had been travelling on the previous night. I walked on, scarcely knowing whither, anxious only to increase my distance from the accursed house, until the day began to break, when almost the first object I could see distinctly was a small body of men approaching me. It was with no small pleasure that I recognised at their head my friend the Capo di Polizia. 'Ah!' he cried, 'unfortunate Inglese, what trouble you have given me! Where have you been? God be praised that I see you safe and sound! But how? What is the matter with you? You look like one possessed.'

"I told him how I had lost my way, and where I had lodged.

"'And what happened to you there?' he cried, with a look of anxiety.

"'I was disturbed in the night. I could not sleep. I made my escape, and here I am. I cannot tell you more.'

"'But you must tell me more, dear sir; forgive me; you must tell me everything. I must know all that passed in that house. We have had it under our surveillance for a long time, and when I heard in what direction you had gone yesterday, and had not returned, I feared you had got into some mischief there, and we were even now upon our way to look for you.'

"I could not enter into particulars, but I told him I had heard strange sounds, and at his request I went back with him to the spot. He told me by the way that the house was known to be the resort of banditti; that the landlord harboured them, received their ill-gotten goods, and helped them to dispose of their booty.

"Arrived at the spot, he placed his men about the premises and instituted a strict search, the landlord and the man who was found in the house being compelled to accompany him. The room in which I had slept was carefully examined; the floor was of plaster or cement, so that no sound could have passed through it; the walls were sound and solid, and there was nothing to be seen that could in any way account for the strange disturbance I had experienced. The room on the ground-floor underneath my bedroom was next inspected; it contained a quantity of straw, hay, firewood, and lumber. It was paved with brick, and on turning over the straw which was heaped together in a corner it was observed that the bricks were uneven, as if they had been recently disturbed.

"'Dig here,' said the officer, 'we shall find something hidden here, I imagine.'

"The landlord was evidently much disturbed. 'Stop,' he cried. 'I will tell you what lies there; come away out of doors, and you shall know all about it.'

"'Dig, I say. We will find out for ourselves.'

"'Let the dead rest,' cried the landlord, with a trembling voice. 'For the love of heaven come away, and hear what I shall tell you.'

"'Go on with your work,' said the sergeant to his men, who were now plying pickaxe and spade.

"'I can't stay here and see it,' exclaimed the landlord once more. 'Hear then! It is the body of my son, my only son—let him rest, if rest he can. He was wounded in a quarrel, and brought home here to die. I thought he would recover, but there was neither doctor nor priest at hand, and in spite of all that we could do for him he died. Let him alone now, or let a priest first be sent for; he died unconfessed, but it was not my fault; it may not be yet too late to make peace for him.'

"'But why is he buried in this place?'

"'We did not wish to make a stir about it. Nobody knew of his death, and we laid him down quietly; one place I thought was as good as another when once the life was out of him. We are poor folk, and could not pay for ceremonies.'

The truth at length came out. Father and son were both members of a band of thieves; under this floor they concealed their plunder, and there too lay more than one mouldering corpse, victims who had occupied the room in which I slept, and had there met their death. The son was indeed buried in that spot; he had been mortally wounded in a skirmish with travellers, and had lived long enough to repent of his deeds and to beg for that priestly absolution which, according to his creed, was necessary to secure his pardon. In vain he had urged his father to bring the confessor to his bedside; in vain he had entreated him to break off from the murderous band with which he was allied and to live honestly in future; his prayers were disregarded, and his dying admonitions were of no avail. But for the strange mysterious warning which had roused me from my sleep and driven me out of the house that night another crime would have been added to the old man's tale of guilt. That gasping attempt to speak, and that awful groaning—whence did they proceed? It was *no living voice*. Beyond that I will express no opinion on the subject. I will only say it was the means of saving my life, and at the same time putting an end to the series of bloody deeds which had been committed in that house.

"I received my passport that evening by the diligence from Rome, and started the next morning on my way to Naples. As we were crossing the frontier a tall figure approached, wearing the long rough cappa of the mendicant friars, with a hood over the face and holes for the eyes to look through. He carried a tin money-box in his hand, which he held out to the passengers, jingling a few coins in it, and crying in a monotonous voice, '*Anime in purgatorio! Anime in purgatorio!*'

"I do not believe in purgatory, nor in supplications for the dead; but I dropped a piece of silver into the box nevertheless, as I thought of that unhallowed grave in the forest, and my prayer went up to heaven in all sincerity—'*Requiescat in pace!*'"

III.

"I jumped awake to the furious ringing of my bell": Sonorous objects and haunting technology

THE LADY'S MAID'S BELL

Edith Wharton

Born Edith Newbold Jones, Edith Wharton (1862–1937) is certainly one of the most famous authors included in this collection. The American writer was extraordinarily productive: she published novels, novellas, short stories, poetry, and a memoir, but also books on design, literary criticism, and travel. Known mostly for her sharp critique of the upper-class, late-nineteenth-century New York of her childhood, she became the first woman to be awarded the Pulitzer Prize in Literature in 1921, for her novel *The Age of Innocence*. She is also remembered for *The House of Mirth* (1905), another social commentary of life in the Gilded Age; but her many spectral stories have long been overlooked, in spite of the fact that the majority of her eighty-five short stories are actually ghost tales. Though Wharton claimed that she had to get rid of books of ghost stories in her youth, frightened to even know of their presence in the downstairs library, she became a master of the genre in her thirties, and went on to write such tales over the following decades and until the end of her life. The year of her death saw the publication of *Ghosts*, a collection of ghost stories that she had herself selected from her works.

"The Lady's Maid's Bell" is one of Wharton's earliest published ghost stories. It appeared in November 1902 in *Scribner's Magazine*, a popular American monthly periodical which had been launched in 1887 and was a competitor of such famous magazines as *Harper's Monthly*. In "The Lady's Maid's Bell", a young woman finds employment in a large Hudson estate as a maid to a lonely mistress in need of a companion. Though warned that it would not be a "cheerful place", young Hartley takes the position and settles in her new home, undisturbed by the odd details she comes across. Until one night, the bell rings.

I

t was the autumn after I had the typhoid. I'd been three months in hospital, and when I came out I looked so weak and tottery that the two or three ladies I applied to were afraid to engage me. Most of my money was gone, and after I'd boarded for two months, hanging about the employment-agencies, and answering any advertisement that looked any way respectable, I pretty nearly lost heart, for fretting hadn't made me fatter, and I didn't see why my luck should ever turn. It did though—or I thought so at the time. A Mrs. Railton, a friend of the lady that first brought me out to the States, met me one day and stopped to speak to me: she was one that had always a friendly way with her. She asked me what ailed me to look so white, and when I told her, "Why, Hartley," says she, "I believe I've got the very place for you. Come in tomorrow and we'll talk about it."

The next day, when I called, she told me the lady she'd in mind was a niece of hers, a Mrs. Brympton, a youngish lady, but something of an invalid, who lived all the year round at her country-place on the Hudson, owing to not being able to stand the fatigue of town life.

"Now, Hartley," Mrs. Railton said, in that cheery way that always made me feel things must be going to take a turn for the better— "now understand me; it's not a cheerful place I'm sending you to. The house is big and gloomy; my niece is nervous, vaporish; her husband—well, he's generally away; and the two children are dead. A year ago, I would as soon have thought of shutting a rosy active girl like you into a vault; but you're not particularly brisk yourself just now, are you? and a quiet place, with country air and wholesome food and early hours, ought to be the very thing for you. Don't mistake me," she added, for I suppose I looked a trifle downcast; "you may find it dull, but you won't be unhappy. My niece is an angel. Her former maid, who died last spring, had been with her twenty years and worshipped the ground she walked on. She's a kind mistress to all, and where the mistress is kind, as you know, the servants are generally good-humoured, so you'll probably get on well enough with the rest of the household. And you're the very woman I want for my niece: quiet, well-mannered, and educated above your station. You read aloud well, I think? That's a good thing; my niece likes to be read to. She wants a maid that can be something of a companion: her last was, and I can't say how she misses her. It's a lonely life... Well, have you decided?"

"Why, ma'am," I said, "I'm not afraid of solitude."

"Well, then, go; my niece will take you on my recommendation. I'll telegraph her at once and you can take the afternoon train. She has no one to wait on her at present, and I don't want you to lose any time."

I was ready enough to start, yet something in me hung back; and to gain time I asked, "And the gentleman, ma'am?"

"The gentleman's almost always away, I tell you," said Mrs. Railton, quick-like—"and when he's there," says she suddenly, "you've only to keep out of his way."

I took the afternoon train and got out at D—— station at about four o'clock. A groom in a dog-cart was waiting, and we drove off at a smart pace. It was a dull October day, with rain hanging close overhead, and by the time we turned into the Brympton Place woods the daylight was almost gone. The drive wound through the woods for a mile or two, and came out on a gravel court shut in with thickets of tall black-looking shrubs. There were no lights in the windows, and the house *did* look a bit gloomy.

I had asked no questions of the groom, for I never was one to get my notion of new masters from their other servants: I prefer to wait and see for myself. But I could tell by the look of everything that I had got into the right kind of house, and that things were done handsomely. A pleasant-faced cook met me at the back door and called the house-maid to show me up to my room. "You'll see madam later," she said. "Mrs. Brympton has a visitor."

I hadn't fancied Mrs. Brympton was a lady to have many visitors, and somehow the words cheered me. I followed the house-maid upstairs, and saw, through a door on the upper landing, that the main part of the house seemed well-furnished, with dark panelling and a number of old portraits. Another flight of stairs led us up to the servants' wing. It was almost dark now, and the house-maid excused herself for not having brought a light. "But there's matches in your room," she said, "and if you go careful you'll be all right. Mind the step at the end of the passage. Your room is just beyond."

I looked ahead as she spoke, and halfway down the passage, I saw a woman standing. She drew back into a doorway as we passed, and the house-maid didn't appear to notice her. She was a thin woman with a white face, and a darkish stuff gown and apron. I took her for the housekeeper and thought it odd that she didn't speak, but just gave me a long look as she went by. My room opened into a square hall at the end of the passage. Facing my door was another which stood open: the house-maid exclaimed when she saw it.

"There—Mrs. Blinder's left that door open again!" said she, closing it.

"Is Mrs. Blinder the housekeeper?"

"There's no housekeeper: Mrs. Blinder's the cook."

"And is that her room?"

"Laws, no," said the house-maid, cross-like. "That's nobody's room. It's empty, I mean, and the door hadn't ought to be open. Mrs. Brympton wants it kept locked."

She opened my door and led me into a neat room, nicely furnished, with a picture or two on the walls; and having lit a candle she took leave, telling me that the servants'-hall tea was at six, and that Mrs. Brympton would see me afterward.

I found them a pleasant-spoken set in the servants' hall, and by what they let fall I gathered that, as Mrs. Railton had said, Mrs. Brympton was the kindest of ladies; but I didn't take much notice of their talk, for I was watching to see the pale woman in the dark gown come in. She didn't show herself, however, and I wondered if she ate apart; but if she wasn't the housekeeper, why should she? Suddenly it struck me that she might be a trained nurse, and in that case her meals would of course be served in her room. If Mrs. Brympton was an invalid it was likely enough she had a nurse. The idea annoyed me, I own, for they're not always the easiest to get on with, and if I'd known, I shouldn't have taken the place. But there I was, and there was no use pulling a long face over it; and not being one to ask questions, I waited to see what would turn up.

When tea was over, the house-maid said to the footman: "Has Mr. Ranford gone?" and when he said yes, she told me to come up with her to Mrs. Brympton.

Mrs. Brympton was lying down in her bedroom. Her lounge stood near the fire and beside it was a shaded lamp. She was a delicate-looking lady, but when she smiled I felt there was nothing I wouldn't do for her. She spoke very pleasantly, in a low voice, asking me my name and age and so on, and if I had everything I wanted, and if I wasn't afraid of feeling lonely in the country.

"Not with you I wouldn't be, madam," I said, and the words surprised me when I'd spoken them, for I'm not an impulsive person; but it was just as if I'd thought aloud.

She seemed pleased at that, and said she hoped I'd continue in the same mind; then she gave me a few directions about her toilet, and said Agnes the house-maid would show me next morning where things were kept.

"I am tired tonight, and shall dine upstairs," she said. "Agnes will bring me my tray, that you may have time to unpack and settle yourself; and later you may come and undress me."

"Very well, ma'am," I said. "You'll ring, I suppose?"

I thought she looked odd.

"No—Agnes will fetch you," says she quickly, and took up her book again.

Well—that was certainly strange: a lady's-maid having to be fetched by the house-maid whenever her lady wanted her! I wondered if there were no bells in the house; but the next day I satisfied myself that there was one in every room, and a special one ringing from my mistress's room to mine; and after that it did strike me as queer that, whenever Mrs. Brympton wanted anything, she rang for Agnes, who had to walk the whole length of the servants' wing to call me.

But that wasn't the only queer thing in the house. The very next day I found out that Mrs. Brympton had no nurse; and then I asked Agnes about the woman I had seen in the passage the afternoon before. Agnes said she had seen no one, and I saw that she thought I was dreaming. To be sure, it was dusk when we went down the passage, and she had excused herself for not bringing a light; but I had seen the woman plain enough to know her again if we should meet. I decided that she must have been a friend of the cook's, or of one of the other women-servants: perhaps she had come down from town for a night's visit, and the servants wanted it kept secret. Some ladies are very stiff about having their servants' friends in the house overnight. At any rate, I made up my mind to ask no more questions.

In a day or two, another odd thing happened. I was chatting one afternoon with Mrs. Blinder, who was a friendly disposed woman, and had been longer in the house than the other servants, and she asked me if I was quite comfortable and had everything I needed. I said I had no fault to find with my place or with my mistress, but I thought it odd that in so large a house there was no sewing-room for the lady's maid.

"Why," says she, "there *is* one: the room you're in is the old sewing-room."

"Oh," said I; "and where did the other lady's maid sleep?"

At that she grew confused, and said hurriedly that the servants' rooms had all been changed about last year, and she didn't rightly remember.

That struck me as peculiar, but I went on as if I hadn't noticed: "Well, there's a vacant room opposite mine, and I mean to ask Mrs. Brympton if I mayn't use that as a sewing-room."

To my astonishment, Mrs. Blinder went white, and gave my hand a kind of squeeze. "Don't do that, my dear," said she, trembling-like. "To tell you the truth, that was Emma Saxon's room, and my mistress has kept it closed ever since her death."

"And who was Emma Saxon?"

"Mrs. Brympton's former maid."

"The one that was with her so many years?" said I, remembering what Mrs. Railton had told me.

Mrs. Blinder nodded.

"What sort of woman was she?"

"No better walked the earth," said Mrs. Blinder. "My mistress loved her like a sister."

"But I mean—what did she look like?"

Mrs. Blinder got up and gave me a kind of angry stare. "I'm no great hand at describing," she said; "and I believe my pastry's rising." And she walked off into the kitchen and shut the door after her.

II

I had been near a week at Brympton before I saw my master. Word came that he was arriving one afternoon, and a change passed over the whole household. It was plain that nobody loved him below stairs. Mrs. Blinder took uncommon care with the dinner that night, but she snapped at the kitchen-maid in a way quite unusual with her; and Mr. Wace, the butler, a serious, slow-spoken man, went about his duties as if he'd been getting ready for a funeral. He was a great Bible-reader, Mr. Wace was, and had a beautiful assortment of texts at his command; but that day he used such dreadful language that I was about to leave the table, when he assured me it was all out of Isaiah; and I noticed that whenever the master came Mr. Wace took to the prophets.

About seven, Agnes called me to my mistress's room; and there I found Mr. Brympton. He was standing on the hearth; a big fair bull-necked man, with a red face and little bad-tempered blue eyes: the kind of man a young simpleton might have thought handsome, and would have been like to pay dear for thinking it.

He swung about when I came in, and looked me over in a trice. I knew what the look meant, from having experienced it once or twice in my former places. Then he turned his back on me, and went on talking to his wife; and I knew what *that* meant, too. I was not the kind of morsel he was after. The typhoid had served me well enough in one way: it kept that kind of gentleman at arm's-length.

"This is my new maid, Hartley," says Mrs. Brympton in her kind voice; and he nodded and went on with what he was saying.

In a minute or two he went off, and left my mistress to dress for dinner, and I noticed as I waited on her that she was white, and chill to the touch.

Mr. Brympton took himself off the next morning, and the whole house drew a long breath when he drove away. As for my mistress, she put on her hat and furs (for it was a fine winter morning) and went out for a walk in the gardens, coming back quite fresh and rosy, so that for a minute, before her colour faded, I could guess what a pretty young lady she must have been, and not so long ago, either.

She had met Mr. Ranford in the grounds, and the two came back together, I remember, smiling and talking as they walked along the terrace under my window. That was the first time I saw Mr. Ranford, though I had often heard his name mentioned in the hall. He was a neighbour, it appeared, living a mile or two beyond Brympton, at the end of the village; and as he was in the habit of spending his winters in the country he was almost the only company my mistress had at that season. He was a slight tall gentleman of about thirty, and I thought him rather melancholy-looking till I saw his smile, which had a kind of surprise in it, like the first warm day in spring. He was a great reader, I heard, like my mistress, and the two were forever borrowing books of one another, and sometimes (Mr. Wace told me) he would read aloud to Mrs. Brympton by the hour, in the big dark library where she sat in the winter afternoons. The servants all liked him, and perhaps that's more of a compliment than the masters suspect. He had a friendly word for every one of us, and we were all glad to think that Mrs. Brympton had a pleasant companionable gentleman like that to keep her company when the master was away. Mr. Ranford seemed on excellent terms with Mr. Brympton too; though I couldn't but wonder that two gentlemen so unlike each other should be so friendly. But then I knew how the real quality can keep their feelings to themselves.

As for Mr. Brympton, he came and went, never staying more than a day or two, cursing the dulness and the solitude, grumbling at everything, and (as I soon found out) drinking a deal more than was good for him. After Mrs. Brympton left the table he would sit half the night over the old Brympton port and madeira, and once, as I was leaving my mistress's room rather later than usual, I met him coming up the stairs in such a state that I turned sick to think of what some ladies have to endure and hold their tongues about.

The servants said very little about their master; but from what they let drop I could see it had been an unhappy match from the beginning. Mr. Brympton was coarse, loud and pleasure-loving; my mistress quiet, retiring, and perhaps a trifle cold. Not that she was not always pleasant-spoken to him: I thought her wonderfully forbearing; but to a gentleman as free as Mr. Brympton I daresay she seemed a little offish.

Well, things went on quietly for several weeks. My mistress was kind, my duties were light, and I got on well with the other servants. In short, I had nothing to complain of; yet there was always a weight on me. I can't say why it was so, but I know it was not the loneliness that I felt. I soon got used to that; and being still languid from the fever, I was thankful for the quiet and the good country air. Nevertheless, I was never quite easy in my mind. My mistress, knowing I had been ill, insisted that I should take my walk regular, and often invented errands for me:—a yard of ribbon to be fetched from the village, a letter posted, or a book returned to Mr. Ranford. As soon as I was out of doors my spirits rose, and I looked forward to my walks through the bare moist-smelling woods; but the moment I caught sight of the house again my heart dropped down like a stone in a well. It was not a gloomy house exactly, yet I never entered it but a feeling of gloom came over me.

Mrs. Brympton seldom went out in winter; only on the finest days did she walk an hour at noon on the south terrace. Excepting Mr. Ranford, we had no visitors but the doctor, who drove over from D—— about once a week. He sent for me once or twice to give me some trifling direction about my mistress, and though he never told me what her illness was, I thought, from a waxy look she had now and then of a morning, that it might be the heart that ailed her. The season was soft and unwholesome, and in January we had a long spell of rain. That was a sore trial to me, I own, for I couldn't go out, and sitting over my sewing all day, listening to the drip, drip of the eaves, I grew so nervous that the least sound made me jump. Somehow, the thought of that locked room across the passage began to weigh on me. Once or twice, in the long rainy nights, I fancied I heard noises there; but that was nonsense, of course, and the daylight drove such notions out of my head. Well, one morning Mrs. Brympton gave me quite a start of pleasure by telling me she wished me to go to town for some shopping. I hadn't known till then how low my spirits had fallen. I set off in high glee, and my first sight of the crowded streets and the cheerful-looking shops quite took me out of myself. Toward afternoon, however, the noise and confusion began to tire me, and I was actually looking forward to the quiet of Brympton, and thinking how I should enjoy the drive home through the dark woods, when I ran across an old acquaintance, a maid I had once been in service with. We had lost sight of each other for a number of years, and I had to stop and tell her what had happened to me in the interval. When I mentioned where I was living she rolled up her eyes and pulled a long face.

"What! The Mrs. Brympton that lives all the year at her place on the Hudson? My dear, you won't stay there three months."

"Oh, but I don't mind the country," says I, offended somehow at her tone. "Since the fever I'm glad to be quiet."

She shook her head. "It's not the country I'm thinking of. All I know is she's had four maids in the last six months, and the last one, who was a friend of mine, told me nobody could stay in the house."

"Did she say why?" I asked.

"No—she wouldn't give me her reason. But she says to me, *Mrs. Ansey*, she says, *if ever a young woman as you know of thinks of going there, you tell her it's not worth while to unpack her boxes.*"

"Is she young and handsome?" said I, thinking of Mr. Brympton.

"Not her! She's the kind that mothers engage when they've gay young gentlemen at college."

Well, though I knew the woman was an idle gossip, the words stuck in my head, and my heart sank lower than ever as I drove up to Brympton in the dusk. There *was* something about the house—I was sure of it now...

When I went in to tea I heard that Mr. Brympton had arrived, and I saw at a glance that there had been a disturbance of some kind. Mrs. Blinder's hand shook so that she could hardly pour the tea, and Mr. Wace quoted the most dreadful texts full of brimstone. Nobody said a word to me then, but when I went up to my room Mrs. Blinder followed me.

"Oh, my dear," says she, taking my hand, "I'm so glad and thankful you've come back to us!"

That struck me, as you may imagine. "Why," said I, "did you think I was leaving for good?"

"No, no, to be sure," said she, a little confused, "but I can't a-bear to have madam left alone for a day even." She pressed my hand hard, and, "Oh, Miss Hartley," says she, "be good to your mistress, as you're a Christian woman." And with that she hurried away, and left me staring.

A moment later Agnes called me to Mrs. Brympton. Hearing Mr. Brympton's voice in her room, I went round by the dressing-room, thinking I would lay out her dinner-gown before going in. The dressing-room is a large room with a window over the portico that looks toward the gardens. Mr. Brympton's apartments are beyond. When I went in, the door into the bedroom was ajar, and I heard Mr. Brympton saying angrily:—"One would suppose he was the only person fit for you to talk to."

"I don't have many visitors in winter," Mrs. Brympton answered quietly.

"You have *me!*" he flung at her, sneering.

"You are here so seldom," said she.

"Well—whose fault is that? You make the place about as lively as a family vault—"

With that I rattled the toilet-things, to give my mistress warning and she rose and called me in.

The two dined alone, as usual, and I knew by Mr. Wace's manner at supper that things must be going badly. He quoted the prophets something terrible, and worked on the kitchen-maid so that she declared she wouldn't go down alone to put the cold meat in the ice-box. I felt nervous myself, and after I had put my mistress to bed

I was half-tempted to go down again and persuade Mrs. Blinder to sit up awhile over a game of cards. But I heard her door closing for the night, and so I went on to my own room. The rain had begun again, and the drip, drip, drip seemed to be dropping into my brain. I lay awake listening to it, and turning over what my friend in town had said. What puzzled me was that it was always the maids who left...

After a while I slept; but suddenly a loud noise wakened me. My bell had rung. I sat up, terrified by the unusual sound, which seemed to go on jangling through the darkness. My hands shook so that I couldn't find the matches. At length I struck a light and jumped out of bed. I began to think I must have been dreaming; but I looked at the bell against the wall, and there was the little hammer still quivering.

I was just beginning to huddle on my clothes when I heard another sound. This time it was the door of the locked room opposite mine softly opening and closing. I heard the sound distinctly, and it frightened me so that I stood stock still. Then I heard a footstep hurrying down the passage toward the main house. The floor being carpeted, the sound was very faint, but I was quite sure it was a woman's step. I turned cold with the thought of it, and for a minute or two I dursn't breathe or move. Then I came to my senses.

"Alice Hartley," says I to myself, "someone left that room just now and ran down the passage ahead of you. The idea isn't pleasant, but you may as well face it. Your mistress has rung for you, and to answer her bell you've got to go the way that other woman has gone."

Well—I did it. I never walked faster in my life, yet I thought I should never get to the end of the passage or reach Mrs. Brympton's room. On the way I heard nothing and saw nothing: all was dark and quiet as the grave. When I reached my mistress's door the silence was so deep that I began to think I must be dreaming, and was half-minded to turn back. Then a panic seized me, and I knocked.

There was no answer, and I knocked again, loudly. To my astonishment the door was opened by Mr. Brympton. He started back when he saw me, and in the light of my candle his face looked red and savage.

"*You?*" he said, in a queer voice. "*How many of you are there, in God's name?*"

At that I felt the ground give under me; but I said to myself that he had been drinking, and answered as steadily as I could: "May I go in, sir? Mrs. Brympton has rung for me."

"You may all go in, for what I care," says he, and, pushing by me, walked down the hall to his own bedroom. I looked after him as he went, and to my surprise I saw that he walked as straight as a sober man.

I found my mistress lying very weak and still, but she forced a smile when she saw me, and signed to me to pour out some drops for her. After that she lay without speaking, her breath coming quick, and her eyes closed. Suddenly she groped out with her hand, and "*Emma,*" says she, faintly.

"It's Hartley, madam," I said. "Do you want anything?"

She opened her eyes wide and gave me a startled look.

"I was dreaming," she said. "You may go, now, Hartley, and thank you kindly. I'm quite well again, you see." And she turned her face away from me.

III

There was no more sleep for me that night, and I was thankful when daylight came.

Soon afterward, Agnes called me to Mrs. Brympton. I was afraid she was ill again, for she seldom sent for me before nine, but I found her sitting up in bed, pale and drawn-looking, but quite herself.

"Hartley," says she quickly, "will you put on your things at once and go down to the village for me? I want this prescription made up—" here she hesitated a minute and blushed—"and I should like you to be back again before Mr. Brympton is up."

"Certainly, madam," I said.

"And—stay a moment—" she called me back as if an idea had just struck her—"while you're waiting for the mixture, you'll have time to go on to Mr. Ranford's with this note."

It was a two-mile walk to the village, and on my way I had time to turn things over in my mind. It struck me as peculiar that my mistress should wish the prescription made up without Mr. Brympton's knowledge; and, putting this together with the scene of the night before, and with much else that I had noticed and suspected, I began to wonder if the poor lady was weary of her life, and had come to the mad resolve of ending it. The idea took such hold on me that I reached the village on a run, and dropped breathless into a chair before the chemist's counter. The good man, who was just taking down his shutters, stared at me so hard that it brought me to myself.

"Mr. Limmel," I says, trying to speak indifferent, "will you run your eye over this, and tell me if it's quite right?"

He put on his spectacles and studied the prescription.

"Why, it's one of Dr. Walton's," says he. "What should be wrong with it?"

"Well—is it dangerous to take?"

"Dangerous—how do you mean?"

I could have shaken the man for his stupidity.

"I mean—if a person was to take too much of it—by mistake of course—" says I, my heart in my throat.

"Lord bless you, no. It's only lime-water. You might feed it to a baby by the bottleful."

I gave a great sigh of relief, and hurried on to Mr. Ranford's. But on the way another thought struck me. If there was nothing to conceal about my visit to the chemist's, was it my other errand that Mrs. Brympton wished me to keep private? Somehow, that thought frightened me worse than the other. Yet the two gentlemen seemed fast friends, and I would have staked my head on my mistress's goodness. I felt ashamed of my suspicions, and concluded that I was still disturbed by the strange events of the night. I left the note at Mr. Ranford's—and, hurrying back to Brympton, slipped in by a side door without being seen, as I thought.

An hour later, however, as I was carrying in my mistress's breakfast, I was stopped in the hall by Mr. Brympton.

"What were you doing out so early?" he says, looking hard at me.

"Early—me, sir?" I said, in a tremble.

"Come, come," he says, an angry red spot coming out on his forehead, "didn't I see you scuttling home through the shrubbery an hour or more ago?"

I'm a truthful woman by nature, but at that a lie popped out ready-made. "No, sir, you didn't," said I, and looked straight back at him.

He shrugged his shoulders and gave a sullen laugh. "I suppose you think I was drunk last night?" he asked suddenly.

"No, sir, I don't," I answered, this time truthfully enough.

He turned away with another shrug. "A pretty notion my servants have of me!" I heard him mutter as he walked off.

Not till I had settled down to my afternoon's sewing did I realise how the events of the night had shaken me. I couldn't pass that locked door without a shiver. I knew I had heard someone come out of it, and walk down the passage ahead of me. I thought of speaking to Mrs. Blinder or to Mr. Wace, the only two in the house who appeared to have an inkling of what was going on, but I had a feeling that if

I questioned them they would deny everything, and that I might learn more by holding my tongue and keeping my eyes open. The idea of spending another night opposite the locked room sickened me, and once I was seized with the notion of packing my trunk and taking the first train to town; but it wasn't in me to throw over a kind mistress in that manner, and I tried to go on with my sewing as if nothing had happened.

I hadn't worked ten minutes before the sewing-machine broke down. It was one I had found in the house, a good machine, but a trifle out of order: Mrs. Blinder said it had never been used since Emma Saxon's death. I stopped to see what was wrong, and as I was working at the machine a drawer which I had never been able to open slid forward and a photograph fell out. I picked it up and sat looking at it in a maze. It was a woman's likeness, and I knew I had seen the face somewhere—the eyes had an asking look that I had felt on me before. And suddenly I remembered the pale woman in the passage.

I stood up, cold all over, and ran out of the room. My heart seemed to be thumping in the top of my head, and I felt as if I should never get away from the look in those eyes. I went straight to Mrs. Blinder. She was taking her afternoon nap, and sat up with a jump when I came in.

"Mrs. Blinder," said I, "who is that?" And I held out the photograph.

She rubbed her eyes and stared.

"Why, Emma Saxon," says she. "Where did you find it?"

I looked hard at her for a minute. "Mrs. Blinder," I said, "I've seen that face before."

Mrs. Blinder got up and walked over to the looking-glass. "Dear me! I must have been asleep," she says. "My front is all over one ear. And now do run along, Miss Hartley, dear, for I hear the clock striking four, and I must go down this very minute and put on the Virginia ham for Mr. Brympton's dinner."

IV

To all appearances, things went on as usual for a week or two. The only difference was that Mr. Brympton stayed on, instead of going off as he usually did, and that Mr. Ranford never showed himself. I heard Mr. Brympton remark on this one afternoon when he was sitting in my mistress's room before dinner.

"Where's Ranford?" says he. "He hasn't been near the house for a week. Does he keep away because I'm here?"

Mrs. Brympton spoke so low that I couldn't catch her answer.

"Well," he went on, "two's company and three's trumpery; I'm sorry to be in Ranford's way, and I suppose I shall have to take myself off again in a day or two and give him a show." And he laughed at his own joke.

The very next day, as it happened, Mr. Ranford called. The footman said the three were very merry over their tea in the library, and Mr. Brympton strolled down to the gate with Mr. Ranford when he left.

I have said that things went on as usual; and so they did with the rest of the household; but as for myself, I had never been the same since the night my bell had rung. Night after night I used to lie awake, listening for it to ring again, and for the door of the locked room to open stealthily. But the bell never rang, and I heard no sound across the passage. At last the silence began to be more dreadful to me than the most mysterious sounds. I felt that *someone* were cowering there, behind the locked door, watching and listening as I watched and listened, and I could almost have cried out, "Whoever you are, come out and let me see you face to face, but don't lurk there and spy on me in the darkness!"

Feeling as I did, you may wonder I didn't give warning. Once I very nearly did so; but at the last moment something held me back. Whether it was compassion for my mistress, who had grown more and more dependent on me, or unwillingness to try a new place, or some other feeling that I couldn't put a name to, I lingered on as if spellbound, though every night was dreadful to me, and the days but little better.

For one thing, I didn't like Mrs. Brympton's looks. She had never been the same since that night, no more than I had. I thought she would brighten up after Mr. Brympton left, but though she seemed easier in her mind, her spirits didn't revive, nor her strength either. She had grown attached to me, and seemed to like to have me about; and Agnes told me one day that, since Emma Saxon's death, I was the only maid her mistress had taken to. This gave me a warm feeling for the poor lady, though after all there was little I could do to help her.

After Mr. Brympton's departure, Mr. Ranford took to coming again, though less often than formerly. I met him once or twice in the grounds, or in the village, and I couldn't but think there was a change in him too; but I set it down to my disordered fancy.

The weeks passed, and Mr. Brympton had now been a month absent. We heard he was cruising with a friend in the West Indies, and Mr. Wace said that was a long way off, but though you had the wings of a dove and went to the uttermost parts of the earth, you couldn't get away from the Almighty. Agnes said that as long as he stayed away from Brympton, the Almighty might have him and welcome; and this raised a laugh, though Mrs. Blinder tried to look shocked, and Mr. Wace said the bears would eat us.

We were all glad to hear that the West Indies were a long way off, and I remember that, in spite of Mr. Wace's solemn looks, we had a very merry dinner that day in the hall. I don't know if it was because of my being in better spirits, but I fancied Mrs. Brympton looked better too, and seemed more cheerful in her manner. She had been for a walk in the morning, and after luncheon she lay down in her room, and I read aloud to her. When she dismissed me I went to my own room feeling quite bright and happy, and for the first time in weeks walked past the locked door without thinking of it. As I sat down to my work I looked out and saw a few snow-flakes falling. The sight was pleasanter than the eternal rain, and I pictured to myself how pretty the bare gardens would look in their white mantle. It seemed to me as if the snow would cover up all the dreariness, indoors as well as out.

The fancy had hardly crossed my mind when I heard a step at my side. I looked up, thinking it was Agnes.

"Well, Agnes—" said I, and the words froze on my tongue; for there, in the door, stood Emma Saxon.

I don't know how long she stood there. I only know I couldn't stir or take my eyes from her. Afterward I was terribly frightened, but at the time it wasn't fear I felt, but something deeper and quieter. She looked at me long and long, and her face was just one dumb prayer to me—but how in the world was I to help her? Suddenly she turned, and I heard her walk down the passage. This time I wasn't afraid to follow—I felt that I must know what she wanted. I sprang up and ran out. She was at the other end of the passage, and I expected her to take the turn toward my mistress's room; but instead of that she pushed open the door that led to the backstairs. I followed her down the stairs, and across the passageway to the back door. The kitchen and hall were empty at that hour, the servants being off duty, except for the footman, who was in the pantry. At the door she stood still a moment, with another look at me; then she turned the handle, and stepped out. For a minute I hesitated. Where was she leading me to? The door had closed softly after her, and I opened it and looked out, half-expecting to find that she had disappeared. But I saw her a few yards off, hurrying across the court-yard to the path through the woods. Her figure looked black and lonely in the snow, and for a second my heart failed me and I thought of turning back. But all the while she was drawing me after her; and catching up an old shawl of Mrs. Blinder's I ran out into the open.

Emma Saxon was in the wood-path now. She walked on steadily, and I followed at the same pace, till we passed out of the gates and reached the high-road. Then she struck across the open fields to the village. By this time the ground was white, and as she climbed the slope of a bare hill ahead of me I noticed that she left no foot-prints behind her. At sight of that, my heart shrivelled up within me, and my knees were water. Somehow, it was worse here than indoors. She made the whole countryside seem lonely as the grave, with none but us two in it, and no help in the wide world.

Once I tried to go back; but she turned and looked at me, and it was as if she had dragged me with ropes. After that I followed her like a dog. We came to the village, and she led me through it, past the church and the blacksmith's shop, and down the lane to Mr. Ranford's. Mr. Ranford's house stands close to the road: a plain old-fashioned building, with a flagged path leading to the door between box-borders. The lane was deserted, and as I turned into it I saw Emma Saxon pause under the old elm by the gate. And now another fear came over me. I saw that we had reached the end of our journey, and that it was my turn to act. All the way from Brympton I had been asking myself what she wanted of me, but I had followed in a trance, as it were, and not till I saw her stop at Mr. Ranford's gate did my brain begin to clear itself. I stood a little way off in the snow, my heart beating fit to strangle me, and my feet frozen to the ground; and she stood under the elm and watched me.

I knew well enough that she hadn't led me there for nothing. I felt there was something I ought to say or do—but how was I to guess what it was? I had never thought harm of my mistress and Mr. Ranford, but I was sure now that, from one cause or another, some dreadful thing hung over them. *She* knew what it was; she would tell me if she could; perhaps she would answer if I questioned her.

It turned me faint to think of speaking to her; but I plucked up heart and dragged myself across the few yards between us. As I did so, I heard the house-door open, and saw Mr. Ranford approaching. He looked handsome and cheerful, as my mistress had looked that morning, and at sight of him the blood began to flow again in my veins.

"Why, Hartley," said he, "what's the matter? I saw you coming down the lane just now, and came out to see if you had taken root in the snow." He stopped and stared at me. "What are you looking at?" he says.

I turned toward the elm as he spoke, and his eyes followed me; but there was no one there. The lane was empty as far as the eye could reach.

A sense of helplessness came over me. She was gone, and I had not been able to guess what she wanted. Her last look had pierced me to the marrow; and yet it had not told me! All at once, I felt more desolate than when she had stood there watching me. It seemed as if she had left me all alone to carry the weight of the secret I couldn't guess. The snow went round me in great circles, and the ground fell away from me...

A drop of brandy and the warmth of Mr. Ranford's fire soon brought me to, and I insisted on being driven back at once to Brympton. It was nearly dark, and I was afraid my mistress might be wanting me. I explained to Mr. Ranford that I had been out for a walk and had been taken with a fit of giddiness as I passed his gate. This was true enough; yet I never felt more like a liar than when I said it.

When I dressed Mrs. Brympton for dinner she remarked on my pale looks and asked what ailed me. I told her I had a headache, and she said she would not require me again that evening, and advised me to go to bed.

It was a fact that I could scarcely keep on my feet; yet I had no fancy to spend a solitary evening in my room. I sat downstairs in the hall as long as I could hold my head up; but by nine I crept upstairs, too weary to care what happened if I could but get my head on a pillow. The rest of the household went to bed soon afterward; they kept early hours when the master was away, and before ten I heard Mrs. Blinder's door close, and Mr. Wace's soon after.

It was a very still night, earth and air all muffled in snow. Once in bed I felt easier, and lay quiet, listening to the strange noises that come out in a house after dark. Once I thought I heard a door open and close again below: it might have been the glass door that led to the gardens. I got up and peered out of the window; but it was in the dark of the moon, and nothing visible outside but the streaking of snow against the panes.

I went back to bed and must have dozed, for I jumped awake to the furious ringing of my bell. Before my head was clear I had sprung out of bed, and was dragging on my clothes. *It is going to happen now*, I heard myself saying; but what I meant I had no notion. My hands seemed to be covered with glue—I thought I should never get into my clothes. At last I opened my door and peered down the passage.

As far as my candle-flame carried, I could see nothing unusual ahead of me. I hurried on, breathless; but as I pushed open the baize door leading to the main hall my heart stood still, for there at the head of the stairs was Emma Saxon, peering dreadfully down into the darkness.

For a second I couldn't stir; but my hand slipped from the door, and as it swung shut the figure vanished. At the same instant there came another sound from below stairs—a stealthy mysterious sound, as of a latchkey turning in the house-door. I ran to Mrs. Brympton's room and knocked.

There was no answer, and I knocked again. This time I heard some one moving in the room; the bolt slipped back and my mistress stood before me. To my surprise I saw that she had not undressed for the night. She gave me a startled look.

"What is this, Hartley?" she says in a whisper. "Are you ill? What are you doing here at this hour?"

"I am not ill, madam; but my bell rang."

At that she turned pale, and seemed about to fall.

"You are mistaken," she said harshly; "I didn't ring. You must have been dreaming." I had never heard her speak in such a tone. "Go back to bed," she said, closing the door on me.

But as she spoke I heard sounds again in the hall below: a man's step this time; and the truth leaped out on me.

"Madam," I said, pushing past her, "there is someone in the house—"

"Someone—?"

"Mr. Brympton, I think—I hear his step below—"

A dreadful look came over her, and without a word, she dropped flat at my feet. I fell on my knees and tried to lift her: by the way she breathed I saw it was no common faint. But as I raised her head there came quick steps on the stairs and across the hall: the door was flung open, and there stood Mr. Brympton, in his travelling-clothes, the snow dripping from him. He drew back with a start as he saw me kneeling by my mistress.

"What the devil is this?" he shouted. He was less high-coloured than usual, and the red spot came out on his forehead.

"Mrs. Brympton has fainted, sir," said I.

He laughed unsteadily and pushed by me. "It's a pity she didn't choose a more convenient moment. I'm sorry to disturb her, but—"

I raised myself up, aghast at the man's action.

"Sir," said I, "are you mad? What are you doing?"

"Going to meet a friend," said he, and seemed to make for the dressing-room.

At that my heart turned over. I don't know what I thought or feared; but I sprang up and caught him by the sleeve.

"Sir, sir," said I, "for pity's sake look at your wife!"

He shook me off furiously.

"It seems that's done for me," says he, and caught hold of the dressing-room door.

At that moment I heard a slight noise inside. Slight as it was, he heard it too, and tore the door open; but as he did so he dropped back. On the threshold stood Emma Saxon. All was dark behind her, but I saw her plainly, and so did he. He threw up his hands as if to hide his face from her; and when I looked again she was gone.

He stood motionless, as if the strength had run out of him; and in the stillness my mistress suddenly raised herself, and opening her eyes fixed a look on him. Then she fell back, and I saw the death-flutter pass over her...

*

We buried her on the third day, in a driving snow-storm. There were few people in the church, for it was bad weather to come from town, and I've a notion my mistress was one that hadn't many near friends. Mr. Ranford was among the last to come, just before they carried her up the aisle. He was in black, of course, being such a friend of the family, and I never saw a gentleman so pale. As he passed me, I noticed that he leaned a trifle on a stick he carried; and I fancy Mr. Brympton noticed it too, for the red spot came out sharp on his forehead, and all through the service he kept staring across the church at Mr. Ranford, instead of following the prayers as a mourner should.

When it was over and we went out to the graveyard, Mr. Ranford had disappeared, and as soon as my poor mistress's body was underground, Mr. Brympton jumped into the carriage nearest the gate and drove off without a word to any of us. I heard him call out, "To the station," and we servants went back alone to the house.

THE CASE OF VINCENT PYRWHIT

Barry Pain

Barry Eric Odell Pain (1864–1928) was an English writer, journalist and humorist. Pain was a prolific contributor to many periodicals and newspapers, such as *The Cornhill Magazine*, *Daily Chronicle*, *Punch*, *The Speaker*, *Black and White* and *The Windsor Magazine*. Though mostly famous for his humorous stories, he published over fifty works, among which novels and short story collections, which covered a wide range of genres from parody to horror and the supernatural. As a result, his bibliography is very eclectic, where disparate titles coexist side by side, such as *The Romantic History of Robin Hood* (1898), *Stories in the Dark* (1901), *Little Entertainments* (1903), *The Shadow of the Unseen* (1907), *Stories in Grey* (1911) or *Innocent Amusements* (1918).

"The Case of Vincent Pyrwhit" was originally published in the collection *Stories in the Dark* (1901), which includes stories that oscillate between the fantastic and the macabre. This short tale of loss suggests an ambivalent relationship with modern technology: a once helpful object, whose sound was a welcome one, can quickly become anxiety-inducing, with a haunting aural quality.

he death of Vincent Pyrwhit, J.P., of Ellerdon House, Ellerdon, in the county of Buckingham, would in the ordinary way have received no more attention than the death of any other simple country gentleman. The circumstances of his death, however, though now long since forgotten, were sensational, and attracted some notice at the time. It was one of those cases which is easily forgotten within a year, except just in the locality where it occurred. The most sensational circumstances of the case never came before the public at all. I give them here simply and plainly. The psychical people may make what they like of them.

Pyrwhit himself was a very ordinary country gentleman, a good fellow, but in no way brilliant. He was devoted to his wife, who was some fifteen years younger than himself, and remarkably beautiful. She was quite a good woman, but she had her faults. She was fond of admiration, and she was an abominable flirt. She misled men very cleverly, and was then sincerely angry with them for having been misled. Her husband never troubled his head about these flirtations, being assured quite rightly that she was a good woman. He was not jealous; she, on the other hand, was possessed of a jealousy amounting almost to insanity. This might have caused trouble if he had ever provided her with the slightest basis on which her jealousy could work, but he never did. With the exception of his wife, women bored him. I believe she did once or twice try to make a scene for some preposterous reason which was no reason at all; but nothing serious came of it, and there was never a real quarrel between them.

On the death of his wife, after a prolonged illness, Pyrwhit wrote and asked me to come down to Ellerdon for the funeral, and to remain at least a few days with him. He would be quite alone, and I *was* his oldest friend. I hate attending funerals, but I *was* his oldest friend, and I was, moreover, a distant relation of his wife. I had no choice and I went down.

There were many visitors in the house for the funeral, which took place in the village churchyard, but they left immediately afterwards. The air of heavy gloom which had hung over the house seemed to lift a little. The servants (servants are always very emotional) continued to break down at intervals, noticeably Pyrwhit's man, Williams, but Pyrwhit himself was self-possessed. He spoke of his wife with great affection and regret, but still he could speak of her and not unsteadily. At dinner he also spoke of one or two other subjects, of politics and of his duties as a magistrate, and of course he made the requisite fuss about his gratitude to me for coming down to Ellerdon at that time. After dinner we sat in the library, a room well and expensively furnished, but without the least attempt at taste. There were a few oil paintings on the walls, a presentation portrait of himself, and a landscape or two—all more or less bad, as far as I remember. He had eaten next to nothing at dinner, but he had drunk a good deal; the wine, however, did not seem to have the least effect upon him. I had got the conversation definitely off the subject of his wife when I made a blunder. I noticed an Erichsen's extension standing on his writing-table. I said:

"I didn't know that telephones had penetrated into the villages yet."

"Yes," he said, "I believe they are common enough now. I had that one fitted up during my wife's illness to communicate with her bedroom on the floor above us on the other side of the house."

234

At that moment the bell of the telephone rang sharply.

We both looked at each other. I said with the stupid affectation of calmness one always puts on when one is a little bit frightened:

"Probably a servant in that room wishes to speak to you."

He got up, walked over to the machine, and swung the green cord towards me. The end of it was loose.

"I had it disconnected this morning," he said; "also the door of that room is locked, and no one can possibly be in it."

He had turned the colour of grey blotting-paper; so probably had I.

The bell rang again—a prolonged, rattling ring.

"Are you going to answer it?" I said.

"I am not," he answered firmly.

"Then," I said, "I shall answer it myself. It is some stupid trick, a joke not in the best of taste, for which you will probably have to sack one or other of your domestics."

"My servants," he answered, "would not have done that. Besides, don't you see it is impossible? The instrument is disconnected."

"The bell rang all the same. I shall try it."

I picked up the receiver.

"Are you there?" I called.

The voice which answered me was unmistakably the rather high staccato voice of Mrs. Pyrwhit.

"I want you," it said, "to tell my husband that he will be with me tomorrow."

I still listened. Nothing more was said.

I repeated, "Are you there?" and still there was no answer.

I turned to Pyrwhit.

"There is no one there," I said. "Possibly there is thunder in the air affecting the bell in some mysterious way. There must be some simple explanation, and I'll find it all out tomorrow."

*

He went to bed early that night. All the following day I was with him. We rode together, and I expected an accident every minute, but none happened. All the evening I expected him to turn suddenly faint and ill, but that also did not happen. When at about ten o'clock he excused himself and said goodnight I felt distinctly relieved. He went up to his room and rang for Williams.

The rest is, of course, well known. The servant's reason had broken down, possibly the immediate cause being the death of Mrs. Pyrwhit. On entering his master's room, without the least hesitation, he raised a loaded revolver which he carried in his hand, and shot Pyrwhit through the heart. I believe the case is mentioned in some of the textbooks on homicidal mania.

THE HAUNTED ORGANIST
OF HURLY BURLY

Rosa Mulholland

Rosa Mulholland (1841–1921), an Irish writer, began her literary career at the young age of fifteen, when she tried to publish her first book. Throughout her life, Mulholland wrote a great many novels and short stories, as well as poems which were praised by her contemporary critics. Some of her works were originally published under the pseudonym of Ruth Murray. She contributed poems and short stories to periodicals such as Charles Dickens's *All The Year Round*, but also *The Cornhill Magazine* and *The Irish Monthly*; and some of her novels, which were first serialised. Her work tended to focus on social issues, such as the lives of the Irish poor or the theme of female autonomy and happiness; but though many of her heroines longed to break away from societal expectations, most of her fiction had a socially appropriate ending instead of defying gender norms. Mulholland's ghost stories were long overlooked, though she wrote many eerie tales; but recent efforts (most notably by editor and scholar Richard Dalby) to recover the work of women writers reclaim her as a 'mistress of the macabre', and draw attention to her strange tales, such as "Not to be Taken at Bed-Time" (1865), "The Ghost at the Rath" (1866), or "The Old Stain on the Floor" (1884).

"The Haunted Organist of Hurly Burly" was originally published in November 1866 in *All the Year Round*, and later reprinted in *The*

Irish Monthly (1886). It also was the title story of a collection of short stories in 1891. The tale is filled with worrying noises: because of thunder, or the sound of rolling wheels, the characters are uneasy from the beginning of the story when they hear acoustic phenomena, whatever their nature. When a strange woman named Lisa turns up in the village asking to play the organ that is in the house of the mistress and master of Hurly Burly, everyone is in shock. Thought to be cursed, the instrument is associated with loss, grief, and potential danger. As Lisa begins to play, the organ's haunting quality, manifested through its sonority, becomes overpowering.

here had been a thunderstorm in the village of Hurly Burly. Every door was shut, every dog in his kennel, every rut and gutter a flowing river after the deluge of rain that had fallen. Up at the great house, a mile from the town, the rooks were calling to one another about the fright they had been in, the fawns in the deer-park were venturing their timid heads from behind the trunks of trees, and the old woman at the gate-lodge had risen from her knees, and was putting back her prayer-book on the shelf. In the garden, July roses, unwieldy with their full-blown richness, and saturated with rain, hung their heads heavily to the earth; others, already fallen, lay flat upon their blooming faces on the path, where Bess, Mistress Hurly's maid, would find them, when going on her morning quest of rose-leaves for her lady's potpourri. Ranks of white lilies, just brought to perfection by today's sun, lay dabbled in the mire of flooded mould. Tears ran down the amber cheeks of the plums on the south wall, and not a bee had ventured out of the hives, though the scent of the air was sweet enough to tempt the laziest drone. The sky was still lurid behind the boles of the upland oaks, but the birds had begun to dive in and out of the ivy that wrapped up the home of the Hurlys of Hurly Burly.

This thunderstorm took place more than half a century ago, and we must remember that Mistress Hurly was dressed in the fashion of that time as she crept out from behind the squire's chair, now that the lightning was over, and, with many nervous glances towards the window, sat down before her husband, the tea-urn, and the muffins. We can picture her fine lace cap, with its peachy ribbons, the frill on the hem of her cambric gown just touching her ankles, the embroidered clocks on her stockings, the rosettes on her shoes, but not so easily the lilac shade of her mild eyes, the satin skin, which still kept its delicate bloom, though wrinkled with advancing age, and the pale, sweet, puckered mouth, that time and sorrow had made angelic while trying vainly to deface its beauty.

The squire was as rugged as his wife was gentle, his skin as brown as hers was white, his grey hair as bristling as hers was glossed; the years had ploughed his face into ruts and channels; a bluff, choleric, noisy man he had been; but of late a dimness had come on his eyes, a hush on his loud voice, and a check on the spring of his hale step. He looked at his wife often, and very often she looked at him. She was not a tall woman, and he was only a head higher. They were a quaintly well-matched couple, despite their differences. She turned to you with nervous sharpness and revealed her tender voice and eye; he spoke and glanced roughly, but the turn of his head was courteous. Of late they fitted one another better than they had ever done in the heyday of their youthful love. A common sorrow had developed a singular likeness between them. In former years the cry from the wife had been, "Don't curb my son too much!" and from the husband, "You ruin the lad with softness." But now the idol that had stood between them was removed, and they saw each other better.

The room in which they sat was a pleasant old-fashioned drawing-room, with a general spider-legged character about the fittings; spinnet and guitar in their places, with a great deal of copied music beside them; carpet, tawny wreaths on pale blue; blue flutings on the walls, and faint gilding on the furniture. A huge urn, crammed with roses, in the open bay-window, through which came delicious airs from the garden, the twittering of birds settling to sleep in the ivy close by, and occasionally the pattering of a flight of rain-drops, swept to the ground as a bough bent in the breeze. The urn on the table was ancient silver, and the china rare. There was nothing in the room for luxurious ease of the body, but everything of delicate refinement for the eye.

There was a great hush all over Hurly Burly, except in the neighbourhood of the rooks. Every living thing had suffered from heat for the past month, and now, in common with all Nature, was receiving the boon of refreshed air in silent peace. The mistress and master of Hurly Burly shared the general spirit that was abroad, and were not talkative over their tea.

"Do you know," said Mistress Hurly, at last, "when I heard the first of the thunder beginning I thought it was—it was—"

The lady broke down, her lips trembling, and the peachy ribbons of her cap stirring with great agitation.

"Pshaw!" cried the old squire, making his cup suddenly ring upon the saucer, "we ought to have forgotten that. Nothing has been heard for three months."

At this moment a rolling sound struck upon the ears of both. The lady rose from her seat trembling, and folded her hands together, while the tea-urn flooded the tray.

"Nonsense, my love," said the squire; "that is the noise of wheels. Who can be arriving?"

"Who, indeed?" murmured the lady, reseating herself in agitation.

Presently pretty Bess of the rose-leaves appeared at the door in a flutter of blue ribbons.

"Please, madam, a lady has arrived, and says she is expected. She asked for her apartment, and I put her into the room that was got ready for Miss Calderwood. And she sends her respects to you, madam, and she'll be down with you presently."

The squire looked at his wife, and his wife looked at the squire.

"It is some mistake," murmured madam. "Some visitor for Calderwood or the Grange. It is very singular."

Hardly had she spoken when the door again opened, and the stranger appeared—a small creature, whether girl or woman it would be hard to say—dressed in a scanty black silk dress, her narrow shoulders covered with a white muslin pelerine. Her hair was swept up to the crown of her head, all but a little fringe hanging over her low forehead within an inch of her brows. Her face was brown and thin, eyes black and long, with blacker settings, mouth large, sweet, and melancholy. She was all head, mouth, and eyes; her nose and chin were nothing.

This visitor crossed the floor hastily, dropped a courtesy in the middle of the room, and approached the table, saying abruptly, with a soft Italian accent:

"Sir and madam, I am here. I am come to play your organ."

"The organ!" gasped Mistress Hurly.

"The organ!" stammered the squire.

"Yes, the organ," said the little stranger lady, playing on the back of a chair with her fingers, as if she felt notes under them. "It was but last week that the handsome signor, your son, came to my little house, where I have lived teaching music since my English father and my Italian mother and brothers and sisters died and left me so lonely."

Here the fingers left off drumming, and two great tears were brushed off, one from each eye with each hand, child's fashion. But the next moment the fingers were at work again, as if only whilst they were moving the tongue could speak.

"The noble signor, your son," said the little woman, looking trustfully from one to the other of the old couple, while a bright blush shone through her brown skin, "he often came to see me before that, always in the evening, when the sun was warm and yellow all through my little studio, and the music was swelling my heart, and I could play out grand with all my soul; then he used to come and say, 'Hurry, little Lisa, and play better, better still. I have work for you to do by-and-by.' Sometimes he said, 'Brava!' and sometimes he said 'Eccellentissima!' but one night last week he came to me and said, 'It is enough. Will you swear to do my bidding, whatever it may be?' Here the black eyes fell. And I said, 'Yes.' And he said, 'Now you are my betrothed.' And I said, 'Yes.' And he said, 'Pack up your music, little Lisa, and go off to England to my English father and mother, who have an organ in their house which must be played upon. If they refuse to let you play, tell them I sent you, and they will give you leave. You must play all day, and you must get up in the night and play. You must never tire. You are my betrothed, and you have sworn to do my work.' I said, 'Shall I see you there, signor?' And he said, 'Yes, you shall see me there.' I said, 'I will keep my vow, signor.' And so, sir and madam, I am come."

The soft foreign voice left off talking, the fingers left off thrumming on the chair, and the little stranger gazed in dismay at her auditors, both pale with agitation.

"You are deceived. You make a mistake," said they in one breath.

"Our son—" began Mistress Hurly, but her mouth twitched, her voice broke, and she looked piteously towards her husband.

"Our son," said the squire, making an effort to conquer the quavering in his voice, "our son is long dead."

"Nay, nay," said the little foreigner. "If you have thought him dead have good cheer, dear sir and madam. He is alive; he is well, and strong, and handsome. But one, two, three, four, five" (on the fingers) "days ago he stood by my side."

"It is some strange mistake, some wonderful coincidence!" said the mistress and master of Hurly Burly.

"Let us take her to the gallery," murmured the mother of this son who was thus dead and alive. "There is yet light to see the pictures. She will not know his portrait."

The bewildered wife and husband led their strange visitor away to a long gloomy room at the west side of the house, where the faint gleams from the darkening sky still lingered on the portraits of the Hurly family.

"Doubtless he is like this," said the squire, pointing to a fair-haired young man with a mild face, a brother of his own who had been lost at sea.

But Lisa shook her head, and went softly on tiptoe from one picture to another, peering into the canvas, and still turning away troubled. But at last a shriek of delight startled the shadowy chamber.

"Ah, here he is! See, here he is, the noble signor, the beautiful signor, not half so handsome as he looked five days ago, when talking to poor little Lisa! Dear sir and madam, you are now content. Now take me to the organ, that I may commence to do his bidding at once."

The mistress of Hurly Burly clung fast by her husband's arm.

"How old are you, girl?" she said faintly.

"Eighteen," said the visitor impatiently, moving towards the door.

"And my son has been dead for twenty years!" said his mother, and swooned on her husband's breast.

"Order the carriage at once," said Mistress Hurly, recovering from her swoon; "I will take her to Margaret Calderwood. Margaret will tell her the story. Margaret will bring her to reason. No, not tomorrow; I cannot bear tomorrow, it is so far away. We must go tonight."

The little signora thought the old lady mad, but she put on her cloak again obediently, and took her seat beside Mistress Hurly in the Hurly family coach. The moon that looked in at them through the pane as they lumbered along was not whiter than the aged face of the squire's wife, whose dim faded eyes were fixed upon it in doubt and awe too great for tears or words. Lisa, too, from her corner gloated upon the moon, her black eyes shining with passionate dreams.

A carriage rolled away from the Calderwood door as the Hurly coach drew up at the steps. Margaret Calderwood had just returned from a dinner-party, and at the open door a splendid figure was standing, a tall woman dressed in brown velvet, the diamonds on her bosom glistening in the moonlight that revealed her, pouring, as it did, over the house from eaves to basement. Mistress Hurly fell into her outstretched arms with a groan, and the strong woman carried her aged friend, like a baby, into the house. Little Lisa was overlooked, and sat down contentedly on the threshold to gloat awhile longer on the moon, and to thrum imaginary sonatas on the doorstep.

There were tears and sobs in the dusk, moonlit room into which Margaret Calderwood carried her friend. There was a long consultation, and then Margaret, having hushed away the grieving woman into some quiet corner, came forth to look for the little dark-faced stranger, who had arrived, so unwelcome, from beyond the seas, with such wild communication from the dead.

Up the grand staircase of handsome Calderwood the little woman followed the tall one into a large chamber where a lamp burned, showing Lisa, if she cared to see it, that this mansion of Calderwood was fitted with much greater luxury and richness than was that of Hurly Burly. The appointments of this room announced it the sanctum of a woman who depended for the interest of her life upon resources of intellect and taste. Lisa noticed nothing but a morsel of biscuit that was lying on a plate.

"May I have it?" said she eagerly. "It is so long since I have eaten. I am hungry."

Margaret Calderwood gazed at her with a sorrowful, motherly look, and, parting the fringing hair on her forehead, kissed her. Lisa, staring at her in wonder, returned the caress with ardour. Margaret's large fair shoulders, Madonna face, and yellow braided hair, excited a rapture within her. But when food was brought her, she flew to it and ate.

"It is better than I have ever eaten at home!" she said gratefully. And Margaret Calderwood murmured, "She is physically healthy, at least."

"And now, Lisa," said Margaret Calderwood, "come and tell me the whole history of the grand signor who sent you to England to play the organ."

Then Lisa crept in behind a chair, and her eyes began to burn and her fingers to thrum, and she repeated word for word her story as she had told it at Hurly Burly.

When she had finished, Margaret Calderwood began to pace up and down the floor with a very troubled face. Lisa watched her, fascinated, and, when she bade her listen to a story which she would relate to her, folded her restless hands together meekly, and listened.

"Twenty years ago, Lisa, Mr. and Mrs. Hurly had a son. He was handsome, like that portrait you saw in the gallery, and he had brilliant talents. He was idolised by his father and mother, and all who knew him felt obliged to love him. I was then a happy girl of twenty. I was an orphan, and Mrs. Hurly, who had been my mother's friend, was like a mother to me. I, too, was petted and caressed by all my friends, and I was very wealthy; but I only valued admiration, riches—every good gift that fell to my share—just in proportion as they seemed of worth in the eyes of Lewis Hurly. I was his affianced wife, and I loved him well.

"All the fondness and pride that were lavished on him could not keep him from falling into evil ways, nor from becoming rapidly more and more abandoned to wickedness, till even those who loved him best despaired of seeing his reformation. I prayed him with tears, for my sake, if not for that of his grieving mother, to save himself before it was too late. But to my horror I found that my power was gone, my words did not even move him; he loved me no more. I tried to think that this was some fit of madness that would pass, and still clung to hope. At last his own mother forbade me to see him."

Here Margaret Calderwood paused, seemingly in bitter thought, but resumed:

"He and a party of his boon companions, named by themselves the 'Devil's Club,' were in the habit of practising all kinds of unholy pranks in the country. They had midnight carousings on the tombstones in the village graveyard; they carried away helpless old men and children, whom they tortured by making believe to bury them alive; they raised the dead and placed them sitting round the tombstones at a mock feast. On one occasion there was a very sad funeral from the village. The corpse was carried into the church, and prayers were read over the coffin, the chief mourner, the aged father of the dead man, standing weeping by. In the midst of this solemn scene the organ suddenly pealed forth a profane tune, and a number of voices shouted a drinking chorus. A groan of execration burst from the crowd, the clergyman turned pale and closed his book, and the old man, the father of the dead, climbed the altar steps, and, raising his arms above his head, uttered a terrible curse. He cursed Lewis Hurly to all eternity, he cursed the organ he played, that it might be dumb henceforth, except under the fingers that had now profaned it, which, he prayed, might be forced to labour upon it till they stiffened in death. And the curse seemed to work, for the organ stood dumb in the church from that day, except when touched by Lewis Hurly.

"For a bravado he had the organ taken down and conveyed to his father's house, where he had it put up in the chamber where it now stands. It was also for a bravado that he played on it every day. But, by-and-by, the amount of time which he spent at it daily began to increase rapidly. We wondered long at this whim, as we called it, and his poor mother thanked God that he had set his heart upon an occupation which would keep him out of harm's way. I was the first to suspect that it was not his own will that kept him hammering at the organ so many laborious hours, while his boon companions tried vainly to draw him away. He used to lock himself up in the room with the organ, but one day I hid myself among the curtains, and saw him writhing on his seat, and heard him groaning as he strove to wrench his hands from the keys, to which they flew back like a needle to a magnet. It was soon plainly to be seen that he was an involuntary slave to the organ; but whether through a madness that had grown within himself, or by some supernatural doom, having its cause in the old man's curse, we did not dare to say. By-and-by there came a time when we were wakened out of our sleep at nights by the rolling of the organ. He wrought now night and day. Food and rest were denied him. His face got haggard, his beard grew long, his eyes started from their sockets. His body became wasted, and his cramped fingers like the claws of a bird. He groaned piteously as he stooped over his cruel toil. All save his mother and I were afraid to go near him. She, poor, tender woman, tried to put wine and food between his lips, while the tortured fingers crawled over the keys; but he only gnashed his teeth at her with curses, and she retreated from him in terror, to pray. At last, one dreadful hour, we found him a ghastly corpse on the ground before the organ.

"From that hour the organ was dumb to the touch of all human fingers. Many, unwilling to believe the story, made persevering endeavours to draw sound from it, in vain. But when the darkened empty room was locked up and left, we heard as loud as ever the well-known sounds humming and rolling through the walls. Night and day the tones of the organ boomed on as before. It seemed that the doom of the wretched man was not yet fulfilled, although his tortured body had been worn out in the terrible struggle to accomplish it. Even his own mother was afraid to go near the room then. So the time went on, and the curse of this perpetual music was not removed from the house. Servants refused to stay about the place. Visitors shunned it. The squire and his wife left their home for years, and returned; left it, and returned again, to find their ears still tortured and their hearts wrung by the unceasing persecution of terrible sounds. At last, but a few months ago, a holy man was found, who locked himself up in the cursed chamber for many days, praying and wrestling with the demon. After he came forth and went away the sounds ceased, and the organ was heard no more. Since then there has been peace in the house. And now, Lisa, your strange appearance and your strange story convince us that you are a victim of a ruse of the Evil One. Be warned in time, and place yourself under the protection of God, that you may be saved from the fearful influences that are at work upon you. Come—"

Margaret Calderwood turned to the corner where the stranger sat, as she had supposed, listening intently. Little Lisa was fast asleep, her hands spread before her as if she played an organ in her dreams.

Margaret took the soft brown face to her motherly breast, and kissed the swelling temples, too big with wonder and fancy.

"We will save you from a horrible fate!" she murmured, and carried the girl to bed.

In the morning Lisa was gone. Margaret Calderwood, coming early from her own chamber, went into the girl's room and found the bed empty.

"She is just such a wild thing," thought Margaret, "as would rush out at sunrise to hear the larks!" and she went forth to look for her in the meadows, behind the beech hedges, and in the home park. Mistress Hurly, from the breakfast-room window, saw Margaret Calderwood, large and fair in her white morning gown, coming down the garden-path between the rose bushes, with her fresh draperies dabbled by the dew, and a look of trouble on her calm face. Her quest had been unsuccessful. The little foreigner had vanished.

A second search after breakfast proved also fruitless, and towards evening the two women drove back to Hurly Burly together. There all was panic and distress. The squire sat in his study with the doors shut, and his hands over his ears. The servants, with pale faces, were huddled together in whispering groups. The haunted organ was pealing through the house as of old.

Margaret Calderwood hastened to the fatal chamber, and there, sure enough, was Lisa, perched upon the high seat before the organ, beating the keys with her small hands, her slight figure swaying, and the evening sunshine playing about her weird head. Sweet unearthly music she wrung from the groaning heart of the organ—wild melodies, mounting to rapturous heights and falling to mournful depths. She wandered from Mendelssohn to Mozart, and from Mozart to Beethoven. Margaret stood fascinated awhile by the ravishing beauty of the sounds she heard, but, rousing herself quickly, put her arms round the musician and forced her away from the chamber. Lisa returned next day, however, and was not so easily coaxed from her post again. Day after day she laboured at the organ, growing paler and thinner and more weird-looking as time went on.

"I work so hard," she said to Mrs. Hurly. "The signor, your son, is he pleased? Ask him to come and tell me himself if he is pleased."

Mistress Hurly got ill and took to her bed. The squire swore at the young foreign baggage, and roamed abroad. Margaret Calderwood was the only one who stood by to watch the fate of the little organist. The curse of the organ was upon Lisa; it spoke under her hand, and her hand was its slave.

At last she announced rapturously that she had had a visit from the brave signor, who had commended her industry, and urged her to work yet harder. After that she ceased to hold any communication with the living. Time after time Margaret Calderwood wrapped her arms about the frail thing, and carried her away by force, locking the door of the fatal chamber. But locking the chamber and burying the key were of no avail. The door stood open again, and Lisa was labouring on her perch.

One night, wakened from her sleep by the well-known humming and moaning of the organ, Margaret dressed hurriedly and hastened to the unholy room. Moonlight was pouring down the staircase and passages of Hurly Burly. It shone on the marble bust of the dead Lewis Hurly, that stood in the niche above his mother's sitting-room door. The organ room was full of it when Margaret pushed open the door and entered—full of the pale green moonlight from the window, mingled with another light, a dull lurid glare which seemed to centre round a dark shadow, like the figure of a man standing by the organ, and throwing out in fantastic relief the slight form of Lisa writhing, rather than swaying, back and forward, as if in agony. The sounds that came from the organ were broken and meaningless, as if the hands of the player lagged and stumbled on the keys. Between the intermittent chords low moaning cries broke from Lisa, and the dark figure bent towards her with menacing gestures. Trembling with the sickness of supernatural fear, yet strong of will, Margaret Calderwood crept forward within the lurid light, and was drawn into its influence. It grew and intensified upon her, it dazzled and blinded her at first; but presently, by a daring effort of will, she raised her eyes, and beheld Lisa's face convulsed with torture in the burning glare, and bending over her the figure and the features of Lewis Hurly! Smitten with horror, Margaret did not even then lose her presence of mind. She wound her strong arms around the wretched girl and dragged her from her seat and out of the influence of the lurid light, which immediately paled away and vanished. She carried her to her own bed, where Lisa lay, a wasted wreck, raving about the cruelty of the pitiless signor who would not see that she was labouring her best. Her poor cramped hands kept beating the coverlet, as though she were still at her agonising task.

Margaret Calderwood bathed her burning temples, and placed fresh flowers upon her pillow. She opened the blinds and windows, and let in the sweet morning air and sunshine, and then, looking up at the newly awakened sky with its fair promise of hope for the day, and down at the dewy fields, and afar off at the dark green woods with the purple mists still hovering about them, she prayed that a way might be shown her by which to put an end to this curse. She prayed for Lisa, and then, thinking that the girl rested somewhat, stole from the room. She thought that she had locked the door behind her.

She went downstairs with a pale, resolved face, and, without consulting any one, sent to the village for a bricklayer. Afterwards she sat by Mistress Hurly's bedside, and explained to her what was to be done. Presently she went to the door of Lisa's room, and hearing no sound, thought the girl slept, and stole away. By-and-by she went downstairs, and found that the bricklayer had arrived and already begun his task of building up the organ-room door. He was a swift workman, and the chamber was soon sealed safely with stone and mortar.

Having seen this work finished, Margaret Calderwood went and listened again at Lisa's door; and still hearing no sound, she returned, and took her seat at Mrs. Hurly's bedside once more. It was towards evening that she at last entered her room to assure herself of the comfort of Lisa's sleep. But the bed and room were empty. Lisa had disappeared.

Then the search began, upstairs and downstairs, in the garden, in the grounds, in the fields and meadows. No Lisa. Margaret Calderwood ordered the carriage and drove to Calderwood to see if the strange little Will-o'-the-wisp might have made her way there; then to the village, and to many other places in the neighbourhood which it was not possible she could have reached. She made inquiries everywhere; she pondered and puzzled over the matter. In the weak, suffering state that the girl was in, how far could she have crawled?

After two days' search, Margaret returned to Hurly Burly. She was sad and tired, and the evening was chill. She sat over the fire wrapped in her shawl when little Bess came to her, weeping behind her muslin apron.

"If you'd speak to Mistress Hurly about it, please, ma'am," she said. "I love her dearly, and it breaks my heart to go away, but the organ haven't done yet, ma'am, and I'm frightened out of my life, so I can't stay."

"Who has heard the organ, and when?" asked Margaret Calderwood, rising to her feet.

"Please, ma'am, I heard it the night you went away—the night after the door was built up!"

"And not since?"

"No, ma'am," hesitatingly, "not since. Hist! hark, ma'am! Is not that like the sound of it now?"

"No," said Margaret Calderwood; "it is only the wind." But pale as death she flew down the stairs and laid her ear to the yet damp mortar of the newly-built wall. All was silent. There was no sound but the monotonous sough of the wind in the trees outside. Then Margaret began to dash her soft shoulder against the strong wall, and to pick the mortar away with her white fingers, and to cry out for the bricklayer who had built up the door.

It was midnight, but the bricklayer left his bed in the village, and obeyed the summons to Hurly Burly. The pale woman stood by and watched him undo all his work of three days ago, and the servants gathered about in trembling groups, wondering what was to happen next.

What happened next was this: When an opening was made the man entered the room with a light, Margaret Calderwood and others following. A heap of something dark was lying on the ground at the foot of the organ. Many groans arose in the fatal chamber. Here was little Lisa dead!

When Mistress Hurly was able to move, the squire and his wife went to live in France, where they remained till their death. Hurly Burly was shut up and deserted for many years. Lately it has passed into new hands. The organ has been taken down and banished, and the room is a bed-chamber, more luxuriously furnished than any in the house. But no one sleeps in it twice.

Margaret Calderwood was carried to her grave the other day a very aged woman.

OVER THE WIRES

H. D. Everett

"Over the Wires" is the second story written by H. D. Everett included in this collection on the acoustic weird. Contrary to "The Whispering Wall", this tale was originally published in one of Everett's short story collections, namely *The Death-Mask, and Other Ghosts* (1920), and under her own name rather than her pseudonym. This time, the story was published two years after the end of the war; and though it is still concerned with this immediate context, it is a more personal tale of separated lovers who yearn to be reunited. Ernest Carrington is on his first leave from the front, and is hoping to trace his betrothed, Isabeau Regnier, whom he lost track of during the Belgian Exodus. Once more, this is a tale of hauntingly sonorous technology, as the object whose sound could be the bearer of good news takes on a potentially spectral quality.

rnest Carrington, captain in the "Old Contemptibles," was in England on his first leave from the front. There he had a special errand, hoping to trace a family of the name of Regnier, which had been swept away in the exodus from Belgium, then of recent date. Two old people, brother and sister, harmless folk who had shown him the kindest hospitality before their home was wrecked and burned; and with them their niece Isabeau, who was his chosen love and his betrothed wife. He had endured agonies in these last weeks, receiving no news of them, though he fully believed they had escaped to England: it was more than strange that Isabeau did not write, as she knew his address, though he was ignorant of hers.

A friend in London had made inquiry for him where the thronging refugees were registered and their needs dealt with, but nothing seemed to be known of the Regniers. Now he would be on the spot, and could himself besiege the authorities. Hay might have been lukewarm over the quest, but it seemed impossible that he, Carrington, could fail. His friend Hay, with whom he was to have stayed, had just been transferred from Middlesex to the coast defence of Scotland, but had placed at Carrington's disposal his small flat, and the old family servant who was caretaker.

The flat was a plain little place, but it seemed luxurious indeed to Carrington that first evening, in sharp contrast to his recent experiences roughing it in the campaign. His brain was still in a whirl after the hurried journey, and it was too late to embark upon his quest that night; but the next morning, the very next morning, he would begin the search for Isabeau.

Only one item in Hay's room demands description. There was a telephone installation in one corner; and twice while Carrington's dinner was being served, there came upon it a sharp summons, answered first by the servant, and secondly by himself. Major Hay was wanted, and it had to be detailed how Major Hay had departed upon sudden orders for Scotland only that morning.

Now the meal was over and cleared away, and the outer door closed, shutting Carrington in for the night. Left alone, his thoughts returned to the channel in which they had flowed for many days and nights. Isabeau—his Isabeau: did the living world still hold his lost treasure, and under what conditions and where? And—maddening reflection—what might she not have suffered of privation, outrage, while he was held apart by his soldier's duty, ignorant, impotent to succour! He could picture her as at their last meeting when they exchanged tokens, the light in her eyes, the sweetness of her lips: the image was perfect before him, down to every fold of her white dress, and every ripple of her hair. His own then, pledged to him, and now vanished into blank invisibility and silence. What could have happened: what dread calamity had torn her from him? Terrible as knowledge might be when gained, it was his earnest prayer that he might know.

A groan burst from his lips, and he cried out her name in a passion of appeal.

"Isabeau, where are you? Speak to me, dead or alive!"

Was it in answer that the telephone call began to ring?—not sharply and loudly, like those demands for Major Hay, but thin and faint like their echo. But without doubt it rang, and Carrington turned to the instrument and took down the receiver.

"Yes," he called back. "What is it?"

Great Heaven! it was Isabeau's voice that answered, a voice he could but just hear, as it seemed to be speaking from far away.

"Ernest—Ernest," she cried, "have you forgotten me? I have forgotten many things since I was tortured, but not you—never you."

"I am here, my darling. I have come to England seeking you, with no other thought in mind. Tell me, for God's sake, where I can find you. Can I come tonight?"

There was a pause, and then the remote voice began again, now a little stronger and clearer.

"Ernest—is it really you? I can die happy, now you tell me that you love me still. That is all I wanted, just the assurance. All I may have in this world—now."

"Darling, of course I love you: you are all in all to me. Where are you speaking from? Tell me, and I will come?"

"No, no: it is all I wanted, what you have just said. It will be easy now to die. I could never have looked you in the face again—after—I am not fit. But soon I shall be washed clean. What does it say—washed? And they gave them white robes—!"

The voice failed, dying away, and when Carrington spoke there was no answer. He called to her by name, begging her to say if she was in London or where, but either the connection had been cut off, or she did not hear. Then after an interval he rang up the exchange. Who was it who had just used the line? But the clerk was stupid or sleepy, thought there had been no call, but was only just on after the shift, and could not say.

It was extraordinary, that she could know where he was to be found that night, and call to him. And how was it that the voice had ceased without giving him a clue? But surely, surely, it would come again.

To seek his bed, tired as he was, seemed now to be impossible. He waited in the living-room, sometimes pacing up and down, sometimes sitting moodily, his head bent on his hands: could he rest or sleep when a further call might come, and, if unheard, a chance be lost. And a call did come a couple of hours later; the same thin reedy vibration of the wire. In a moment he was at the instrument, the receiver at his ear, and again it was Isabeau's voice that spoke.

"Ernest, can you hear me? Will you say it over again: say that you love me still, in spite of all?"

"Dearest, I love you with all my heart and soul. And I entreat you to tell me where you are, so that I can find you."

"You will be told—quite soon. They are so kind—the people here, but they want to know my name. I cannot tell them any more than Isabeau; I have forgotten what name came after. What was my name when you knew me?"

"My darling, you were Isabeau Regnier. And you were living at Martel, with your old uncle Antoine Regnier, and his sister, Mademoiselle Elise. Surely you remember?"

"Yes; yes. I remember now. I remember all. I was Isabeau Regnier then, and now I am lost—lost—lost! Poor old uncle Antoine! They set him up against the wall and shot him, because they said he resisted; and they dragged the Tante and me away. But the Tante could not go fast enough to please them. They stabbed her in the back with their bayonets, and left her bleeding and moaning, lying in the road to die. Oh, if only they had killed me too. Don't ask me—never ask me—what they did to me!"

"Do not think of it, Isabeau dearest. Think only that I have come to seek you, and that you are safe in England and will be my wife. But I must know where you are, and when I can come to see you."

"I will tell you some time, but not now. The nurse says I must not go on talking; that I am making myself more ill. She's wrong, for it cannot make me ill to speak to you; but I must do as I am bidden.

Tell me that you love me; just once again. That you love what I was: you cannot love what I have become."

"Darling, I loved you then, I love you now, and shall love you always. But tell me—you must tell me where—"

She did not answer. This seemed to be the end, for, though he still watched and listened, the wire did not vibrate again that night, nor for many following hours.

He did not spend those hours in inaction. He was early at the London office, and then took the express to Folkestone, but at neither place was there knowledge of the name of Regnier. Nor had he better fortune at the other seaports, which he visited the day following. But where there had been such thronging numbers, despite the organisation vigilance, was it wonderful that a single name had dropped unnoted? And if what had been told him was correct, about the murder of her uncle and aunt, she must have reached England alone.

His next resort was to a private inquiry office, and there an appointment was arranged for him at three o'clock on Friday afternoon.

He had arrived in London on the Monday, and it was on Monday evening and night that those communications from Isabeau came over the wire. Each of the following nights, Tuesday, Wednesday and Thursday, he had spent in Hay's rooms, but from the installed telephone there was no sound or sign.

No sign came until mid-day on Friday, when he was just debating whether to go out to lunch, or have it brought to him from the service down below. The thin, echo-like call sounded again, and he was at once at the receiver.

"Isabeau! Is it you? Speak!"

"Yes, it is I." It was Isabeau's voice that answered, and yet her voice with a difference: it was firmer and clearer than on Monday night, although remote—so remote!

"Where are you? Tell me, that I may come to you. I am seeking you everywhere."

"I do not know where I am. It is all strange and new. But I rejoice in this: I have left behind what was soiled. I would tell you more, but something stops the words. I want you to do something for me: I have a fancy. You have done much, dear Ernest, but this is one thing more."

"What is it, dearest? You have only to ask."

"Go to the end of this street at two o'clock. That is in an hour from now; and wait there till I pass by. I shall not look as I used to do, but I will give you a flower—"

Here the voice failed; he could scarcely distinguish the last words. Strange, that one thing could be said and not another, never what he craved to know. But in an hour he would see her—speak to her, and their separation would be at an end. Not as she used to look! Did she mean changed by what she had suffered? But not so changed, surely, that he would not know, that she would need to identify herself by the gift of a flower. And was the change she spoke of, of the body or the mind? A chill doubt as to the latter, which had assailed him before, crept over him again. But even if it were so, there would be means of healing. She was ill now, shaken by what she had suffered: with love and care, and returning health, all would be well.

He was punctual at the place of appointment. A draughty corner this street-end; but what did he, campaign-hardened, care for chill winds, or for the flying gusts of rain? The passers-by were few for a London street; but each one was carefully scrutinised and each umbrella looked under—that is, if a woman carried it. There was not one, however, that remotely resembled Isabeau. Taxis went by, now and then horse-drawn vehicles; presently a funeral came up the crossing street. A glass hearse with a coffin in it, probably a woman's coffin by its size. A cross of violets lay upon it within, but a couple of white wreaths had been placed outside, next to the driver's seat. A hired brougham was the only following.

They had done better to put the wreaths under shelter, but perhaps no one was in charge who greatly cared. As the cortège came level with the corner, a sharper gust than before tore a white spray from the exposed wreath, and whirled it over towards him; it struck him on the chest, and fell on the wet pavement at his feet. He stooped to pick it up: he loved flowers too well to see it trodden in the mud: and as he did so, a great fear for the first time pierced him through. What might it not signify, this funeral flower? But no, death was not possible: scarcely an hour ago he had heard her living voice.

He waited long at the rendezvous, the flower held in his hand, but no one resembling her came by. Then, chilled and dispirited, but still holding the flower, he turned back to his lodging. It was time and over for his appointment at the inquiry office, but the rain had soaked him through, and he must change to a dry coat.

The servant met him as he came in.

"A letter for you, sir. I am sorry for the delay. You should have had it before, but it must have been brushed off the table and not seen. I found it just now on the floor."

Could it be from Isabeau?—but no, the address was not in her writing. Carrington tore it open: it was from the Belgian central office, and bore date two days back.

"We have at last received information respecting Mademoiselle Regnier. A young woman who appeared to have lost her memory, was charitably taken in by Mrs. Duckworth, in whose house she has remained through a recent serious illness, the hospitals being over full. She recovered memory last night, and now declares her name to be Isabeau Regnier, formerly of Martel. Mrs. Duckworth's address is 18, Silkmore Gardens, S. Kensington, and you will doubtless communicate with her."

Here at last was the information so long vainly sought, and it must have been from the Kensington house that Isabeau telephoned, though her voice sounded like a long-distance call. He would go thither at once; his application to the inquiry office was no longer needed: but still there was a chill at his heart as he looked at the white flower. Was some deep-down consciousness aware, in spite of his surface ignorance; and had it begun to whisper of the greater barrier which lay between?

As he approached the house in Silkmore Gardens, he might have noticed that a servant was going from room to room, drawing up blinds that had been lowered. At the door he asked for Mrs. Duckworth.

"I am not sure if my mistress can see you, sir," was the maid's answer. "She has been very much upset."

"Will you take in my card, and say my business is urgent. I shall be grateful if she will spare me even five minutes. I am a friend of Mademoiselle Regnier's."

Carrington was shown into a sitting-room at the back of the house, with windows to the ground and a vision of greenery beyond. It was not long before Mrs. Duckworth came to him; she wore a black gown, and looked as if she had been weeping.

"You knew Isabeau Regnier," she began with a certain abruptness. "Are you the Ernest of whom she used to speak?"

"I am. She is my affianced wife, so you see I inquire for her by right. I have been searching for her in the utmost distress, and until now in vain. I have but just heard that you out of your charity took her in, also that she has been ill. May I see her now, today?"

The lady's eyes filled again with tears, and she shrank back.

"Ah, you do not know what has happened. O, how sad, how dreadful to have to tell you! Isabeau is dead."

"What, just now, within this hour? She was speaking to me on the telephone only at mid-day."

"No—there is some mistake. That is impossible. She died last Tuesday, and was buried this afternoon. Her coffin left the house at a quarter before two, and my husband went with it to the cemetery. I would have gone too, only that I have been ill."

At first he could only repeat her words: "Dead—Tuesday—Isabeau dead!" She was frightened by the look of his face—the look of a man who is in close touch with despair.

"Oh, I'm so sorry. Oh do sit down, Mr. Carrington. This has been too much for you."

He sank into a chair, and she went hurriedly out, and returned with a glass in her hand.

"Drink this: nay, you must. I am sorry; oh, I am sorry. I wish my husband were here; he would tell you all about it better than I. It has been a grief to us all, to every one in the house; we all grew fond of her. And we began quite to hope she would get well. When she came to us her memory was a blank, except for the wrong that had been done her. That seemed to have blotted out all that was behind, except her love for Ernest—you. But she said she could never look Ernest in the face again, and she wanted to be lost. She took an interest in things here after a while, and she was kind and helpful, like a daughter in the house—we have no children. And then her illness came on again; it was something the matter with the brain, caused by the shock she had sustained. She was very ill, but we could not get her into any hospital, all were too full. But she had every care with us, you may be sure of that, and I think she was happier to be here to the last. So it went on, up and down, sometimes a little better, sometimes worse. Last Monday evening delirium set in. She fancied Ernest was here—you—and she was talking to you all the time. It was as if she heard you answering."

"Have you a telephone installed? Could she get up and go to the telephone?"

"We have a telephone—yes, certainly. But she had not strength enough to leave her bed, and the installation is downstairs in the study."

"I declare to you on my most solemn word that she spoke to me over the telephone—twice on Monday night, and once today. It is beyond comprehension. Can you tell me what she said, speaking as she thought to Ernest?"

"She asked you to remind her of her forgotten name. We did not get Regnier till then, nor Martel where she lived; it was as if she heard the words spoken by you. I wrote at once to the organising people to say we had found out: I had no idea then that her death was so near. With the recollection of her name came back—horrors, and she was telling them to you. It seems she lived with an old uncle and aunt: would that be right for the girl you knew? They shot her uncle, the Germans did, when they burnt the house, and stabbed her poor old aunt and left her to die. I can show you a photograph of Isabeau, if that will help to identify. It is only an amateur snapshot, taken in our garden, at the time she was so much better, and, we hoped, recovering. It is very like her as she was then."

Mrs. Duckworth opened the drawer of a cabinet, and took out a small square photograph of a girl in a white dress sitting under a tree, and looking out of the picture with sad appealing eyes.

Carrington looked at it, and at first he could not speak. Presently he said, answering a question of Mrs. Duckworth's:

"Yes, there can be no doubt."

He had heard enough. Mrs. Duckworth would fain have asked further about the marvel of the voice, but he got up to take leave.

"I will come again if you will permit," he said. "Another day I shall be able to thank you better for all you did for her—for all your kindness. You will then tell me where she is laid, and let me take on myself—all expense. Now I must be alone."

There was ready sympathy in the little woman's face; tears were running down, though her words of response were few. Carrington still held the photograph.

"May I take this?" he said, and she gave an immediate assent. Then he pressed the hand she held out in farewell, and in another moment was gone.

The sequel to this episode is unknown. Carrington sat long that night with the picture before him, the pathetic little picture of his lost love; and cried aloud to her in his solitude: "Isabeau, speak to me, come to me. Death did not make it impossible before: why should it now? Do not think I would shrink from you or fear you. Nothing is in my heart but a great longing—a great love—a great pity. Speak again—speak!"

But no answer came. The telephone in the corner remained silent, and that curious far-off tremor of the wire sounded for him no more.

IV.

*Sounds and silence: Acoustic
weird beyond the ghostly*

SIOPE — A FABLE

Edgar Allan Poe

The American writer of mystery and the macabre Edgar Allan Poe (1809–1849) is a central figure of early weird fiction and of Gothic horror. In the span of his relatively short life, Poe made significant contributions to literary fiction: an early practitioner of the short story, his works have also influenced the development of detective fiction and of science fiction, though they mostly belong to the dark romanticism genre. Additionally, Poe wrote humorous and satirical pieces, but also literary criticism, as he famously reflected on the art of writing in several essays. His short stories have often been anthologised, including by British Library Publishing as *The Tell-Tale Heart and Other Tales* (2016)—which bears the title of Poe's most sonorous tale.

"Siope—A Fable" is one of Poe's lesser-known stories, and was first published in W. H. Carpenter and T. S. Arthur's *The Baltimore Book* at the end of 1837. It was later consistently republished under the title "Silence—A Fable". In fact, "siope" is a transliteration of the Greek for silence, "σωπή", into English. The tale's connections with silence are strengthened by its epigraph, which is a quotation from Poe's longest poem, "Al Aaraaf", first published in 1829.

The last section of this volume proposes to expand the boundaries of the acoustic weird beyond the ghostly, which is why I have selected Poe's tale, as an early exploration of sounds and silence. Told by a demon, it is a fable in which silence, or sound removed, is terror.

> *Ours is a world of words: Quiet we call*
> *Silence—which is the merest word of all*

AL AARAAF.

isten to *me*," said the Demon, as he placed his hand upon my head. "There is a spot upon this accursed earth which thou hast never yet beheld. And if by any chance thou *hast* beheld it, it must have been in one of those vigorous dreams which come like the Simoom upon the brain of the sleeper who hath lain down to sleep among the forbidden sunbeams—among the sunbeams, I say, which slide from off the solemn columns of the melancholy temples in the wilderness. The region of which I speak is a dreary region in Libya, by the borders of the river Zaire. And there is no quiet there, nor silence.

"The waters of the river have a saffron and sickly hue—and they flow not onwards to the sea, but palpitate forever and forever beneath the red eye of the sun with a tumultuous and convulsive motion. For many miles on either side of the river's oozy bed is a pale desert of gigantic water-lilies. They sigh one unto the other in that solitude, and stretch towards the heaven their long ghastly necks, and nod to and fro their everlasting heads. And there is an indistinct murmur which cometh out from among them like the rushing of subterrene water. And they sigh one unto the other.

"But there is a boundary to their realm—the boundary of the dark, horrible, lofty forest. There, like the waves about the Hebrides, the low underwood is agitated continually. But there is no wind throughout the heaven. And the tall primæval trees rock eternally hither and thither with a crashing and mighty sound. And from their high summits, one by one, drop everlasting dews. And at the roots strange poisonous flowers lie writhing in perturbed slumber. And overhead, with a rustling and loud noise, the grey clouds rush westwardly forever, until they roll, a cataract, over the fiery wall of the horizon. But there is no wind throughout the heaven. And by the shores of the river Zaire there is neither quiet nor silence.

"It was night, and the rain fell; and, falling, it was rain, but, having fallen, it was blood. And I stood in the morass among the tall lilies, and the rain fell upon my head—and the lilies sighed one unto the other in the solemnity of their desolation.

"And, all at once, the moon arose through the thin ghastly mist, and was crimson in colour. And mine eyes fell upon a huge grey rock which stood by the shore of the river, and was litten by the light of the moon. And the rock was grey, and ghastly, and tall,—and the rock was grey. Upon its front were characters engraven in the stone; and I walked through the morass of water-lilies, until I came close unto the shore, that I might read the characters upon the stone. But I could not decypher the characters. And I was going back into the morass, when the moon shone with a fuller red, and I turned and looked again upon the rock, and upon the characters—and the characters were DESOLATION.

"And I looked upwards, and there stood a man upon the summit of the rock, and I hid myself among the water-lilies that I might discover the actions of the man. And the man was tall and stately in form, and was wrapped up from his shoulders to his feet in the toga of old Rome. And the outlines of his figure were indistinct—but his features were the features of a Deity; for the mantle of the night, and of the mist, and of the moon, and of the dew, had left uncovered the features of his face. And his brow was lofty with thought, and his eye wild with care; and, in the few furrows upon his cheek I read the fables of sorrow, and weariness, and disgust with mankind, and a longing after solitude. And the moon shone upon his face, and upon the features of his face, and oh! they were more beautiful than the airy dreams which hovered about the souls of the daughters of Delos!

"And the man sat down upon the rock, and leaned his head upon his hand, and looked out upon the desolation. He looked down into the low unquiet shrubbery, and up into the tall primæval trees, and up higher at the rustling heaven, and into the crimson moon. And I lay close within shelter of the lilies, and observed the actions of the man. And the man trembled in the solitude—but the night waned and he sat upon the rock.

"And the man turned his attention from the heaven, and looked out upon the dreary river Zaire, and upon the yellow ghastly waters, and upon the pale legions of the water-lilies. And the man listened to the sighs of the water-lilies, and of the murmur that came up from among them. And I lay close within my covert and observed the actions of the man. And the man trembled in the solitude—but the night waned and he sat upon the rock.

"Then I went down into the recesses of the morass, and waded afar in among the wilderness of the lilies, and called unto the hippopotami which dwelt among the fens in the recesses of the morass. And the hippopotami heard my call, and came, with the behemoth, unto the foot of the rock, and roared loudly and fearfully beneath the moon. And I lay close within my covert and observed the actions

275

of the man. And the man trembled in the solitude—but the night waned and he sat upon the rock.

"Then I cursed the elements with the curse of tumult; and a frightful tempest gathered in the heaven where before there had been no wind. And the heaven became livid with the violence of the tempest—and the rain beat upon the head of the man—and the floods of the river came down—and the river was tormented into foam—and the water-lilies shrieked within their beds—and the forest crumbled before the wind—and the thunder rolled,—and the lightning fell—and the rock rocked to its foundation. And I lay close within my covert and observed the actions of the man. And the man trembled in the solitude—but the night waned and he sat upon the rock.

"Then I grew angry and cursed, with the curse of silence, the river, and the lilies, and the wind, and the forest, and the heaven, and the thunder, and the sighs of the water-lilies. And they became accursed and *were still*. And the moon ceased to totter in its pathway up the heaven—and the thunder died away—and the lightning did not flash—and the clouds hung motionless—and the waters sunk to their level and remained—and the trees ceased to rock—and the water-lilies sighed no more—and the murmur was heard no longer from among them, nor any shadow of sound throughout the vast illimitable desert. And I looked upon the characters of the rock, and they were changed—and the characters were SILENCE.

"And mine eyes fell upon the countenance of the man, and his countenance was wan with terror. And, hurriedly, he raised his head from his hand, and stood forth upon the rock, and listened. But there was no voice throughout the vast illimitable desert, and the characters upon the rock were SILENCE. And the man shuddered, and turned his face away, and fled afar off, and I beheld him no more."

*

Now there are fine tales in the volumes of the Magi—in the iron-bound, melancholy volumes of the Magi. Therein, I say, are glorious histories of the Heaven, and of the Earth, and of the mighty Sea—and of the Genii that overruled the sea, and the earth, and the lofty heaven. There was much lore too in the sayings which were said by the sybils; and holy, holy things were heard of old by the dim leaves that trembled around Dodona—but, as Allah liveth, that fable which the Demon told me as he sat by my side in the shadow of the tomb, I hold to be the most wonderful of all! And as the Demon made an end of his story, he fell back within the cavity of the tomb and laughed. And I could not laugh with the Demon, and he cursed me because I could not laugh. And the lynx which dwelleth forever in the tomb, came out therefrom, and lay down at the feet of the Demon, and looked at him steadily in the face.

THE HOUSE OF SOUNDS

M. P. Shiel

Matthew Phipps Shiell (1865–1947) was a late-Victorian writer of supernatural horror, so-called "future history" science-fiction, and later in his career, romantic novels. Writing under the pen name M. P. Shiel, his speculative fiction and rich prose were characterised by the fact that they often drew on contemporary scientific and philosophical developments. He is best remembered for his novel *The Purple Cloud* (1901), a post-apocalyptic tale about a man who discovers upon his return from an expedition to the North Pole that a massive volcanic eruption has left him the last man alive. Shiel's fiction contributed to the development of British weird fiction, and the master of the genre H. P. Lovecraft himself was fascinated by Shiel's work. However, it must be noted that, like Lovecraft, Shiel's personal life and views were problematic, which is sometimes reflected in his stories through storylines with racist or anti-Semitic undertones, or through their controversial characterisation of young women.

"The House of Sounds" is a masterpiece of the acoustic weird, and has often been compared to Edgar Allan Poe's 1839 short story "The Fall of the House of Usher". The narrator of Shiel's tale is called for by a friend, who resides on an isolated island off the coast of Norway. The story is brimming with sounds, as the house is on top of a cliff which is constantly battered by waves, and the overbearing sonority of the sea constitutes the backdrop of most of the story. The characters communicate via written notes, as the noise drowns conversation and renders it almost impossible. It is a tale of destruction: while the narrator discovers the curse on his friend's family and on his home, the story also stages the mental and physical destruction of the characters, through its use of noises—whether they are within the story itself, or in its narrative techniques and in its prose. "The House of Sounds" concludes this anthology by proposing a different form of acoustic weird, with overwhelming sound(s) beyond the ghostly.

"E caddi come l'uom cui sonno piglia."—Dante.

A good many years ago, when a young man, a student in Paris, I knew the great Carot, and witnessed by his side many of those cases of mind-malady, in the analysis of which he was such a master. I remember one little maid of the Marais who, until the age of nine, did not differ from her playmates; but one night, lying abed she whispered into her mother's ear: "Mama, can you not hear *the sound of the world*?" It appears that her geography had just taught her that our globe reels with an enormous velocity on an orbit about the sun; and this *sound of the world* of hers was merely a murmur in the ear, heard in the silence of night. Within six months she was as mad as a March-hare.

I mentioned the case to my friend, Haco Harfager, then occupying with me an old mansion in St. Germain, shut in by a wall and jungle of shrubbery. He listened with singular interest, and during a good while sat wrapped in gloom.

Another case which I gave made a great impression upon my friend: A young man, a toy-maker of St. Antoine, suffering from consumption—but sober, industrious—returning one gloaming to his garret, happened to purchase one of those factious journals which circulate by lamplight over the Boulevards. This simple act was the beginning of his doom. He had never been a reader: knew little of the reel and turmoil of the world. But the next night he purchased another journal. Soon he acquired a knowledge of politics, the huge

281

movements, the tumult of life. And this interest grew absorbing. Till late into the night, every night, he lay poring over the roar of action, the printed passion. He would awake sick, but brisk in spirit—and bought a morning paper. And the more his teeth gnashed, the less they ate. He grew negligent, irregular at work, turning on his bed through the day. Rags overtook him. As the grand interest grew upon his frail soul, so every lesser interest failed in him. There came a day when he no more cared for his own life; and another day when he tore the hairs from his head.

As to this man the great Carot said to me:

"Really, one does not know whether to chuckle or to weep over such a business. Observe, for one thing, how diversely men are made! There are minds precisely so sensitive as a thread of melted lead: *every* breath will fret and trouble them: and how about the hurricane? For such this scheme of things is clearly no fit habitation, but a Machine of Death, a baleful Immense. *Too* cruel to some is the rushing shriek of Being—they *cannot* stand the world. Let each look well to his own little shred of existence, I say, and leave the monstrous Automaton alone! Here in this poor toy-maker you have a case of the ear: it is only the neurosis, Oxyecoia. Grand was that Greek myth of 'the Harpies'—by *them* was this creature snatched away—or say, caught by a limb in the wheels of the universe, and so perished. It is quite a ravishing exit—translation in a chariot of flame! Only remember that the member first seized was *the pinna*—he bent *ear* to the howl of the world, and ended by himself howling. Between chaos and our shoes swings, I assure you, the thinnest film! I knew a man who had this aural peculiarity: that every sound brought him some knowledge of the matter causing the sound: a rod for instance, of mixed copper and tin striking upon a rod of mixed iron and lead, conveyed to him not merely the proportion of each metal in each rod, but some knowledge of the essential meaning and spirit, as it were, of copper, of tin, of iron and of lead. Him also did the Harpies snatch aloft!"

I have mentioned that I related some of these cases to my friend, Harfager: and I was astonished at the obvious pains which he gave himself to hide his interest, his gaping nostrils...

From first days when we happened to attend the same seminary in Stockholm an intimacy had sprung up between us. But it was not an intimacy accompanied by the ordinary signs of friendship. Harfager was the shyest, most isolated, of beings. Though our joint house-keeping (brought about by a chance meeting at a midnight *séance*) had now lasted some months, I knew nothing of his plans. Through the day we read together, he rapt back into the past, I engrossed with the present; late at night we reclined on sofas within the vast cave of a hearth-place *Louis Onze*, and smoked over the dying fire in silence. Occasionally a *soirée* or lecture might draw me from the house; except once, I never understood that Harfager left it. On that occasion I was hurrying through the Rue St. Honoré, where a rush of traffic rattles over the old pavers retained there, when I came upon him. In this tumult he stood in a listening attitude; and for a moment did not know me.

Even as a boy I had seen in my friend the genuine patrician—not that his personality gave any impression of loftiness or opulence: on the contrary. He did, however, suggest an incalculable *ancientness;* and I have known no nobleman who so bore in his expression the assurance of the essential Prince, whose pale blossom is of yesterday, and will perish tomorrow, but whose root shoots through the ages. This much I knew of Harfager; also that on one or other of his islands north of Zetland lived his mother and an aunt; that he was somewhat deaf; but liable to a thousand torments or delights at certain sounds, the whine of a door, the note of a bird...

He was somewhat under the middle height; and inclined to portliness. His nose rose highly aquiline from that sort of brow called "the musical"—that is, with temples which incline *outward* to the cheek-bones, making breadth for the base of the brain; while the direction of the heavy-lidded eyes and of the eyebrows was a downward *droop* from the nose of their outer ends. He wore a thin chin-beard. But the feature of his face were the ears, which were nearly circular, very small and flat, without that outer curve called "the helix." I came to understand that this had long been a trait of his race. Over the whole wan face of my friend was engraved an air of woeful inability, utter gravity of sorrow: one said "Sardanapalus," frail last of the race of Nimrod.

After a year I found it necessary to mention to Harfager my intention of leaving Paris, as we reclined one night in our nooks within the fireplace. He replied to my tidings with a polite "Indeed!" and continued to gloat over the grate: but after an hour turned to me and observed: "Well, it seems to be a hard world."

Truisms uttered in just such a tone of discovery I occasionally heard from him; but his earnest gaze, his despondency now, astonished me.

"Apropos of what?" I asked.

"My friend, do not leave me!" He spread his arms.

I learned that he was the object of a devilish malice; that he was the prey of a horrible temptation. That a lure, a becking hand, a lurking lust, which it was the effort of his life to escape (and to which he was especially liable in solitude) perpetually enticed him; and that so it had been almost from the day when, at the age of five, he had been sent by his father from his desolate home in the ocean.

And whose was this malice?

He told me his mother's and aunt's.

And what was this temptation?

He said it was the temptation to go back—to hurry with the very frenzy of hunger—back to that home.

I demanded with what motives, and in what way, the malice of his mother and aunt manifested itself. He answered that there was, he fancied no definite motive, but only a fated malevolence; and that the respect in which it manifested itself was the prayers and commands with which they plagued him to go again to the hold of his ancestors.

All this I could not understand, and said so. In what consisted this magnetism, and this peril, of his home? To this Harfager did not reply, but rising from his seat, disappeared behind the hearth-curtains, and left the apartment. When he returned, it was with a quarto tome bound in hide, which proved to be Hugh Gascoigne's "Chronicle of Norse Families" in English black-letter. The passage to which he pointed I read as follows:

"Now of these two brothers the older, Harold, being of seemly personage and prowess, did go a pilgrimage into Danemark, where-from he repaired again home to Hjaltland (Zetland), and with him fetched the amiable Thronda for his wife, who was a daughter of the sank (blood) royal of Danemark. And his younger brother, Sweyn, that was sad and debonair, but far surpassed the other in cunning, received him with all good cheer.

"But eftsoons (soon after) fell Sweyn sick for all his love that he had of Thronda, his brother's wife. And while the worthy Harold ministered about the bed where Sweyn lay sick, lo, Sweyn fastened on him a violent stroke with a sword, and with no longer tarrying enclosed his hands in bonds, and cast him in the bottom of a deep hold. And because Harold would not deprive himself of the gov-ernance of Thronda his wife, Sweyn cut off both his ear[s], and put out one of his eyes, and after divers such torments was ready to slay him. But on a day the valiant Harold, breaking his bonds, and embracing his adversary, did by the sleight of wrestling overthrow him, and escaped. Notwithstanding, he faltered when he came to the Somburg Head, not far from the Castle, and, albeit that he was swift-foot, could no farther run, by reason that he was faint with the long plagues of his brother. And whilst he there lay in a swoon, did Sweyn come upon him, and when he had stricken him with a dart, cast him from Somburg Head into the sea.

"Not long hereafterward did the lady Thronda (though she knew not the manner of her lord's death, nor, verily, if he was dead or alive) receive Sweyn into favour, and with great gaudying and blowing of beamous (trumpets) did become his wife. And right soon they two went thence to sojourn in far parts.

"Now, it befell that Sweyn was minded by a dream to have built a great mansion in Hjaltland for the home-coming of the lady Thronda; wherefore he called to him a cunning Master-workman, and sent him to England to gather men for the building of this lusty House, while he himself remained with his lady at Rome. Then came this Architect to London, but passing thence to Hjaltland was drowned, he and his feers (mates), all and some.

"And after two years, which was the time assigned, Sweyn Harfager sent a letter to Hjaltland to understand how his great House did: for he knew not of the drowning of the Architect: and soon after he received answer that the House *did well,* and was building on the Isle of Rayba. But that was not the Isle where Sweyn had appointed the building to be: and he was afeard, and near fell down dead for dread, because, in the letter, he saw before him the manner of writing of his brother Harold. And he said in this form: 'Surely Harold is alive, else be this letter writ with ghostly hand.' And he was wo many days, seeing that this was a deadly stroke.

"Thereafter he took himself back to Hjaltland to know how the matter was, and there the old Castle on Somburg Head was break down to the earth. Then Sweyn was wode-wroth, and cried: 'Jhesu mercy, where is all the great house of my fathers gone? alas! this wicked day of destiny!' And one of the people told him that a host of workmen from far parts had break it down. And he said: 'Who hath bid them?' but that could none answer. Then he said again: 'nis (is not) my brother Harold alive? for I have behold his writing': and that, too, could none answer. So he went to Rayba, and saw there a great House stand, and when he looked on it, he said: 'This, sooth, was y-built by my brother Harold, be he dead or be he on-live.' And there he dwelt, and his lady, and his sons' sons until now: for that the House is ruthless and without pity; wherefore 'tis said that upon all who dwell there falleth a wicked madness and a lecherous anguish; and that by way of the ears do they drinck the cup of the furie of the earless Harold, till the time of the House be ended."

After I had read the narrative half-aloud, I smiled, saying: "This, Harfager, is very tolerable romance on the part of the good Gascoigne, but has the look of indifferent history."

"It is, nevertheless, *history*," he replied.

"You believe that?"

"The house stands solidly on Rayba."

"But you believe that mediæval ghosts superintended the building of their family mansions?"

"Gascoigne nowhere says that," he answered: "for to be 'stricken with a darte,' is not necessarily to die; nor, if he did say it, have I any knowledge on the subject."

"And what, Harfager, is the nature that 'wicked madness,' that 'lecherous anguish,' of which Gascoigne speaks?"

"Do you ask me?"—he spread his arms—"what do I know? I know nothing! I was banished from the place at the age of five. Yet the cry of it still rings in my mind. And have I not *told* you of anguishes—even in myself—of inherited longing and loathing..."

Anyway, I *had to go* to Heidelberg just then: so I said I would compromise by making my absence short, and rejoin him in a few weeks. I took his moody silence to mean assent; and soon afterwards left him.

But I was detained: and when I got back to our old house found it empty. Harfager was gone.

It was only after twelve years that a letter was forwarded me—a rather wild letter, an awfully long one—in the writing of my friend. It was dated at Rayba. From the writing I understood that it had been dashed off *with furious haste*, so that I was the more astonished at the very trivial nature of the contents. On the first half page he spoke of our old friendship, and asked if I would see his mother, who was dying; the rest of the epistle consisted of an analysis of his mother's family-tree, the apparent aim being to show that she was a genuine Harfager, and a distant cousin of his father. He then went on to comment on the great prolificness of his race, stating that since the fourteenth century over *four millions* of its members had lived; three only of them, he believed, being now left. This settled, the letter ended.

Influenced by this, I travelled northward; reached Caithness; passed the stormy Orkneys; reached Lerwick; and from Unst, the most bleak and northerly of the Zetlands, contrived, by dint of bribes, to pit the weather-worthiness of a lug-sailed "sixern" (identical with the "langschips" of the Vikings) against a flowing sea and an ugly sky. The trip, I was told, was at such a season of some risk. It was the sombre December of those seas; and the weather, they said, although never cold, is seldom other than tempestuous. A mist now lay over the billows, enclosing our boat in a dome of doleful gloaming; and there was a ghostly something in the look of the silent sea and brooding sky which produced upon my nerves the mood of a journey out of nature, a cruise beyond the world. Occasionally, however, we ran past one of those "skerries," or sea-stacks, whose craggy seawalls, disintegrated by the struggles of the Gulf Stream with the North Sea, had a look of awful ruin and havoc. But I only noticed three of these: for before the dun day had well run half its course, sudden darkness was upon us; and with it one of those storms of which the winter of this semi-Arctic sea is one succession. During the haggard glimpses of the following day the rain did not stop; but before darkness had quite fallen, my skipper (who talked continuously to a mate of seal-maidens, and water-horses, and *grülies*), paused to point me out a mound of gloomier grey on the weather-bow, which, he said, should be Rayba.

Rayba, he said, was the centre of quite a nest of those *rösts* (eddies) and cross-currents which the tidal wave hurls with complicated swirlings among all the islands: but at Rayba they ran with more than usual angriness, owing to the row of sea-crags which garrisoned the land around: approach was therefore at all times difficult, and at night foolhardy. With a running sea, however, we came sufficiently close to see the mane of foam which railed round the coast-wall. Its shock, according to the captain, had often more than all the efficiency of artillery, tossing tons of rock to heights of six hundred feet upon the island.

When the sun next pried above the horizon, we had closely approached the coast; and it was then that for the first time the impression of some *spinning* motion of the island (due probably to the swirling movements of the water) was produced upon me. We affected a landing at a *voe*, or sea-arm, on the west coast—the east, though the point of my aim, was out of the question on account of the swell. Here I found in two *skeoes* (or sheds), thatched with feal, five or six seamen, who gained a livelihood by trading for the groceries of the great house on the east: and, taking one of them for a guide, I began the climb of the island.

Now, during the night in the boat, I had been aware of a booming in the ears for which even the roar of the sea round the coast seemed insufficient to account; and this now, as we went on, became immensely augmented—and with it, once more, that conviction within me of *spinning* motions. Rayba I found to be a land of precipices of granite and flaggy gneiss; at about the centre, however, we came upon a tableland, sloping from west to east, and covered by a lot of lochs, which sullenly flowed into one another. I could see no shore eastward to this chain of waters, and by dint of shouting to my leader, and bending ear to his shoutings, I came to know that there *was* no such shore—I say *shout,* for nothing less could have sounded through the steady bellowing as of ten thousand bisons that now resounded on every side. A certain trembling, too, of the earth became distinct. In vain, meantime, did the eye in its dreary survey seek a tree or shrub—for no kind of vegetation, save peat, could brave for a day the perennial tempest of this benighted island. Darkness, half an hour after noon, commenced to fall upon us: and it was soon afterwards that my guide, pointing down a defile near the east coast, hurriedly started back upon the way he had come. I bawled a question after him, as he went: but at this point the voice of mortals had ceased to be in the least audible.

Down this defile, with a sinking of the heart, and a singular sickness of giddiness, I passed; and, on reaching its end, emerged upon a ledge of rock which shuddered to the immediate onsets of the sea—though all this part of the island was, besides, in the grip of an ague not due to the great guns of the sea. Hugging a crag of cliff for steadiness from the gusts, I gazed forth upon a scene not less eerily dismal than some drear district of the dreams of Dante. Three "skerries," flanked by stacks as fantastic and twisted as a witch's finger, and giving a home to hosts of osprey and scart, seal and walrus, lay at some fathoms distance; and from its rush among them, the sea in blanched, tumultuous, but inaudible wrath, like an army with banners, ranted toward the land. Letting go my crag, I staggered some distance to the left: and now all at once an amphitheatre opened before me, and there broke upon my view a panorama of such appalling majesty as had never entered my heart to fancy.

"An amphitheatre," I said: but it was rather the form of a Norman door that I saw. Fancy such a door, half a mile wide, flat on the ground, the rounded part farthest from the sea; and all round it let a wall of rock tower perpendicular forty yards: and now down this rounded door-shape, and *over its whole extent*, let a roaring ocean roll its tonnage in hoary fury—and the stupor with which I looked, and then the shrinking, and then the instinct of flight, will find comprehension.

This was the disemboguement of the lochs of Rayba.

And within the curve of this Norman cataract, robed in the world of its smokes and far-excursive surfs, stood a fabric of brass.

The last beam of the day had now nearly passed; but I could still see through the mist which bleakly nimbused it as in tears, that the building was low in proportion to the hugeness of its circumference; that it was roofed with a dome; and that round it ran two rows of Norman windows, the upper smaller than the lower. Certain indications led me to infer that the house had been founded upon a bed of rock which lay, circular and detached, within the curve of the cataract; but this nowhere emerged above the flood: for the whole floor which I had before me dashed one reeking deep river to the beachless sea—passage to the mansion being made possible by a massive causeway-bridge, with arches, all bearded with seaweed.

Descending from my ledge, I passed along it, now drenched in spray; and, as I came nearer, could see that the house, too, was to half its height more thickly bearded than an old hull with barnacles and every variety of bright seaweed; also—what was very surprising—that from many spots near the top of the brazen wall ponderous chains, dropping beards, reached out in rays: so that the fabric had the aspect of a many-anchored ark. But without pausing to look closely, I pushed forward, and rushing through the smooth waterfall which poured all round from the roof, by one of its many porches I entered the dwelling.

Darkness now was around me—and sound. I seemed to stand in the centre of some yelling planet, the row resembling the resounding of many thousands of cannon, punctuated by strange crashing and breaking uproars. And a sadness descended on me; I was near to tears. "Here," I said, "is the place of weeping; not elsewhere is the vale of sighing." However, I passed forward through a succession of halls, and was wondering where to go next, when a hideous figure, with a lamp in his hand, stamped towards me. I shrank from him! It seemed the skeleton of a lank man wrapped in a winding-sheet, till the light of one tiny eye, and a film of skin over a portion of the face reassured one. Of ears he showed no sign. His name, I afterwards learned, was Aith; and his appearance was explained by his pretence (true or false), that he had once suffered *burning*, almost to the cinder-stage, but had somehow recovered. With an expression of malice, and agitated gestures, he led the way to a chamber on the upper stage, where, having struck light to a taper, he made signs toward a spread table, and left me.

For a long time I sat in solitude, conscious of the shaking of the mansion, though every sense was swallowed up and confounded in the one impression of sound. Water, water, was the world—a nightmare on my breast, a desire to gasp for breath, a tingling on my nerves, a sense of being infinitely drowned and buried in boundless deluges; and when the feeling of giddiness, too, increased, I sprang up and paced—but suddenly stopped, angry, I scarce knew why, with myself. I had, in fact, caught myself walking with a certain *hurry*, not usual with me, not natural to me. So I forced myself to stand and take note of the hall. It was large, and damp with mists, so that its tattered, but rich, furniture looked lost in it, its centre occupied by a tomb bearing the name of a Harfager of the fourteenth century, and its walls old panels of oak. Having drearily seen these things, I waited on with an intolerable consciousness of solitude; but a little after midnight the tapestry parted, and Harfager with a rapid stalk walked in.

In twelve years my friend had grown old. He showed, it is true, a tendency to portliness: yet, to a knowing eye he was in reality tabid, ill-nourished. And his neck stuck forward from his chest; and the lower part of his back had quite a forward bend of age; and his hair floated about his face and shoulders in a wildness of awful whiteness, while a white chin-beard hung to his chest. His dress was a robe of bauge, which, as he went, waved aflaunt from his bare and hairy shins; and he was shod in those soft slippers called *rivlins*.

To my astonishment, he spoke. When I passionately shouted that I could gather no fragment of sound from his moving mouth, he clapped both his palms to his ears, and then anew besieged mine: but again without result: and now, with an angry throw of the hand, he caught up his taper, and walked from the apartment.

There was something strikingly unnatural in his manner—something which reminded me of the skeleton, Aith: an excess of zeal, a fever, a rage, *a loudness*, an eagerness of gait, a great extravagance of gesture. His hand constantly dashed wiffs of hair from a face which, though of the saffron of death, had red eyes—thick-lidded eyes, fixed in a downward and sideward gaze. When he came back to me, it was with a leaf of ivory, and a piece of graphite, hanging from the cord tied round his garment; and he rapidly wrote a petition that, if not too tired, I would take part with him in the funeral of his mother.

I shouted assent.

Once more he clapped his palms to his ears; then wrote: "Do not shout: no whisper in any part of the building is inaudible to me."

I remembered that in early life he had been slightly *deaf*.

We passed together through many apartments, he shading the taper with his hand—a necessary action, for, as I quickly discovered, in no nook of the quivering building was the air in a state of rest, but was for ever commoved by a curious agitation, a faint windiness, like an echo of tempests, which communicated a universal nervousness to the curtains. Everywhere I met the same past grandeur, present raggedness and decay. In many of the rooms were tombs; one was a museum thronged with bronzes, but broken, grown with fungoids, dripping with moisture—it was as if the mansion, in ardour of travail, sweated; and a miasma of decomposition tainted all the air.

I followed Harfager through the maze of his way with some difficulty, for he went headlong—only once stopping, when with a face ungainly wild over the glare of the light, he tossed up his fingers, and gave out a single word: from the form of his lips I guessed the word "*Hark!*"

Presently we entered a very long chamber, in which, on chairs beside a bed, lay a coffin flanked by a file of candles. The coffin was very deep, and had this singularity—that the foot-piece was absent, so that the soles of the corpse could be seen as we approached. I saw too, three upright rods secured to a side of the coffin, each rod fitted at its top with a little silver bell of the sort called *morrice*, pendent from a flexible spring. And at the head of the bed, Aith, with an air of irascibility, was stamping to and fro within a narrow area.

Harfager deposited the taper upon a stone table, and stood poring with a crazy intentness over the body. I, too, stood and looked at death so grim and rigorous as I think I never saw. The coffin looked angrily full of tangled grey locks, the lady being of great age, bony and hook-nosed; and her face shook with solemn constancy to the quivering of the building. I noticed that over the body had been fixed three bridges, like the bridge of a violin, their sides fitting into grooves in the coffin's sides, and their tops of a shape to fit the slope of the two coffin-lids when closed. One of these bridges passed over the knees of the dead lady; another bridged her stomach; the third her neck. In each of them was a hole, and across each of the three holes passed a string from the morrice-bell above it—the three holes being thus divided by the three tight strings into six semi-circles. Before I could guess the significance of all this, Harfager closed the folding coffin-lids, which had little holes for the passage of the three strings. He then turned the key in the lock, and uttered a word which I took to be "come."

Aith now took hold of the handle at the coffin's head; and out of the dark parts of the hall a lady in black walked forward. She was tall, pallid, of imposing aspect; and from the curvature of her nose, and her circular ears, I guessed her the lady Swertha, aunt of Harfager. Her eyes were quite red—if with crying I could not tell.

Harfager and I taking each a handle near the coffin-foot, and the lady bearing before us one of the black candlesticks, the obsequies began. When I got to the doorway, I noticed in a corner there two more coffins, engraved with the names Harfager and his aunt. Thence we wound our way down a wide stairway winding to a lower floor; and descending thence still lower by narrow brass steps, came to a portal of metal, where the lady, depositing the candlestick, left us.

The chamber of death into which we now bore the body had for its outer wall the brazen outer wall of the whole house at a spot where this closely approached the cataract, and was no doubt profoundly drowned in the world of surge without: so that the earthquake there was urgent. On every side the place was piled with coffins, ranged high and wide upon shelves; and the huge rush and scampering which ensued on our entrance proved it the paradise of troops of rats. As it was inconceivable that these could have eaten a way through sixteen brazen feet—for even the floor here was brazen—I assumed that some fruitful pair must have found in the house, on its building, an ark from the waters. Even this guess, though, seemed wild; and Harfager afterwards confided to me his suspicion that they had for some reason been *placed* there by the original builder.

We deposited our load upon a stone bench in the centre; where-upon Aith made haste to be away. Harfager then repeatedly walked from end to end of the place, scrutinising with many a stoop and peer and upward stretch, the shelves and their props. Could he, I was led to wonder, have any doubts as to their soundness? Damp, in fact, and decay pervaded everything. A bit of timber which I touched crumbled to dust under my thumb.

He presently beckoned to me, and, with yet one halt and "*Hark!*" from him, we passed through the house to my chamber; where, left alone, I paced about, agitated with a vague anger; then tumbled to an agony of slumber.

In the far interior of the mansion even the bleared day of this land of bleakness never rose upon our gloom; but I was able to regulate my gettings-up by a clock which stood in my chamber; or I was called by Harfager, with whom in a short time I renewed more than all our former friendship. That I should say *more* is curious: but so it *was*: and this was proved by the fact that we grew to take, and to excuse, freedoms of speech and of manner which, as two persons of more than usual reserve, we had once never dreamed of permitting to ourselves in respect of each other. Once, for example, in our pacings of aimless haste down passages that vanished in shadow and length of perspective remoteness, he wrote that my step was very slow. I replied that it was just such a step as suited my then mood. He wrote: "You have developed a tendency to *fret*." I was very offended, and said: "Certainly, there are more fingers than one in the world which *that* ring will fit!"

Another day he was no less than rude to me for seeking to reveal to him the secret of the unhuman keenness of his hearing—and of mine! For I, too, to my dismay, began, as time passed, to catch hints of shouted sounds. The cause might be found, I asserted, in a fervour of the auditory nerve, which, if the cataract were absent, the roar of the ocean, and the row of the perpetual tempest round us, might by themselves be sufficient to bring about; his own ear-interior, I said, must be inflamed to an exquisite pitch of fever; and I named the disease to him as the "Paracusis Wilisü." When he frowned dissent, I, quite undeterred, proceeded to relate the case (that had occurred within my own experience) of a very deaf lady who could hear the drop of a pin in a railway-train*; and now he made me the reply: "Of

---

* Such cases are known to many medical men. The concussion on the deaf nerve is the cause of the acquired sensitiveness; nor is there any limit to that sensitiveness when the tumult is immensely augmented.

ignorant people I am accustomed to consider the mere scientist the most ignorant!"

But I, for my part, regarded it as merely far-fetched that he should pretend to be in the dark as to the morbid state of his hearing! He himself, indeed, confessed to me his own, Aith's, and the lady Swertha's proneness to paroxysms of *vertigo*. I was startled! for I had myself shortly previously been roused out of sleep by feelings of reeling and nausea, and an assurance that the room furiously flew round with me. The impression passed away, and I attributed it, perhaps hastily, to some disturbance in the nerve-endings of "the labyrinth," or inner ear. In Harfager, however, the conviction of whirling motions in the house, in the world, got to so horrible a degree of certainty, that its effects sometimes resembled those of lunacy or energumenal possession. Never, he said, was the sensation of giddiness altogether dead in him; seldom the sensation that he gazed with stretched-out arms over the brink of abysms which wooed his half-consenting foot. Once, as we walked, he was hurled as by unearthly powers to the ground, and there for an hour sprawled, bathed in sweat, with distraught bedazzlement and amaze in his stare, which watched the racing walls. He was constantly racked, moreover, with the consciousness of sounds so peculiar in their character, that I could account for them on no other supposition than that of a *tinnitùs* infinitely sick. Through the roar there sometimes visited him, he told me, the lullaby of some bird, from the burden of whose song he had the consciousness that she derived from a very remote country, was of the whiteness of foam, and crested with a comb of mauve. Or else he knew of accumulated human tones, distant, yet articulate, busily contending in volubility, and in the end melting into a medley of musical movements. Or, anon, he was shocked by an infinite and imminent crashing, like the monstrous racket of the crackling of a cosmos of crockery round his ears. He told me, moreover, that he could frequently see, rather than hear, the parti-coloured wheels of a mazy sphere-music deep, deep within the black dark of the cataract's roar. These impressions, which I protested *must* be merely entotic had sometimes a pleasing effect upon him, and he would stand long to listen with a lifted hand to their seduction: others again inflamed him to a mad anger. I guessed that they were the cause of those "*Harks!*" that at intervals of about an hour did not fail to break from him. But in this I was wrong: and it was with a thrill of dismay that I soon came to know the truth.

For, as we were once passing by an iron door on the lower floor, he stopped, and for some minutes stood listening with a leer most keen and cunning. Presently the cry "*Hark!*" escaped him; and he then turned to me and wrote on the tablet: "Did you not hear?" I had heard nothing but the roar; and he howled into my ear in sounds now audible to me as an echo caught far off in dreams: "You shall see."

He took up the candlestick; produced from the pocket of his robe a key; unlocked the iron door; and we passed into a room very loftily domed in proportion to its area, and empty, save that a pair of steps lay against its wall, and that in the centre of its marble floor was a pool, like a Roman "impluvium," only round like the room—a pool evidently profound in depth, full of a thick and inky fluid. I was very perturbed by its present aspect, for as the candle burned upon its surface, I observed that this had been quite recently *disturbed*, in a style for which the shivering of the house could not account, since *ripples* of slime were now rounding out from its middle to its brink. When I glanced at Harfager for explanation, he gave me a signal to wait; and now for about an hour, with his hands behind his back, paced the chamber; but then paused, and we two stood together by the pool's margin, gazing into the water. Suddenly his clutch tightened on my arm, and I saw, with a touch of horror, a tiny ball, probably of lead, but daubed blood-red by some chemical, fall from the roof, and sink into the middle of the pool. It hissed on contact with the water a whiff of mist.

"In the name of all that is sinister," I whispered, "what thing is this?"

Again he made me a busy and confident signal to wait, moved the ladder-steps toward the pool, handed me the taper. When I had mounted, holding high the light, I saw hanging out of the fogs in the dome a globe of old copper, lengthened into balloon-shape by a neck, at the end of which I could spy a tiny hole. Painted over the globe was barely visible in red print-letters:

"HARFAGER-HOUS: 1389—188."

I was down quicker than I went up!

"But the meaning?" I panted.

"Did you see the writing?"

"Yes. The meaning?"

He wrote: "By comparing Gascoigne with Thrunster, I find that the house was *built* about 1389."

"But the last figures?"

"After the last 8," he replied, "there is another figure not quite obliterated by a tarnish-spot."

"What figure?" I asked.

"It cannot be read, but may be surmised. As the year 1888 is now all but passed, it can only be the figure 9."

"Oh, you are depraved in mind!" I cried, very irritated: "you assume—you *state*—in a manner which no mind trained to base its conclusions on facts can bear with patience."

"And you are irrational," he wrote. "You know, I suppose, the formula of Archimedes by which, the diameter of a globe being known, its volume also is known? Now, the diameter of that globe in the dome I know to be four and a half feet; and the diameter of the leaden balls about the third of an inch. Supposing, then, that 1389 was the year in which the globe was full of balls, you may readily calculate that not many fellows of the four million and odd which have since dropped at the rate of one an hour are now left within. The fall of the balls *cannot* persist another year. The figure 9 is therefore forced upon us."

"But you assume, Harfager!" I cried: "Oh, believe me, my friend, this is the very wantonness of wickedness! By what algebra of despair do you know that each ball represents one of the scions of your house, or that the last date was intended to correspond with the stoppage of the horologe. And, even if so, what is the significance of it? It can have *no significance!*"

"Do you want to madden me?" he shouted. Then furiously writing; "I swear that I know nothing of its significance! But it is not evident to you that the thing is a big hour-glass, intended to count the hours, not of a day, but of a cycle; and of a cycle of five hundred years?"

"But the whole contrivance," I passionately cried, "is a baleful phantasm of our brains! How is the fall of the balls regulated? Ah, my friend, you wander—your mind is debauched in this brawl of waters."

"I have not ascertained," he replied, "by what internal works, or clammy medium, or spiral coil, dependent probably for its action upon the vibration of the mansion, the balls are retarded in their fall: that was a matter well within the skill of the mediæval mechanic, the inventor of the clock; but this at least is clear, that one element of their retardation is the smallness of the aperture through which they have to pass; that this element, by known laws of statics, will cease to operate when no more than three balls remain; and that, consequently, the last three will fall at almost the same instant."

"In Heaven's name!" I exclaimed, careless now what folly I poured out, "but your mother is dead, Harfager! Do you deny that there remain but you and the Lady Swertha?"

A glance of disdain was all the answer he then gave me as to this.

But he confessed to me a day later that the leaden drops were a constant sorrow to his ears; that from hour to hour his life was a keen waiting for their fall; that even from his brief sleeps he infallibly started awake at each descent; that in whatever region of the mansion he chanced to be, they found him out with a crashing *loudness*; and that each crash tweaked him with a twinge of anguish within the ear. I was therefore shocked at his declaration that these droppings had now become as the life of life to him; had acquired an entwining so close with the tone of his mind, that their ceasing might even mean for him the reeling of Reason: at which confession he sobbed, with his face buried, as he leant upon a column. When this paroxysm was past, I asked him if it was out of the question that he should once for all cast off the fascination of the horologe, and escape with me from the place. He wrote in mysterious reply: "A *three*-fold cord is not easily broken." I started, asking—"How three-fold?" He wrote with a bitter smile: "To be in love with pain—to pine after aching—is not that a wicked madness?" I stood astonished that he had unconsciously quoted Gascoigne! "a wicked madness!" "a lecherous anguish!" "You have seen my aunt's face," he proceeded; "your eyes were dim if you did not see in it an impious calm, the glee of a blasphemous patience, a grin behind her daring smile." He then spoke of a prospect at the terror of which his whole soul trembled, yet which sometimes laughed in his heart in the form of a *hope*. It was the prospect of any considerable increase in the volume of sound about his ears. At *that*, he said, the brain must totter. On the night of my arrival the noise of my boots, and, since then, my voice occasionally raised, had produced acute pain in him. To such an ear, I understood him to say, the luxury of torture involved in a large sound-increase around was an allurement from which no human virtue could turn: and when I said that I could not even conceive such an increase, much less the means by which it could be effected, he brought out from the archives of the mansion some annals kept by the heads of his family. From these it appeared that the tempests that ever lacerated the latitude of Rayba did not fail to give place, at intervals of some years, to one mammoth madness, one Samson among the merry men, and Sirius among the suns. At such periods the rains descended—and the floods came—even as in the first world-deluge; those *rösts*, or eddies, which ever encircled Rayba, spurning then the bands of lateral space, burst aloft into a whirl of water-spouts, to dance about the little land, upon which, converging, some of them discharged their waters: and the locks which flowed to the cataract thus redoubled their volume, and crashed with redoubled roar. Harfager said it was miraculous that for eighteen years no such grand event had transacted itself at Rayba.

"And what," I asked "in addition to the dropping balls, and the prospect of an increase of sound, is the third strand of that '*threefold cord*' of which you have spoken."

For answer he led me to a circular hall which, he said, he had ascertained to be the centre of the circular mansion. It was a very large hall—so large as I think I never saw—so large that the amount of wall lighted at one time by the candle seemed nearly flat: and nearly the whole of its area, from floor to roof, was occupied by a column of brass, the space between the wall and column being only such as to admit of a stretched-out arm.

"This column," Harfager wrote, "goes up to the dome and passes beyond it; it goes down to the lower floor, and passes through that; it goes down thence to the brazen flooring of the vaults and *passes through that* into the bed-rock. Under each floor it spreads out, helping to support the floor. What is the precise quality of the impression which I have made upon your mind by this description?"

"I do not know," I answered, turning from him: "ask me none of your enigmas, Harfager: I feel a giddiness..."

"But answer me," he said: "consider *the strangeness* of that brazen lowest floor, which I have discovered to be some six feet thick, and whose under-surface, I have reason to think, is somewhat *above* the bed-rock; remember that the fabric is at no point *fastened* to the column; think of the *chains* which ray out from the outer wall, apparently *anchoring* the house to the ground. Tell me, what impression have I *now* made?"

"And is it for *this* you wait?" I cried. "Yet there may have been no malevolent intention! You jump at conclusions! Any fixed building in such a land and spot as this would at any time be liable to be broken up by some sovereign tempest! What if it was the intention of the builder that in such a case the chains should break, and the building, by yielding, be saved?"

"You have no lack of charity at least," he replied; and we then went back to the book we were reading together.

He had not wholly lost the old habit of study, although he could no longer get himself to *sit* to read; so with a volume (often tossed down) he would stamp about within the region of the lamplight; or I, unconscious of my voice, might read to him. By a whim of his mood the few books which now lay within the limits of his patience had all for their motive something of the *picaresque*, or the foppishly speculative: Quevedo's "Tacaño;" or the system of Tycho Brahe; above all, George Hakewill's "Power and Providence of God." One day, however, as I read, he interrupted me with the sentence, *à propos* of nothing: "What I cannot understand is that you, a scientist, should believe that life ceases with the ceasing of breathing"—and from that moment the tone of our reading changed. For he led me to the crypts of the library in the lowest part of the building, and hour after hour, with a *furore* of triumph overwhelmed me with books proving the length of life after "death." What, he asked, was my opinion of Baron Verulam's account of the dead man who was heard to utter words of prayer? or of the bounding bowels of the dead convict? On my expressing unbelief, he seemed surprised, and reminded me of the writhings of dead cobras, of the long beating of a frog's heart after "death." "She is not dead," he quoted, "but *sleepeth*." The idea of Bacon and Paracelsus that the principle of life resides in a spirit or fluid was proof to him that such fluid could not, from its very nature, undergo any *sudden* annihilation, while the organs which it pervades remain. When I asked what limit he, then, set to the persistence of "life" in the "dead," he answered that when decay had so far advanced that the nerves could no longer be called nerves, or when the brain had been disconnected at the neck from the body, as by rats gnawing, then the king of terrors was king verily. With an indiscretion strange to me before my residence at Rayba, I now blurted out the question whether in all this he could be referring to his mother? For a while he stood thoughtful, then wrote: "Even if I had not had reason to believe that my own and Swertha's life in some way hung upon the final cessation of hers, I should still have taken precautions to ascertain the march of the destroyer on her frame: as it is, I shall not lack even the exactest information." He then explained that the rats which ran riot in the place of death would in time do their full work upon her; but would be unable to reach to the region of the throat without first gnawing their way through the three strings stretched across the holes of the bridges within the coffin, and thus, one by one, liberating the three morrisco-bells to tinklings.

The winter solstice had gone; another year began. I was sleeping a deep sleep by night when Harfager came into my chamber, and shook me. His face was ghastly in the taper's glare. A change within a short time had taken place upon him. He was hardly the same. He was like some poor wight into whose surprised eyes in the night have pried the eyes of Affright.

He said that he was aware of strainings and creakings, which gave him the feeling of being suspended in airy spaces by a thread which must break to his weight; and he begged me, for God's sake, to accompany him to the coffins. We passed together through the house, he craven, haggard, his gait now laggard, into the chamber of the dead, where he stole to and fro examining the shelves. Out of the footless coffin of the dowager trembling on its bench I saw a water-rat crawl; and as Harfager passed beneath one of the shortest of the shelves which bore one coffin, it suddenly dropped from a height to dust at his feet. He screamed the cry of a frighted creature; tottered to my support; and I bore him back to the upper parts of the palace.

He sat, with his face buried, in a corner of a small chamber, doddering, overtaken, as it were, with the extremity of age, no longer marking with his "*Hark!*" the fall of the leaden drops. To my remonstrances he responded only with the moan, "so soon!" Whenever I looked for him, I found him there, his manhood now collapsed in an ague. I do not think that during this time he slept.

On the second night, as I was approaching him, he sprang suddenly upright with the outcry: "The first bell is tinkling!"

And he had scarcely screamed it when, from some long way off, a faint wail, which at its origin must have been a fierce shriek, reached my now feverish ears. Harfager, for his part, clapped his palms to his ears, and dashed from his place, I following in hot chase through the black breadth of the mansion: till we came to a chamber containing a candelabrum, and arrased in faded red. On the floor in swoon lay the lady Swertha, her dark-grey hair in disarray wrapping her like an angry sea; tufts of it scattered, torn from the roots; and on her throat prints of strangling fingers. We bore her to her bed in an alcove; and, having discovered some tincture in a cabinet, I administered it between her fixed teeth. In her rapt countenance I saw that death was not; and, as I found something appalling in her aspect, shortly afterwards left her to Harfager.

When I next saw him his manner had undergone a kind of change which I can only describe as gruesome. It resembled the officious self-importance seen in a person of weak intellect who spurs himself with the thought, "to business! the time is short!" while his walk sickened me with a hint of *ataxie locomotrice*. When I asked him as to his aunt, as to the meaning of the marks of violence on her body, bending ear to his deep and unctuous tones, I could hear: "An attempt has been made upon her life by the skeleton, Aith."

He seemed not to share my astonishment at this thing! nor could give me any clear answer as to his reason for retaining such a servant, or as to the origin of Aith's service. Aith, he told me, had been admitted into the palace during the period of his own absence in youth, and he knew little of him beyond the fact that he was extraordinarily strong. *Whence* he had come, or how, no person except the lady Swertha was aware: and she, it seems, feared, or at least persistently flinched from admitting him into the mystery. He added that, as a matter of fact, the lady, from the day of his coming back to Rayba, had with some object imposed upon herself a dumbness on all subjects, which he had never once known her to break through, except by an occasional note.

With an ataxic strenuousness, with the airs of a drunken man constraining himself to ordered action, Harfager now set himself to the doing of a host of trivial things: he collected chronicles and arranged them in order of date; he docketed or ticketed packets of documents; he insisted upon my assistance in turning the faces of paintings to the wall. He was, however, now constantly stopped by bursts of vertigo, six times in a single hour being hurled to the ground, while blood frequently guttered from his ears. He complained to me in a tone of piteous wail of the wooing of a silver *piccolo* that continually seduced him. As he bent, sweating, over his momentous nothings, his hands fluttered like aspen. I noted the movements of his whimpering lips, the rheum of his sunken eyes: sudden doting had come upon his youth.

On a day he threw it utterly off, and was young anew. He entered my room; roused me from dreams; I observed the lunacy of bliss in his eyes, heard his hiss in my ear:

"Up! *The storm!*"

Ah! I had known it—in the nightmare of the night. I felt it in the air of the room. It had come. I saw it lurid by the lamplight on the hell of Harfager's face.

A glee burst at once into birth within me, as I sprang from my couch, glancing at the clock: it was eight—in the morning. Harfager, with the naked stalk of some maniac prophet, had already taken himself away; and I started out after him. A deepening was clearly felt in the quivering of the edifice; anon for a second it stopped still, as if, breathlessly, to listen; its air was troubled with a vague gustiness. Occasionally there came to me as it were the noising of some far-off lamentation and voice in Ramah, but whether this was in my ear or the screaming of the gale I could not tell; or again I could hear one clear chord of an organ's vaunt. About noon I spied Harfager, lamp in hand, running along a corridor, with naked soles. As we met he looked at me, but hardly with recognition, and passed by; stopped, however, and ran back to howl into my ear the question: "Would you *see*?" He then beckoned before me, and I followed to a very small opening in the outer wall, closed with a slab of brass. As he lifted the latch, the slab dashed inward with instant impetuosity and tossed him a long way, while the breath of the tempest, braying through the brazen tube with a brutal bravura, caught and pinned me upon a corner of a wall, and all down the corridor a long crashing racket of crowds of pictures and couches followed. I nevertheless managed to push my way on the belly to the opening. Hence the sea should have been visible; but my senses were met by nothing but a vision of tumbled tenebrousness, and a general impression of the letter O. The sun of Rayba had gone out. In a moment of opportunity our two forces got the shutter shut again.

"Come!"—he had obtained a fresh glimmer, and beckoned before me—"let's go see how the dead fare in the great desolation:" and we ran, but had hardly got to the middle of the stairway, when I was thrilled by the consciousness of some great shock, the bass of a dull thud, which nothing save the thumping to the floor of the whole lump of the coffins could have caused. I looked for Harfager, and for a moment only saw his heels skedaddling, panic-hounded, his ears stopped, his mouth round! Then, indeed, fear reached me—a tremor in the audacity of my heart, a thought that now at any rate I must desert him in his extremity, and work out my own salvation. Yet it was with hesitancy that I turned to search for him for the last farewell—a hesitancy which I felt to be not unselfish, but selfish, and unhealthy. I rambled through the night, seeking light, and having happened upon a lamp, proceeded to seek for Harfager. Several hours went by in this way, during which I could not doubt from the state of the air in the house that the violence about me was being wildly heightened. Sounds as of screams—unreal, like the shriekings of demons—now reached my ears. As the time of night came on, I began to detect in the greatly augmented baritone of the cataract a fresh character—a shrillness—the whistle of a rapture—a malice— the menace of a rabies blind and deaf. It must have been at about the hour of six that I found Harfager. He sat in an obscure room, with his brow bowed down, his hands on his knees, his face covered with hair, and with blood from the ears. The right sleeve of his robe had been rent away in some renewed attempt, I imagined, to manage a window; and the rather crushed arm hung lank from the shoulder. For some time I stood and eyed him mouthing his mumblings; but now that I had found him uttered nothing as to my departure. Presently he looked sharply up with the call "*Hark!*"—then with impatience, "Hark! Hark!"—then with a shout, "The second bell!" And *again*, in immediate sequence upon his shout, there sounded a wail, vague yet real, through the house. Harfager at the instant dropped reeling with giddiness; but I, snatching up a lamp, dashed out, shivering but eager. For some while the wild wailing went on (either actually, or by reflex action of my ear); and as I ran for the lady's apartment, I saw opposite to it the open door of an armoury, into which I passed, caught up a battle-axe, and was now about to dart in to her aid, when Aith, with a blazing eye, shied out of her chamber. I cast up my axe, and, shouting, dashed forward to down him: but by some chance the lamp fell from me, and before I knew anything more, the axe sprang from my grasp, and I was cast far backward by some most grim vigour. There was, however, enough light shining out of the chamber to show that the skeleton had darted into a door of the armoury, so I instantly slammed and locked the door near me by which I had procured the axe, and hurrying to the other, secured it, too. Aith was thus a prisoner. I then entered the lady's chamber. She lay over the bed in the alcove, and to my bent ear grossly croaked the ruckle of death. A glance at her mangled throat convincing me that her last moments were come, I settled her on the bed, curtained her within the loosened festoons of the hangings of black, and turned from the cursedness of her aspect. On an *escritoire* near I noticed a note, intended apparently for Harfager: "I mean to defy, and fly; not from fear, but for the delight of the defiance itself. *Can* you come?" Taking a flame from the candelabrum, I left her to her loneliness, and throes of her death.

I had passed some way backward when I was startled by a queer sound—a crash—resembling the crash of a tamboureen; and as I could hear it pretty clearly, and from a distance, this meant some prodigious energy. In two minutes it again broke out; and thenceforth at regular intervals—with an effect of pain upon me; and the conviction grew gradually within me that Aith had unhung two of the old brass shields from their pegs, and holding them by their handles, and dashing them viciously together, thus expressed the frenzy that had now overtaken him. When I found my way back to Harfager, very anguish was now stamping in him about the chamber; he shook his head like a tormented horse, brushing and barring from his hearing each crash of the brass shields. "Ah, when—when—" he hoarsely groaned into my ear, "will that ruckle cease in her throat? I will myself, I tell you—*with my own hand*—oh God..." Since the morning his auditory fever (as indeed my own also) appeared to have increased in steady proportion with the roaring and screeching chaos round; and the death-struggle in the lady's throat bitterly filled for him the intervals of the grisly cymbaling of Aith. He presently sent twinkling fingers into the air, and, with his arms cast out, darted into the darkness.

And again I sought him, and long again in vain. As the hours passed, and the day deepened toward its baleful midnight, the cry of the now redoubled cataract, mixed with the mass and majesty of the now climatic tempest, took on too intentional a *shriek* to be longer tolerable to any reason. My own mind escaped my sway, and went its way: for here in the hot-bed of fever I was fevered. I wandered from chamber to chamber, precipitate, dizzy on the upbuoyance of a joy. "As a man upon whom sleep seizes," so I had fallen. Even yet, as I passed near the region of the armoury, the rapturous shields of Aith did not fail to smash faintly upon my ear. Harfager I did not see, for he, too, was doubtless roaming a hurtling Ahasuerus round the world of the house. However, at about midnight, observing light shining from a door on the lower stage, I entered and saw him there—the chamber of the dropping horologe. He sat hugging himself on the ladder-steps, gazing at the gloomy pool. The final lights of the riot of the day seemed dying in his eyes; and he gave me no glance as I ran in. His hands, his bare arm, were all washed with new-shed blood; but of this, too, he looked unconscious; his mouth was hanging open to his pantings. As I eyed him, he suddenly leapt high, smiting his hands with the yell, "The last bell tinkling!" and ran out raving. He therefore did not see (though he may have understood by hearing) the thing which, with cowering awe, I now saw: for a ball slipped from the horologe with a hiss and mist of smoke into the pool; and while the clock once ticked another: and while the clock yet ticked, another! and the smoke of the first had not perfectly thinned, when the smoke of the third, mixing with it, floated toward the dome. Understanding that the sands of the mansion were run, I, too, throwing up my arm, rushed from the spot; but was suddenly stopped in my flight by the sense of some stupendous destiny emptying its vials upon the edifice; and was made aware by a crackling racket, like musketry, above, and the downpour of a world of waters, that some waterspout, in the waltz and whirl, had hurled its broken summit upon us, and burst through the dome. At that moment I beheld Harfager running toward me, his hands buried in his hair; and, as he raced past, I caught him, crying: "Harfager, save yourself! the very fountains, Harfager—by the grand God, man"—I hissed it into his inmost ear—"*the very fountains of the Great Deep...!*" He glared at me, and went on his way, while I, whisking myself into a room, closed the door. Here for some time with weak knees I waited; but the eagerness of my frenzy pressed me, and I again stepped out, to find the corridors everywhere thigh-deep with water; while rags of the storm, bragging through the hole in the dome, were now blustering about the house. My light was at once puffed out; but I was surprised by the presence of *another* light—most ghostly, gloomy, bluish—mild, yet wild—which now gloated every-where through the house. I was standing in wonder at this when a gust of auguster passion galloped up the mansion; and, with it, I was made aware of the *snap* of something somewhere. There was a minute's infinite waiting—and then—quick—ever quicker—came the throb, snap, pop, in spacious succession, of the anchoring chains of the mansion before the hurried shoulder of the hurricane. And *again* a second of breathless stillness—and then—deliberately—its hour came—the house moved. My flesh worked like the flesh of worms which squirm. Slowly moved, and stopped—then there was a sweep—and a swirl—and a pause! then a swirl—and a sweep—and a pause! then steady labour on the brazen axis as the labourer tramps by the harrow; then a heightening of zest—then intensity—then the final light liveliness of flight. And now once again, as, staggering and plunging, I spun, the notion of escape for a moment came to me, but this time I shook an impious fist. "No, but, God, no, no," I gasped, "I will no more go from here: here let me waltzing pass in this carnival of the vortices, anarchy of the thunders!"—and I ran staggering. But memory gropes in a greyer gloaming as to all that followed. I struggled up the stairway, now flowing a river, and for a good while ran staggering and plunging, full of wild rantings, about, amid the downfall of roofs, and the ruins of walls. The air was thick with splashes, the whole roof now, save three rafters, having been snatched by the wind away; and in the blush of that bluish moonshine the tapestries were flapping and trailing wildly out after the flying place, like the streaming hair of some ranting fakir stung reeling by the tarantulas of distraction. At one point, where the largest of the porticoes protruded, the mansion began at every revolution to bump with grum shudderings against some obstruction: it bumped, and while the lips said one-two-three it three times bumped again. It was the mænadism of mass! Swift—still swifter—in an ague of flurry it raced, every portico a sail to the gale, racking its great frame to fragments. I, running by the door of a room littered with the ruins of a wall, saw through that livid moonlight Harfager sitting on a tomb—a drum by him, upon which, with a club in his bloody fist, he feebly, but persistingly, beat. The speed of the leaning house had now attained the *sleeping* stage, that last pitch of the spinning-top; and now all at once Harfager dashed away the mat of hair which wrapped his face, sprang, stretched his arms, and began to spin—giddily—in the same direction as the mansion—nor less sleep-embathed, with lifted hair, with quivering cheeks... From such a sight I shied with retching; and, staggering, plunging, presently found myself on the lower floor opposite a porch, where an outer door chancing to crash before me, the breath of the tempest smote freshly upon me. On this an impulse, partly of madness, more of sanity, spurred in my soul; and I spurted out of the doorway, to be whirled far out into the limbo without.

The river at once rushed me deep-drenched toward the sea—though even there, in that depth of whirlpool, a shrill din, like the splitting of a world, reached my ears. It had hardly passed when my body butted in its course upon one of the arches, cushioned with seaweed, of the not all demolished causeway. Nor had I utterly lost consciousness. A clutch freed my head from the drench; and in the end I heaved myself to the level of the summit. Hence to the ledge of rock by which I had come, the bridge being intact, I rowed myself on my face under the thumps of the wind, and under a rushing of rain, like a shimmering of silk through the air. Noticing the same wild shining about me which had blushed through the broken dome into the mansion, I glanced backward—and saw that the dwelling of the Harfagers was a memory of the past; then upward—and the whole north heaven, to the zenith, shone one ocean of variegated glories—the *aurora borealis*, which was being fairly brushed and flustered by the gale. At the augustness of which sight, I was touched to a gush of tears. And with them the dream broke! the infatuation passed! a palm seemed to skin back from my brain the films and media of delusion; and on my knees I threw my hands to heaven in thankfulness for the marvel of my rescue from all the temptation, the tribulation, and the breakage, of Rayba.

ALSO AVAILABLE

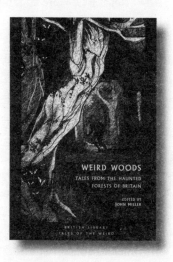

*But foliage surrounded him, branches blocked the
way; the trees stood close and still; and the sun dipped
that moment behind a great black cloud. The entire
wood turned dark and silent. It watched him.*

Woods play a crucial and recurring role in horror, fantasy, the gothic
and the weird. They are places in which strange things happen, where
it is easy to lose your way. Supernatural creatures thrive in the thickets.
Trees reach into underworlds of pagan myth and magic. Forests are full
of ghosts.

Lining the path through this realm of folklore and fear are twelve stories
from across Britain, telling tales of whispering voices and maddening
sights from deep in the Yorkshire Dales to the ancient hills of Gwent
and the eerie quiet of the forests of Dartmoor. Immerse yourself in this
collection of classic tales celebrating the enduring power of our natural
spaces to enthral and terrorise our senses.

There was a faint rustling sound, like some small silk thing
blown in a gentle breeze. He sat up straight, stark and
scared, and a small wooden voice spoke in the stillness.
'Pa-pa,' it said, with a break between the syllables.

From living dolls to spirits wandering in search of solace or vengeance, the ghostly youth is one of the most enduring phenomena of supernatural fiction, its roots stretching back into the realms of folklore and superstition. In this spine-tingling new collection Jen Baker gathers a selection of the most chilling hauntings and encounters with ghostly children, expertly paired with notes and extracts from the folklore and legends which inspired them.

Reviving obscure stories from Victorian periodicals alongside nail-biting episodes from master storytellers such as Elizabeth Gaskell, M. R. James and Margery Lawrence, this is a collection by turns enchanting, moving and thoroughly frightening.

ALSO AVAILABLE

Where the indescribable thrills of music and the arts, piercing early psychology and terrifying supernatural beings find their meeting place, so dwell the startlingly original weird tales of Vernon Lee.

In this collection, fiction expert Mike Ashley selects the writer's eeriest dark fantasies: stories which blend the shocking, the sentimental, the beautiful and the unnerving into an atmosphere and style still unmatched in the field of supernatural writing.

From the modernised folktales "Marsyas in Flanders" and "The Legend of Madame Krasinska" to ingenious psychological hauntings such as "A Phantom Lover" and "A Wicked Voice", Lee's captivating voice rings out just as distinctively now as in her Fin-de-Siècle heyday.

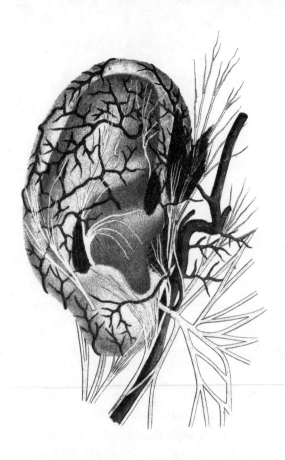

For more Tales of the Weird titles
visit the British Library Shop (shop.bl.uk)

We welcome any suggestions, corrections or feedback you may have, and will
aim to respond to all items addressed to the following:

The Editor (Tales of the Weird), British Library Publishing,
The British Library, 96 Euston Road, London NW1 2DB

We also welcome enquiries through our Twitter account, @BL_Publishing.